Don't let Shaggy run the show !

JOHNNY LYCAN
& THE VEGAS BERSERKER

WAYNE TURMEL

Black Rose Writing | Texas

ISBN: 978-1-68513-075-6
PUBLISHED BY BLACK ROSE WRITING
www.blackrosewriting.com

Printed in the United States of America
Suggested Retail Price (SRP) $21.95

Johnny Lycan & the Vegas Berserker is printed in Calluna

*As a planet-friendly publisher, Black Rose Writing does its best to eliminate
unnecessary waste to reduce paper usage and energy costs, while never compromising
the reading experience. As a result, the final word count vs. page count may not meet
common expectations.

PRAISE FOR
JOHNNY LYCAN
& THE VEGAS BERSERKER

"Compelling characters, fast-paced action, magic crystals and a berserker. It's Johnny Lupul in Vegas baby! As always, Wayne Turmel has created a compulsively readable action packed story with a unique take on the werewolf mythos. An enjoyable read and I can't wait for the next installment!"

—G Clatworthy, author of the *Rise of the Dragons* series

"*Johnny Lycan and the Las Vegas Berserker* is a riveting Sin City romp like I've never seen before. Aliens, covens, and magic of all stripes rocket across every page, with the reader (and sometimes Johnny, too) holding on for dear life. Harry Dresden better watch his back—Johnny Lycan is the snarky, shapeshifting badass you've been waiting for."

—S.G. Tasz, author of the *Dead Mall* series

"Get a flashlight, because you'll be reading *Johnny Lycan and the Vegas Berserker* well into the night. Johnny's world is full of mischief, mayhem, and magic—excuse me, magick—and I can't wait to read more."

—Luke Swanson, author of *Spectators of War* and *The Other Hamlet Brother*

"The stakes are high—life and death high—as werewolf private detective Johnny Lupul goes to Las Vegas to take custody of a mysterious ancient artifact. It's a full moon, and the fur is about to fly!"

—Jill Hand, author of the *Trapnell Thrillers, White Oaks* and *Black Willows*

"I loved this book. A rollicking, clever ride with a story so good you forget it's a genre novel. If Jack Reacher was a werewolf, he'd be Johnny Lycan."

—John Wing, Jr., comedian and author of *A Car to Die For*

"Witches, a Werewolf, and a Berserker. Only in Vegas, Baby! Johnny, Shaggy and the gang are back in this page turning, magic-infused thriller of epic proportions. Beware: *Johnny Lycan and the Vegas Berserker* will cast a spell on you!"

—Jean M. Roberts, author of *The Heron* and *The Frowning Madonna*

"As usual, Wayne's fast-paced writing style draws you in immediately. Johnny Lupul is in fine form once again as he tries to keep some of Shaggy's darker instincts in check and help those who can't help themselves. If you're hankering for a hairy good time, pick this novel up now!"

–Katie Berry, author of the *Claw* and *Abandoned* series

*To all the writers who corrupted me,
and those of us corrupting future generations*

JOHNNY LYCAN
& THE VEGAS BERSERKER

CHAPTER 1

Night of the full moon.

Two sets of wide brown eyes watched me, clearly horrified. I'm big and hairy and freaky enough even before I change, so no wonder. Still, this was no time for subtlety.

"Get into that closet and don't open that door, no matter what you hear. Understand?" My vocal cords still worked, even if the muscles in my arms and legs spasmed and twitched under my clothes, adding to the general freakiness.

The girl, the older of the pair, looked up. Locking eyes with me she asked, "Are you going to hurt these guys?" Her baby brother clung to her shirt, sucking his thumb.

"Probably. Yup." *Not as much as they deserve.* Shaggy, the beast living inside me, wouldn't be satisfied. But yeah.

Amy Tong nodded and took her crying brother by his free hand, cooing to him in Mandarin. Even at ten years old, she played mother. Kids in foster care do that. The little girl looked up at me with trusting eyes. I closed the door to the same room I'd sprung them from moments ago.

Trying to sound as rational as possible with a werewolf clawing and chomping its way out of my skin, I put my mouth against the heavy wooden door. "Stay there and don't open up for anyone unless you hear a woman's voice. Please. Don't look and don't open the door unless you hear a nice older lady. Okay?"

1

Through the barrier came a sniff. "Yes, sir."

That's when the baseball bat hit me between the shoulder blades, knocking me face first into the door panel. Whichever of the two dickwads it was let out a high-pitched cackle. I ducked and rolled to my left. Strike two put a hole in the plaster wall.

In a low crouch, I looked around the basement room. Two very angry men closed in. The skinny, meth head-looking guy with long hair slapped the bat in his hand menacingly. The other guy, not much more than a beer gut with legs, shouted, "Get him."

It's always good to identify the weak link early.

The room wasn't big, and it was jam-packed with video equipment and computer gear. The only open space was on either side of a ratty futon on the floor. Since only one of these guys actually posed any real threat, it was enough. Crouching on all fours, I sprung to the middle of the room. That way, I could face them both at the same time.

Since it was a full moon, I was having a hell of a time keeping Shaggy under control. There was rage at what these perverts were doing. Stir in the fact that my hairy alter ego hadn't had any real release in a couple of months. All that meant I felt him tugging on my brain, aching for a chance to vent all that rage and pent-up violence.

God help me, I wanted to let him do his thing. I really, *really,* did.

Fortunately, I didn't need to. When I'm in the middle of a full-blown high cycle, the urge to beat the hell out of someone is almost irresistible. In this case, there was no reason to resist. In fact, it would be fun.

A high-volume howl-scream burst from my chest and out of my mouth. My jaw and canine teeth expanded along with it, and I damn near lost control. Before going full Lycan, I wrenched control back, retracting them and feeling the electric burn from the exertion.

That sight alone was enough to scare the hell out of Meth Boy. He locked up with fear, aluminum weapon held high over his head. His knees knocked together, too shaky to provide any kind of leverage. That's when I leaped at him.

My hair-covered hand grabbed his pale, skinny wrist. Through more concentration than I could afford, I kept the claws retracted. Twisting my wrist, I savored the watery, submissive look in his eyes and the satisfying scream as his arm snapped. *He should stop whining. I could've eaten him, instead.*

Incapacitated and yelling to beat hell, the jerk fell to the ground, crying and calling out to a God who wanted nothing to do with him. Then I turned on the fat one.

This slug was wearing a wife beater and stained gray sweatpants. A new stain appeared at the crotch and spread slowly as he backed away from me. The stink of his fear and fresh urine—I wouldn't have picked him for an asparagus fan—filled my nostrils, registered in my brain and caused Shaggy to make a surge for control.

Nah, big guy. I got this.

Responding to the labored breathing rushing up behind me, I kicked backwards at the skinny guy, catching him square in the jaw with my steel-toed work boots. That knocked him onto his back and out of commission.

The sound of his teeth clicking together made me laugh. At least, it was supposed to be a laugh. Whatever awful sound actually emerged from my throat made the fat guy go even paler. He dropped his head to his chest, babbling and crying.

"Jesus Christ, Mister. Don't kill me. We weren't..."

"Yeah, you were, you fat sack of shit. Were you supposed to be the star of this operation? I leaned forward, knowing he saw Shaggy in my eyes. All he could manage was to whimper and nod.

"You're in luck. You still get your camera time."

I grabbed him by the back of his undershirt and shoved him to his knees on the stained futon with orders not to fucking move. He took direction well, squirming and sniffling, but staying put.

One reason I needed to maintain my Johnny form was because it's tough to operate video equipment with seven-inch fingernails. I slipped on surgical gloves so I wouldn't leave fingerprints, hit record, and slowly swung the camera around the room, taking in the entire scene. The time stamp in the viewfinder showed the correct time and date.

Perfect.

First, I panned the table full of high-tech recording equipment, then zoomed in on the bottle of roofies and pitcher of Kool Aid, along with two small solo cups. There was a baggie of something crystalline and a vial of white powder for the grownups.

Then it was show time. I moved the camera left to the skinny guy, still dazed in the corner but flipping me the bird. Slowly, the lens turned on the kneeling kidnapper. "What's your name, handsome?"

Fat boy had recovered from his shock enough to play the tough guy. He stuck his chin up and spat at me. It only took one fake lunge at him to stop that BS. He shouted, "Nathan. Evans. Nathan Evans."

"And your co-conspirator over there, Nathan?"

He couldn't throw his friend under that bus fast enough. "David Nelson. David Arthur Nelson."

Meth Boy muttered, "Asshole," under his breath, but didn't bother trying to get up.

Keeping Beer Gut's face unmarked—I'd hate for anyone to think he was coerced—clearly in frame I asked questions. Everything the cops would want to know.

Who else was part of this?

Who at Child Services gave them the kids? Turns out it was ICE. *Yeah. Not at all disturbing to know it was the immigration service.*

What websites were the videos intended for?

None of the names meant anything to me, but I'm sure there were entire divisions of Chicago cops and FBI that would make careers on the information.

At last, I turned the camera off. I looked down at Nathan Evans.

"We done now?" he asked.

"Not even close." Now I pulled a handful of zip ties out of my pocket.

I started with David Arthur Nelson. With a single pull and a *ziiiiiip,* his hands were immobilized. His broken wrist must have hurt like hell. I grabbed a handful of greasy hair and slammed his face three times on the cracked hardwood floor. The amount of blood in the air was enough to make Shaggy shiver inside me. Fortunately for Nelson, it wasn't enough to be life-threatening. He needed to be taken alive. Pity.

The second jerk looked up at me from the floor, tears staining his face, liver-colored lips trembling. "Please, I'm sorry. I'm so sorry."

"Yeah. Okay."

I followed that up with three vicious, very cathartic punches to his fat, evil face. HIs orbital bone cracked, and the fleshed swelled under my fist.

I felt better. A bit. It would have to do.

Zip-tying his hands as well, I pulled out my phone and hit number one on my speed dial.

A woman's voice answered. Calm and professional. "Can I come down now?"

"Yup. Can you take the kids to the police station? I was never here."

"Who was where, now?"

I grinned. It would take Francine Ball less than five minutes to be in and out and have the little ones safe and under wraps. She was a nurse, and the best woman in a crisis I ever knew. I trusted her completely.

Arriving at the bottom of the stairs, she stopped and surveyed the scene. Seeing the wounded, groaning men, she uttered a quick, "Jesus, Johnny."

She took in the rest of the scene, glowered back at the scumbags on the floor, and back at me. Her green eyes turned colder than a January night.

"Good thing you got to them before I did." Her voice was cold and terrifying as her eyes. She wasn't kidding. They don't know how lucky they were. They only had to deal with a werewolf.

From the closet came a scuffling sound. Francine kneeled and placed her ear to the door. In a surprisingly maternal voice, she asked,

"Amy, are you alright in there? It's okay. My name is Francine Ball. We're going to get you out of here."

After a sniff, Amy asked, "Are you the older lady?"

"Am I the *what?*" She turned and glared at me now.

I winked at her. "I'll call the cops soon as you're gone."

She turned the laser beams on me for a moment, then sighed. "You're a good man, Johnny. A bit of a dick, but a good man."

I wasn't, but God knows I tried. Now I needed to let Shaggy run wild and take out a couple of deer just to get it out of his, well, my, system.

CHAPTER 2

One day past full moon- waning gibbous.

If Chicago has an official card game, it's euchre. It's simple. More importantly, it gives you an excuse to stay inside, warm and dry, with family and friends. Much as I love this town, six or seven months of the year, the weather tries to kill you. Playing euchre, a guy can bet a little money if that's your thing. You can cuss out your relatives with impunity. Some folks drink heavily while doing it.

None of us were imbibing. It was still a little too close to my high cycle to loosen the reins, and Bill was never much of a drinker. Meaghan was in the fourth month at her sober house, and Gramma was plying her with tea—or whatever that brew really was—keeping the kid on the straight and narrow. It worked, so nobody cared all that much.

"Queen trump. Suck it boys." Gramma leaned across the table to fist-bump her younger partner and Bill just glared at me while writing a precise "4" under the women's names. That was two dollars and fifty cents he'd never get back. Quarter a point can add up when you're on the schneid like we were.

"Dude, you led a nine?" Like Mister Accountant Guy never accidentally played a nine instead of a face card before. In all honesty, he probably hadn't. Bill played euchre like he did everything else—

cautious and methodical. Gramma threw cards around, cursed every play, and loved to torture her grandson and me at every possible moment. As for Meaghan–her old man was an Irish bookie. It was a safe bet she'd been reading card players since she was holding tea parties and playing Go Fish in her Barbie Explorer tent. Now that her eyes and mind were clear, she never missed even the littlest things. It was good to see. And a little creepy.

I have my talents, but attention to detail wasn't one of them. Truth is, most of the time I was too sulky and ADD-addled to be a decent card player. Having a homicidal animal try to burst through your skin every four weeks can be a distraction when trying to plan which cards to play. In fact, I may have been the worst player in the world, but tried in vain to mount a defense. "We're playing with a couple of psychics. Hardly seems fair."

My buddy shifted in his chair, nearly knocking his crutch to the floor, but caught it without looking. "First, they're not psychics, they're con artists. Second, maybe they know what you have because your eyes bug out like Sponge Bob every time you have something higher than a Jack."

Ouch.

Meaghan snort-laughed, enjoying my misery too much to dignify my partner's dig at her abilities. "Seriously, man, never go to Vegas. You'd come back naked." She paused momentarily. Her eyebrows rose and came together as if remembering something, but a split second later, her face returned to normal.

The old lady couldn't help herself. "I came back naked from Vegas once. In a convertible all the way to L.A. But that was a whole different thing." We sat in appalled silence, wondering which of us was supposed to comment. Then Gramma Mostoy cackled to let us know she was kidding. Most likely. This was a woman with a past. And she was never shy about telling a good story.

She relished the horror on Bill's face. "Lighten the hell up. You're such a tight-ass it's taking all the fun out of being an old lady. Deal, kid."

I took my time, successfully handing out five cards each, counting out loud, trying not to flip any of them over and force a re-deal, which was kind of my signature move. As everyone picked up their hands, I took a long look at Meaghan O'Rourke.

She'd come a long way since the night I saved her from the Russians; padded on ten much-needed pounds, let her hair return to a color found in nature, and cut it short and spiky. Most important, she'd gotten straight, unless you consider her dependence on Gramma's mystery tea a problem. Her powers with the Tarot deck were growing just as Gramma predicted they would, despite Bill's skepticism of anything that smacked of Old-World Gypsy hucksterism. The less savory parts of the Mostoy family's Roma background were always an embarrassment. It was one more reason his self-esteem was in the toilet. My boy had issues enough for three people, but he was my friend. Gimpy leg and all. He always had my back.

Nice thing about playing cards. It gives you the chance to have conversations without getting too intense, and I knew they were all dying for the details of the previous night's adventure. I nodded to Meaghan to play next. "You were right about the house, you know."

Her and her Tarot deck had been a big part of rescuing the Tong kids. She deserved to hear it.

"For real?" Her eyes lit up.

"I mean, your dad gave you the tip to pass on to me." Big Neil O'Rourke had a tolerance for vice, but no love for anyone who'd hurt a kid. He'd told me about the missing Tong kids.

The fat bookie knew what I was capable of, even if he didn't really understand some of the salient details. He'd been throwing me the odd collection gig for a couple of months, partly because I was good at it, and mostly because Gramma and I kept an eye on his baby girl. His daughter scheduled most of my work, so there was no way for them to avoid each other. They were at least on speaking terms again. Baby steps.

JOHNNY LYCAN & THE VEGAS BERSERKER

I continued, knowing it went straight up Bill's craw. "Almost to the exact house."

Her face broke out in a proud grin, making her look more like a high school kid than a twenty-one-year-old. "No shit? It didn't seem too clear."

It hadn't been, but a little exaggeration for a good cause was no sin. She got me to the right block at least, where the spire of St Susanna's was clearly visible. That was the key. I found the rest by the sight of unmown grass, blankets for curtains, and neglected paint. Shaggy confirmed it through the reek of meth and children's terror emanating from the basement window. "It was enough."

The ungrateful brat rewarded my kindness by taking every single trick. Bill cursed and threw his cards at me, then dutifully added up the score.

"God dammit. As your accountant, I need to warn you. Keep losing money like this and you won't be able to keep doing freebies. Especially when you give it to the help."

Meaghan gave him her best sneer—the one reserved for when he accused her of being overhead. One lip curled up and her blue eyes rolled to the top of her skull. Their truce was particularly precarious tonight. After all, she was my only employee, and part-time at that. She wasn't much of a burden. Plus, you know, saving kids should count for something. That she'd endeared herself to his grandmother bugged the hell out of him more than anything else.

Bill pushed himself away from the table. He rose unsteadily to his feet and braced himself on his arm-crutch. "Whatever. I'm going out for a bit." Then he turned and clomped out of the room. The three of us watched him go.

"Is he ever going to tell you?" Meaghan asked once he was safely out of earshot.

Gramma clucked her tongue. "When he's ready. How can the boy not know I know? Does he think I'm some kind of *gorger dinlow?*" She always slipped into Romani when she was especially annoyed, and "non-Romani idiot" was one of her favorites. "He's thirty, I ain't got no grandkids, and he lives with his grandmother. How can I not know? Not that I get decent intel from anyone else." That last was aimed at me.

Discretion was part of my job, and I never told her anything about Bill's love life. But since I lived in her basement apartment, this was a good time for me to keep my mouth shut and my head down. I wasn't blood, but knew what it was like to be a victim of that sharp tongue. Time to light out before it turned on me.

After a hard night's werewolfing, I hadn't slept well. The Blackhawks were playing on the West Coast, so I could catch the last couple of periods in my apartment downstairs, blessedly alone. Meaghan's phone buzzed and interrupted my escape. She looked at me and held up a finger. "It's him."

I didn't have to ask, 'him who?'

She put on her best secretary's voice. "J Lupul and Associates. Yes, sir. Ten o'clock. I'll tell him."

"Why's he calling you?" Gramma asked.

Meaghan stared daggers at me. "Because he's Johnny's biggest client. And I actually pick up when he calls."

She had a point. I was forever losing my phone when I wasn't ignoring it. I hated the damned electronic umbilical cord. "Ten. Got it."

Time for my monthly chat with Malcolm Cromwell.

Crap.

CHAPTER 3

3 days past full moon. Waning gibbous.

I knew better than to be late, so it was nine fifty-five when the ultra-shiny brass elevator doors opened outside Cromwell's penthouse. At nine fifty-six, I pressed the buzzer. At nine fifty-six and three seconds, the door opened.

"Come on in. He's expecting you." Nurse Ball answered the door. Sure, I knew the woman in the starched white uniform in front of me was the same Francine Ball who'd helped rescue the kids and, several times a month, engaged in some of the most intense sex of my life. When working she was Nurse Ball; dark hair pulled tight back, hospital ward shoes, white seamed stockings. She was not to be trifled with.

On the clock for Malcolm Cromwell, I was simply The Help, and she treated me that way. Of course, that was one of her favorite little games to play other times, but at the moment she meant it in the traditional sense.

"Mr. Cromwell told me to bring you right in," she said loudly enough to be heard in the office at the end of the hall. Then she dropped her voice. "He's not having one of his better days. Try not to upset him."

Rather than make a promise I couldn't keep, I just nodded. It's not like I tried to make the old fart cranky every time we talked, it just worked out that way half the time. Not a great business best-practice when you've got exactly one regular paying client.

From the corridor, I saw his polished aircraft carrier of a desk, but not Old Man Cromwell. That meant he was in his hospital bed, and his kidneys were acting up. As Nurse Ball ushered me in, it was clear today was indeed a rough one. My odds against pissing him off dropped.

He was sitting on the edge of the bed. Cromwell was head-down over some papers, his feet dangling over the side in leather slippers. The old man raised his eyes when he heard us come in. The watery blue orbs sunk into fleshy blue-black rings. Not one of his better days, for sure.

The old man tugged the plush robe about himself to cover up his bony, gray-haired chest and forced his chapped lips into what was intended to be a smile. It wound up more like a creepy sneer. He did that a lot, so I just smiled back, as if I wasn't a little freaked out.

"Lupul. Good, good. Glad you're here," he said like he conducted business from a hospital bed every day of the week.

Sticking out his hand to shake mine, Nurse Ball intercepted the bony, almost transparent wrist. She intended to take his pulse, but he waved her away like a petulant brat. "You can do that later. I'm not going anywhere, goddammit."

She looked over at me for help, but I knew better than to get between those two. This duet had been playing long before I showed up. I shoved my hands into my pockets and waited to see who was going to take this round. To my surprise, it was Cromwell.

"Fine, sir. Can I at least check your readings?"

For an answer, she got a dismissive wave, and Cromwell turned his attention to me. "Ready to get back to work, or are you too busy saving the goddamned world?"

Over his shoulder, Francine shrugged to let me know she had said nothing about our extracurricular project, but my boss knew anyway. Not at all creepy. I wondered for a moment if he knew I'd been playing

JOHNNY LYCAN & THE VEGAS BERSERKER

doctor with his nurse for the last couple of months. Probably. Even creepier.

I kept my game face on. "Of course, sir. What can I do for you?"

"I need you to go to London for me. Is that going to be a problem?"

My heart pounded a bit, a mix of excitement and disappointment. I'd never been overseas, much as I'd always wanted to, but this was a conversation I didn't want to have yet. "Ummm. Yeah, it is, actually."

"You still haven't got your passport yet, have you?"

Great, the I'm-disappointed-in-you voice. My favorite.

"I've tried. The name change isn't legal yet, and I can't get my passport until it's done." The State of Illinois website promised it would take eight to ten weeks to change my adopted name, McPherson, to my birth name, Lupul. Illinois being Illinois, I was into week fourteen and counting.

Cromwell scowled. "The passport I can help expedite. God himself can't help this clusterfuck of a state." He wasn't wrong. When bribery and influence can't get the job done, the bureaucracy was beyond hope. "Alright, fine. Plan B."

He turned to his attending angel. "Excuse us."

Nurse Ball took an obvious moment jotting down some numbers from the dialysis machine, then slammed the notebook shut. Her voice was more compliant than the look in her eyes. "Of course, sir."

Hating the tension, I tried to help. "Hey, if she's doing something important there, that's fine. I don't mind."

Cromwell's voice was icy. "This, you don't want anyone to hear."

Given the kinds of jobs she did for him after hours, not to mention what she and I had been up to, that was a little ominous. After all, it was Francine who'd been responsible for removing Kozlov's half-werewolf corpse from the warehouse as Cromwell's price for helping me. She'd also stitched me back together after that fight. Other than my Social Security Number, there wasn't a lot left she didn't know. I was only guessing about that one.

With more crashing and banging than necessary, she put everything away. As she brushed past, she put an arm on mine.

Knowing my hearing was far better than the old man's, she whispered, "I need to talk when you're done."

If Cromwell suspected anything, he didn't show it. His impatient hands waved me towards him. "Help me to my desk, please."

We shuffle-walked to his desk chair, where he plunked down with an "oof" and a grimace. His claws dug into my bicep when I moved to get around to the other side. "No, I need you to see something."

Bony fingers stabbed furiously at the keyboard, and a familiar-looking spreadsheet popped up on the screen. "Recognize this?"

I did. It was a list of cities, code names for objects he coveted, and numbers with so many commas it was hard to believe they were prices. I'd seen the list before. Some items had changed position since I'd looked last. There was no need to list the Anubis Disk, for one thing. It was in The Archives, wherever they were. Hopefully miles underground encased in concrete. There weren't any more Chicago items listed.

"That's the wish list of stuff you're trying to collect, right?"

He harrumphed. "Not trying. Have to. But you'll notice that most of them are overseas. London, Budapest, Jakarta. You're useless to me without a passport."

Nice. He wasn't wrong, but it still stung. I pointed halfway down the page. "What's that Las Vegas one? That's in the U.S."

"And that's Plan B. We can check it off the list while we get your little bureaucratic snafu handled. It's not critical, but it's—what's your word for it?—nonfuckupable. Just pick up an item and bring it back. It's all bought and paid for, but I'd like to make sure it actually arrives. I presume you can fly to Las Vegas in three weeks?"

Oh boy. Another conversation I'd been avoiding. "I could, sure. Of course, sir. Do you think I'd be able to drive out instead?"

"You don't fly?" His voice was more tired than angry. Francine would be pissed. I was ruining his day. It takes a lot of talent to be more stressful than organ failure.

"Not if I can help it."

"Nervous flier?"

'Something like that, yeah." *Locking a hairy, homicidal, rage monster in a metal tube at thirty-six thousand feet with flight delays, a bunch of crying babies, entitled carry-on clutchers, and smelly lavatories for five or six hours over open water. What could go wrong?*

His breath reeked of halitosis and resignation. "In this case, it's not critical. The Egg's likely a fake, anyway. Purely decorative. Unlike these other items. Sure. You can drive out. But I want it here first of the month. You pay for your own gas. It's a tax write-off. Mostoy can explain it to you."

Bill would, indeed, but that wasn't my question. "An egg?"

He nodded and held his hands a foot apart. "Probably Native American. Crystal. About the size of a football. More decorative than anything. But I have to make you earn your money this month."

"If this one's a fake, why the rush?"

Cromwell steepled his fingers and bowed his head for a second. He raised it and looked at the closed window blinds across the room. "I'm dying, is the rush. Oh, Nurse Ball and modern medicine are doing their best, but I'm not stupid. What I am is determined. I need to try some... less orthodox methods of preserving my life. I'm not ready to go without a fight. This won't keep me alive, but until you can travel, I'll have to settle for what I can get."

Desperate, determined. Potato, potahto. He wasn't beyond taking a dead Lycan for examination and stripping him for parts. "That's why you wanted Kozslov's body?" I'd never given much thought to what he did with the Russian's corpse. I was too busy being grateful it wasn't mine.

He ignored my question. "You seem to have recovered nicely, by the way."

"I heal fast."

"That's another thing I wanted to talk to you about. The part you probably don't want to share with anyone." More click-clacking and a popular genealogy site appeared on the screen. After log-in, he called up a list of very science-y looking words.

Cromwell spun his chair towards me, the light in his eyes growing along with his energy. "One of the tests we ran on your—friend— looked at his DNA. Of course, part of the challenge was to separate his from yours. All that blood, hair, what have you. So, I figured what the hell? I ran your DNA as well. Know what we found?"

"You ran a DNA test on me without asking? Is that legal?"

"Is killing a fellow human being with an Egyptian relic legal? Stay focused, for Chrissake. I found something you're going to want to know. Can I continue?"

My head nodded without my brain's permission. What the holy hell I was getting into this time?

"Good man. As you know, your... gift... can be transmitted through a bite. Probably bacterial or viral, but transmittable, nonetheless. In your case, though, you were born with it. It's genetic. One test we ran was the geographic dispersal of your particular traits. With me so far?"

"Barely."

"Good enough." He waved his spotty, wrinkled hand like a magician. "Ta da."

With a single click, a map of the world appeared. It had a couple of pale pink dots in North America, two or three in what looked like China, and a bright red circle somewhere in the middle of Europe. A couple of mouse taps, and the map expanded.

"Do you ever wonder how many people share that particular genetic trait? As you can see, not all that many. That's probably a good thing, I suppose. A few people have scattered hither and yon, but look at this. Nearly everyone on your family tree is here. And has been for hundreds of years without leaving or spreading out.

I leaned in, my pissiness replaced with curiosity. "Where's that?"

Now he studied me, aching to see my reaction when he sprung his surprise. "Cluj-Napoca. Romania."

I was too stunned to worry if my face betrayed me or not. Cluj. Where I was born. Where Shaggy recalled more clearly than I did the scene: children in isolation wards and filthy cribs. Signs that read

"AIDS," and *"Riscantă."* Where the orphanage couldn't hand me over to the McPhersons fast enough, and my folks were so happy to find a white baby, they didn't ask questions about his origins.

All my spinning head could muster up was, "Huh."

Cromwell's response to my response was a hacking cough that shook his entire body and forced him to clutch his stomach. I stood, helpless, as he gasped for breath. I turned to yell for Francine, but he waved at me not to call her.

When he could speak, he choked out, "Seems nearly all your family has lived there for generations, keeping the bloodline pure. If, of course, pure bloodlines were of interest to, uh, researchers."

Despite not really getting all of that, the hairs on the back of my neck stood up, anyway. I've seen enough movies and read enough science fiction to know when people talk about bloodlines and purity, let alone actively research the subject, things can get ugly in a hurry. I needed to say something clever and change the subject.

"Huh."

Frigging brilliant comeback. That'll show him.

"None of which matters much if you can't get there, so... Plan B it is. I'll make all the arrangements with the owner in Vegas and let you know."

"Yeah, okay. Yes, sir."

Cromwell dropped his voice, "Help me get back to that goddamned bed so the warden doesn't lose her mind."

We'd barely accomplished that feat and pulled the blanket over his knees when the door flew open and Hurricane Francine blew in. Twenty bucks says she was listening at the door. After some fussing and pretend-compliance from Cromwell, she offered to see me out.

Once we were in the living room, she whispered, "I didn't tell him anything about those kids."

I believed her. "Does he know about... everything else?"

"He didn't hear it from me."

"But he knows?"

"What do you think?" That meant she knew I knew he knew. *Great.*

Taking my elbow, she directed me towards the door, her eyes searching for cameras we both knew were there.

Francine's voice dropped even lower. "Speaking of which, care to come by tonight?"

It hadn't been a week yet since the full moon. "I want to, but it's probably not safe yet."

"You take all the fun out of it. But I've been doing some thinking about that. Do you think we wouldn't have to worry about that if we used some restraints?"

At first, I thought she'd said, 'use some restraint,' and it was a little late for that. Then I realized what she was asking.

"Wait. You want to tie me up?"

Francine mistook confusion for resistance.

"Scared, big fella?"

"I just... I've never done that. Like handcuffs or what?"

She grinned. "Relax, they're not regulation handcuffs. That's a rookie mistake."

"I'm a rookie."

She grinned, and the tip of her tongue caressed the corner of her mouth. "I'm not."

How did she always manage to turn me on and scare the bejeezus out of me at the same time?

A delicious thought occurred to me. "I don't suppose you could come to Vegas, could you?"

CHAPTER 4

7 Days before the full moon- First quarter moon

"You got a minute?" Meaghan stood in my doorway in her traditional hoodie and Blackhawks cap. She seldom came down here. It was just simpler for me to go up to Gramma and Bill's apartment, since Meaghan spent more time up there. More than that, it was clean and sunny. I lived in a basement apartment that was not very inviting, for starters. Plus, I kept my place about as clean as you'd imagine a single guy who was half wild animal did. It was far more hygienic upstairs.

I motioned her inside. Something about her was different. She smelled like something besides drug store shampoo. "Are you wearing makeup?" I was pretty sure her lashes weren't always that dark, and I smelled the slightly bitter scent of cruelty-free mascara. Her eyes, now that they weren't constantly bloodshot, were her best feature. I also forgot how skinny she was, although after hanging around Gramma for so long, she'd gone from emaciated to "could-use-a-few-pounds."

"No. Well, yeah. I have.... This thing later."

I wasn't a legally licensed private eye for nothing. "What's his name?"

"Ha ha." She paused. "Shut up. I need to talk to you."

"Do you want to go upstairs? I mean it's..."

"No, I don't want Gramma to know I'm here." Keeping anything from the old girl was a neat trick, and usually Meaghan knew better than to even try. This was weird, but intriguing.

I pulled out a chair from my recently acquired kitchen set and motioned her to sit. She looked surprised.

"You actually bought furniture?" For someone five months out of rehab and dressed like a ten-year-old gym teacher, it was pretty judge-y.

"You know me. Adulting like a boss. What's going on?"

She sat down and picked at the laces of her hoody. "When do you go to Las Vegas?"

I had to be back by the end of the month. I figured three long days there, two days in Las Vegas to pick up whatever it was, and three back. "Wednesday, Thursday at the latest. Why?"

"Do you have to go?" I just looked at her.

"If I want to get paid, I do. What's going on, Megs?"

She bit her lip and avoided my eyes. "Don't tell Gramma I'm here. Okay?"

Now it was getting weird. "O-o-kay. Why not? Is it because you don't want her to know you have a date?"

She laughed. "Hell no. She says it's high time I... and I quote... got my ashes hauled. Old people talk so weird."

"So, what's the problem?"

"She thinks I'm making a big deal out of nothing, but I don't think you should go."

"Are the cards talking to you again? Because you know those things hate me, anyway."

She shook her head. "Just a feeling. Every time I hear you and Las Vegas in the same sentence, I get the jeebies." A few months ago, I'd have chalked a nervous reaction like that up to drugs or immaturity. Now I knew better than to just ignore when she got a vibe about something.

"What can go wrong? I don't gamble, don't drink much, or chase women—"

"Except *her*." Meaghan had a serious problem with Francine and my—well, it wasn't a relationship exactly—but whatever it was, the young woman didn't approve.

JOHNNY LYCAN & THE VEGAS BERSERKER

"If it makes you feel better, she's not going with me, so my virtue is safe." I wiggled my eyebrows, knowing dirty jokes made the kid uncomfortable, which was half the fun.

"Ew." *Mission accomplished.* She reached into the pouch on her sweatshirt and pulled out her Tarot deck. It was brand new just a couple of months ago, but was already looking a little ratty. "Can I do a reading on you? Just to make sure?"

"If you can." My Lycan abilities have the same impact on psychic energy that lemon juice has on paper cuts.

"I just need you to shuffle them up, then you can step back." Her black-outlined eyes were deadly serious. I nodded. She relaxed a bit and put the deck on the table and spread the cards out face down. I reached over and messed them up for a minute. Then I stepped back and rested my ass against the kitchen sink. The further away, the less static she got on her spiritual receiver.

Shaggy whimpered from a dark space in the back of my head. He had an animal's distrust of the unusual, and he wasn't happy. I told him to sit down and shut up. I'd seen Meaghan and Gramma do this a hundred times and recognized the basic moves. She ignored me, focusing as she peeled off ten cards. A simple reading used five. Ten was going nuclear.

"A Celtic Cross spread? You're not messing around, are you?"

"Shush." I listened as she mumbled to herself the position and purpose of each card. "Internal, external, fears, outcome." That was the last card, and she slapped it down and studied the layout.

Knowing better than to open my yap, I studied her as she worked the Tarot cards. She'd become more proficient and confident in the months under Gramma Mostoy's tutelage. Much as the old girl would never admit, Meaghan might actually be better with the cards than she was, although Gramma was a grandmaster with the crystal ball.

Being young and not great at self-control, Meaghan usually spewed the first thing that entered her head. That was supposedly a rule of Tarot. Don't second guess yourself, just say what the cards tell you. Now she was taking an awfully long time, using her finger to indicate one card, then the other. Whether I believed in it or not, I was dying to know what she found. I bit my lip and waited.

Finally, she looked up, paler than usual. "This is really messed up. You really have to go, right?"

"Yeah. What's it telling you?"

She held her hand over the first couple of cards. "There's chaos. Like a thunderstorm, only it's..." She struggled for the words. "It's like a storm of magic."

I thought I disguised the snort pretty well, but she glared at me. "Shut up. That's what it says. A storm of magic. And women."

That was statistically likely. Fifty percent of the people I meet there will probably not be men. Doesn't seem like such a big deal.

"Women, plural? Cool." This was accompanied by more eyebrow wiggling.

"Yes, plural. And don't be such a guy. I'm serious."

"Are they good women or bad women?"

"Neither. Both. I don't know." Meaghan looked off into the distance as she spoke.

"So, a storm of magic we don't know what and a bunch of women that might or might not be bad. Thanks for stopping by."

"That's just the appetizer. The worst thing makes no sense at all. What are you going to do there?"

I shrugged. "I'll know all the details tomorrow, but it's just some old Indian relic, made out of crystal. Cromwell says it's just a replica— a fake. That's all I know. What do you see?"

"Cold light." She said it like there was going to be organ music. Didn't mean squat to me.

"Cold light." She said it again, slower, like I didn't understand the first time.

"Okay." Repeating it didn't make it clearer or scarier.

She bit her lip. "And Johnny. Whatever it is? It's not a fake."

CHAPTER 5

Six days before the full moon- waxing gibbous

Say this for Malcolm Cromwell. When he had to, he scrubbed up okay. Today, the old codger wore a suit that cost more than my car and shoes so polished the reflected light hurt my eyes.

"Board meeting. Whiny bastards think I'm not up to running the place anymore." He stood without help and offered himself for inspection.

I might not have a medical degree, but this looked like improvement. "That's great. All that dialysis is working?"

He cackled. "Nah. This is some of Nurse Ball's magic juju juice. Full of vitamins and crap that's illegal in five states. She shoots me full of it, rolls me out in front of the weasels. It's enough to get me out, get me through, get me home. I'll be useless for two days after, but I'll still have control of my company."

I wasn't that surprised to hear Francine was doing something medically sketchy. I didn't think for a second she'd do anything that would permanently hurt him, even if she was probably in the old guy's will. No. Her ethical code was like a bungee cord, flexible and stretchy as hell, but ultimately unbreakable. There were limits she wouldn't exceed. She was good at her job, as evidenced by how chipper he was.

Cromwell called me in to give me all the last-minute details of my trip to Las Vegas. He still wasn't happy that I wasn't flying out, but wasn't overly concerned. Time wasn't the big problem.

"By agreement, the current owner has it until the end of the month. Then she turns it over to me. She runs some rinky-dink tourist trap and uses it in her stage show. There's no rush. It's not perishable or dangerous. My guy in Vegas says I've definitely bought a fake. But hell, I paid for it. I want it."

I couldn't argue with that logic. One thing didn't make sense. "Why did you pay so much for it if it's a fake?"

"Because somebody else wanted it. Dumb bastard kept running up the bid until I finally pulled a number out of my ass that he couldn't match."

"You bought it out of spite?" How much had he spent on something just to tick someone else off?

"Mostly. Clive Bowden and I have history. And the thing has a hell of a backstory, shame it's all horseshit. You'll see when you get there."

Cromwell took a couple of long, confident steps towards his desk. Two strides away, he paused and his body shook, then he reached out and staggered forward til he reached his chair. His eyes were wide with surprise. Whatever just happened, he didn't expect it. I ran to him and grabbed his arm, which he shook until I let him go.

"Get the hell off me. Dammit. If I can't fool an amateur like you, I sure as hell won't be able to bamboozle those idiots. Gimme a second." He dropped his head, sucked in a breath, and held it a moment. Then he lifted his head with clearer eyes and took his seat, like nothing happened. If Malcolm Cromwell had a superpower, it was pure stubborn denial. It was kind of impressive.

Francine would never forgive me if he died on my watch. "Where's Nurse Ball? Shouldn't she be watching you? "

Cromwell dismissed the notion with an impatient gesture. "Sent her to do something else. She's always hovering. Man needs his privacy, sometimes."

Cromwell waved a manila envelope at me. "Here are all the details—addresses and such. Hotel, meals, all paid for once you get there. Since you insist on going by horse and buggy, you pick up your own expenses on the way there and back. Hopefully, your name change will come through in the meantime and you can start acting like a functioning adult."

Again. Ouch. Accurate, but still.

"This is pretty simple. I want you to meet with my provenance guy. He'll give you proof of authenticity—or not, also help supervise the handoff with the owner. Lemuel's like a notary public, only not so public, if you get my meaning."

"Your providence guy—"

He rolled his watery eyes at me. "Pro-ve-nance. It means he's—"

"I know what provenance is. Does he have a name besides Provenance Guy?" I'd been there ten minutes, which was three minutes longer than it usually took for him to grate on me. I was building up a tolerance for his asshole attitude. Signs of growth.

"Ah. Lemuel Collins. He lives in Vegas. Has for years. I use him on all my important acquisitions. He has a… a knack… for finding out the truth about objects. Their history and what all. I wouldn't use him on this one except he already lives there. Plus, you should know him. He's a good man."

There was always a "but," when he described people. He didn't say anything more, so I did. "He's a good man but..."

"But nothing. He's a good man. Known him for more years than either of us cares to admit." This Lemuel must be some kind of saint with that kind of recommendation. Or the old man was going soft.

"This is a simple pickup and retrieval. Don't make it a, what do the kids call it? A thing. You tend to complicate matters unnecessarily. You're not saving the world, you're bringing a souvenir back from Vegas."

Definitely not going soft. I'd never met a real saint before, something to look forward to.

CHAPTER 6

One thing I learned in those years building Waffle Huts is that, while beautiful, this country is inconveniently large. No matter which way you drive coast-to-coast, there will be at least one day that's just a long-ass drive through miles and miles of nothing. I knew the Midwest and northern states pretty well, so figured I'd switch things up and do the whole Southwest, Route Sixty-Six thing.

They built the Charger for trips like this, at least on paper. Flat roads for hours at a stretch sounded like muscle-car heaven. In reality, the Mother Road has mostly been replaced by interstate highways with identical off-ramp fast food every thirty miles separated by the most boring countryside ever. And I'd driven through downstate Illinois. Still, you could safely go eighty for most of it, which has been scientifically proven to be the ideal speed for listening to AC/DC.

I was five days away from the full moon, and Shaggy should have been present but curled up waiting for the big night. Instead, he was itchy and pissed off, leaving me permanently grumpy. The good news was I'd gotten better at keeping him under control when I needed to. The problem, it turned out, is that when he doesn't get to go full-Lycan each cycle, it's like he banks energy, and has to find other ways to let go of all that nastiness. This resulted in my getting really snappy with people, making me look like an asshole. On the road, at least, I

JOHNNY LYCAN & THE VEGAS BERSERKER

could take all the anger and frustration out on the gas pedal, roaring past all the trucks and RVs that were minding their own business.

I checked the route multiple times. If you're going from Chicago to the Pacific by that route, it's pretty hard to avoid Amarillo, Texas. There's nothing but cows, scrub brush and truck stops for hours in any direction and if you overshoot it, the next stop is New Mexico. What the hell, I thought. I'd never been to Texas. What could go wrong?

Amarillo is exactly like the hundreds of square miles around it... flat, colorless, and ideal for cattle. People were a secondary consideration and just made do. They compensated for the lack of reason for civic pride by latching onto the one thing they did lay claim to. They lived in Texas.

Boy, were they in Texas. Everywhere you went, there were Lone Star flags in places that sold Lone Star beer displaying, "Don't Mess with Texas," signs. That, plus the hats and belt buckles the size of hubcaps, all served to remind me I wasn't in Chicago anymore. Even the waffle iron at the cheap hotel I was spending the night in turned out half-raw, half-burned creations in the shape of the state. It said so right at the top of the website. Clearly that was more of a selling feature than the hot tub and two-treadmill gym.

It was a bit early to be off the road, but I had to stop somewhere and at least this town I had heard of. Truthfully, I got sucked in by the multiple billboards for the Big Texan Steak Ranch—Home of the Seventy-Two Ounce Steak. I toyed with the notion of going for it—if you finished the sucker it was free—but I'd have had to go full Shaggy. While turning into a hairy, slobbering monster wasn't technically against the rules, it wasn't really worth finding out.

Instead, after settling in, I asked the pretty Latina behind the registration desk for food recommendations. At first she rattled off a bunch of chain restaurants, before I held my hand up. "No, I mean the good stuff. This is Texas, right? Where's the best Tex-Mex in town?"

"I don't know. I'm, like, vegan? But my aunt has a place—"

Jackpot. If you live in Chicago long enough, you'll learn two phrases that will make your life worth living. The first is "I got a guy." No matter what you need, someone has the hook-up for anything you need cheap. And probably legal, if that matters to you. Car repairs, plumbing, pest removal of all kinds, find someone with a "guy."

The second is "My aunt has a place." That guarantees the best ethnic food in town. It will be cheap and not much for décor. Screw the health department, it will be the real deal, and probably the best you ever ate. Pro-tip: park somewhere you can see your car.

Lupe didn't steer me wrong. The place was sketchy as hell, and the Chile Rellenos the gooiest and best ever. They lasted about two minutes. To the shock of the waitress, who looked like someone had put an air hose in her cousin Lupe and turned it on high, I ordered a second dish of Carnitas—hold the rice and beans—just to keep Shaggy happy. Plus, they were absolutely delicious.

I waddled out of the place, rubbing my furry belly. The Blackhawks were playing the Stars tonight in a meaningless game since both were long out of the playoff hunt, but it might be fun to watch in enemy territory. Time to find an appropriate dive bar.

Any good resident of the Second City knows that you really get to know a place from its taverns and local joints. At home, the scarier the place looked, the friendlier the people in it.

This wasn't home. First, the minute I walked in, I felt terribly under-dressed. I was the only person not carrying a gun for all the world to see. In a fit of civic responsibility, I'd left my Ruger in my room safe. Now I might as well have worn a gigantic neon sign that said, "Not from here."

Second, I had to ask for one of the TVs to be turned from a replay of the Two Thousand and Ten Red River bowl—Texas and Oklahoma—to the live hockey game. Amarillo might be in the Stars' media market. It sure wasn't the target demographic.

"Must be your car with the Illinois plates," the big guy in the Dallas Cowboys cap—a giant star, of course—pronounced it *Illinoise*. His holster rode on his hip, cowboy-style. His two buddies, much smaller guns also visible, laughed like that was hysterical. I immediately connected him to the brand-new Silverado with the giant rims and the shiny dual exhausts parked in front of the bar.

Crap.

I nodded politely to the Cowboys fan and asked for a Shiner Bock, the only alternative being Lone Star. A middle-aged woman with gray hair and a Toby Keith tee-shirt slapped down a napkin, placed the bottle on top and slapped the bar. "Here ya go, hon. Welcome to Amarilla."

Toasting her with the bottle, I offered a half-hearted, "Thanks," and looked around. I wasn't feeling the place and figured on having one beer, watch the Hawks give up another power-play goal, and head back. If I got an early enough start, it would be twelve hours to Vegas straight through.

Shaggy's super-hearing wasn't helping my mood. The juke box blared country music, but at least some old, good stuff. The nasal twang was compounded by the drone from the television, the clatter of bottles and ice poured into wells, and the loud *har-har-har* of the big guy and his two skinny flunkies. All in all, the recipe for a whopper of a headache.

One beer and out is a pretty good rule when drinking by myself and it kept me out of a lot of situations in which a guy with a bad temper and control issues shouldn't find himself. "How much do I owe you?" I asked the bartender.

"Four fifty, sugar."

"Martha." The big guy's voice boomed down the bar.

"Keep yer shirt on."

He waggled his whiskey glass back and forth. "Since when do the tourists drink first? Another one."

"Since they say please and thank you, you fat bastard." That was when I made my mistake. I laughed. Not even a good chuckle, just a single, "Ha." It was enough.

"Something funny?"

Shaggy perked up, and I felt him sniff the air, sensing trouble.

Not here. Just walk away.

I put a five and a single on the bar. "Thanks, Martha. You have a good night."

Five steps from the door, I heard a "Hey," but kept walking.

A bell rang over the door as I left. Two seconds later, I heard it again. Someone was right behind me, and I didn't need Lycan senses to know who it was. Cowboy fan and his buddies stood on the concrete doorstep. "I asked you a question, asshole. You find something funny?"

The hair on my arms stood up like it always did when violence was in the air. I tried to avoid fights whenever possible, but sometimes it just felt so good to hit someone. This guy's face was eminently punchable.

Walk away, just ignore him. "Nope. It's all good."

The two skinny guys were enjoying this more than necessary. I heard a whoop, then boots on concrete, and one of them brushed past me. He turned and leaned against the Charger's rear fender, crossing his arms.

Rationally, getting in a fight in Amarillo, Texas, on a Monday night when I had work to do was a terrible idea. Scrapping with an armed idiot was no smarter. Didn't matter, it had been a while since I'd really worked out my issues on someone, and these guys were intent on dragging me into a fight whether I wanted to cooperate or not.

"Get off my car. Please." It wouldn't do any good. It wasn't supposed to. Street fights have a format and rhythm to them. Most normal people think fights are *about* something. Some are, but most times guys who like to fight decide they're going to fight, they just need an excuse. Then there's the half-assed attempt to avoid violence, which doesn't fool anyone but frees your conscience. *Hey, I asked him nicely.*

There's even less reason for polite attempts at reconciliation when both parties want to fight and I wanted it as bad as this guy did. There's a toxic chemical cocktail that gets stirred up when there's violence afoot. Sure, there's the same "mine is bigger than yours" that men have always enjoyed, but you can get that in sports, or beating a guy at cards. It's purely garden-variety testosterone.

The feeling's like having a beer versus moonshine. A good fight builds up all those macho chemicals with a shot of "it's forbidden," and tosses in a dash of potential death or injury. The male mind—at least those of us on the Cro-Magnon end of the spectrum—come as close as we can to overdosing on the rush of cortisol, adrenaline, plus a giant shot of dopamine. And that's assuming you don't have a werewolf cheering you on, waiting for their chance at the other guy.

The social niceties having been observed, it was time to move on. I breathed as deeply as I could without obviously bracing for an attack. When you're getting jumped by more than one guy, there were two scenarios. One, the boss could send his flunkies in first to soften you up and test your mettle before he steps in and finishes the job. The other is for him to get his shots in, weaken you, then let the others finish you off. Kind of like a lion stepping aside for the hyenas. A gang leader does this when he wants to toss his boys a bone and make them feel like they're tougher than they are.

Best guess was, Cowboys Fan was a sacrifice-his-pawns kind of guy. That was fine with me. It wouldn't take much to remove this first guy from the board. Plus, his stupid belt buckle was scratching my Charger's orange paint job. I guess part of me still needed that reason.

Skinny Jerk Number One must have expected more preamble, because my hands flew out and grabbed him by his shirt. I growled at him, "I said please." Then, with a little Shaggy assistance, I flung him across the sidewalk into the wall. His head made a lovely crunching sound and set off the first drip of dopamine. Before he could say anything else, he crumpled up, rubbing his head and moaning at the sight of his own blood.

The second, crazier looking guy had been expecting to come at me—likely from behind—while his buddy distracted me. Now he had my undivided attention and wasn't sure what to do with it. He sent a quick look over his shoulder, checking in with the leader, then back at me. He was a tad cockeyed, so his eyes looked in slightly different directions, but both were equally wide with fear.

I felt the feral grin spread across my face. This was so. Much. Fun. In general, I had the decency to feel bad about hurting anyone who didn't deserve it. But when they did... that's why I was good muscle for guys like O'Rourke. By the time they had to deal with me, the jury had convicted them and I was just doing my job.

Number Two clenched his fists, thumbs inside. I let him take the first swing, gambling he'd hurt his hand worse than me. Sure enough, he landed a glancing blow to my cheek, but let out a shout and held his hand, shaking it and cursing.

Ignoring his whining, I elbowed the loser aside and focused on the only guy that worried me. Cowboy Fan had gone quiet, which made me take him more seriously. He had the same nasty look on his face I did. The odds weren't as good with this one.

That would make it more fun.

"Come on, asshole." His voice was steady as he beckoned me forward.

Good strategy.

Countering an attack told you more about your opponent than going at him, and he'd already misread me once. Unfortunately for him, I'd read the same textbook.

I upset my head. "Nah, you started this. Show me what you got or get the hell out of my way." From the way he squinted, he momentarily considered the second option, but by then, his boys had risen to their feet. They looked to him for vengeance. Good sense was no longer an option for him.

He was big, he was not too bright, and he was from Texas. Odds were good he'd played football and wasn't smart enough to be a quarterback. Defensive linebacker, then. I lifted my fists nice and high, covering my face but exposing my gut. Predictably, he lowered his head like a bull and charged.

The dumb bastard thought I was going to fight fair. My brain was already exploding like pop rocks by now and the usual rules didn't matter.

When he was two steps away, I lifted my knee and caught him under the chin. His head snapped up and he let out a bovine grunt as he hit the ground. Now that I had his attention, it was time to teach him a lesson.

The big guy rolled on his back, probably trying to clear his head. I straddled his chest and got right in his face. It was all I could do not to snap my teeth at him. Shaggy wanted his turn, but this was all me. "You know what was funny? That a dumb-ass hick like you thought you could beat me." Then I hammered a short right to the nose.

I don't know who was happier to see the blood spurt, me or Shaggy. He was adding his own Lycan -specific neurochemicals to mine, and I was high as hell on the violence. A left to one side of the guy's head rewarded me with a healthy thud. Then a right to the other side of his head. If this scrap had been about something, it would have ended right there. But the fight itself was the point, and I wasn't done.

For the hell of it, I grabbed his bloody face and head-butted him just to feel the burn on my scalp. My eyes saw everything through a red film, and I think I let out a whoop.

It could have gone a lot worse for Cowboy Fan, but my Shaggy ears picked up a thick metallic click. That was a safety catch on a shotgun.

"Okay, stop this shit." I let go of my opponent and turned to see Martha standing in the doorway. The lamplight formed a halo around her head, but that sawed-off Remington in her hand was anything but angelic.

The stupid, out-of-control part of me would gladly have charged her too, but there were enough embers of good sense left. I lifted my hands, although I let out a very non-human growl.

Her face was a mixture of admiration and disgust. "*Goddamn,* boy."

I looked at the guy on the ground. Yeah, goddamn about summed it up. I got myself under control enough to speak. "I... he started it."

WAYNE TURMEL

"I know who started it. But he's going to be back in here in a night or two. And you aren't." She lifted her head and pointed the gun at the sidewalk. "Are you?"

I raised both hands and stepped back. "No ma'am. I sure won't."

She raised the gun again, and I caught my breath.

"And you two idiots. Get him out of here before the cops show up."

Jerk One just mumbled, "Yes'm."

I dug into my pocket for my keys, then moved without turning my back to the bartender and unlocked my car.

"Uh, thanks."

Martha raised her head at the distant sound of sirens, then looked from the guy on the ground back to me. "I have no idea who did this to him, but you'd best not be here when the cops arrive."

It was my turn to say, "Yes, ma'am."

"Goddamn, boy."

She was right. I had to get moving. My body throbbed with unspent energy, but this was no time to speed through a strange town and attract attention. I drove off in the opposite direction from the blue and red flashing lights.

Jesus H Christ on a sofa, Lupul. What the hell are you thinking?

35

CHAPTER 7

Three days before the full moon- waxing gibbous.

After three days of driving along what was left of Route 66, it was a
relief to see the glow of Las Vegas appear over the hills ahead like the
Northern Lights. Truthfully, I'd have been just as happy to see
Topeka, Kansas, or Winslow, Arizona. While driving across the desert
sounds romantic, it's empty and boring, especially by yourself. That's
why it's called a desert, duh. Lesson learned.

On the other hand, driving at eighty miles an hour, "Kashmir,"
blaring on the satellite radio with the lights getting nearer and
brighter almost made the last three days' worth it. Nearly.

It looked douchey, but I had my sunglasses on even as the sky
turned purple and orange above the Eiffel tower and that big-ass
balloon. Being three days from high tide, my eyes were sensitive as
hell to the brightness of the billboards and all those lights flashing.
Part of me—the big dumb kid from Downers Grove—was dazzled.
The rest of me was pretty much done with Vegas by the time I got to
the pull-in at Caesar's Palace.

I may or may not have gunned the engine unnecessarily in the
valet line. My dusty, bug-splattered muscle car looked wildly out of
place among the Porsches, Benzes, Lexuses—Lexi? I don't know—in
the queue but the dirty looks from the snooty assholes were balanced
out by the thumbs up and grins from the bell guys and valet drivers.

A Latino kid in a buzz cut, bow tie and black vest bent low to my window. "Whoa." Then he caught himself and replaced the warm grin with the official, cheesy version. "Welcome to Caesar's, sir."

If the kid was surprised by the dusty, low-rent guy wearing sunglasses and a Sox cap at night, it didn't show. He was too dazzled by the car. "What do you have in this thing? Oh, sorry. Here." He reached into the back seat for the duffle bag that was all the luggage I had.

"A five point seven hemi."

His face lit up like it was Christmas. "V-8, really? Gas mileage must be for shit, but then chicks don't care about miles per gallon, am I right?"

"Got that right." I didn't say that to his face because I was staring like a rube at the white and gold monstrosity that was Caesar's fricking Palace.

This was a mistake. Cromwell knew it was my first time in Las Vegas and probably thought he was doing me a big favor by putting me in its most famous hotel. Or maybe he just assumed that everyone would stay at the most expensive place given the opportunity and someone else picking up the tab. Either way, this fish was way out of water.

The lobby was all white marble and gold paint, big fake statues and way too many people milling around. It was just barely sundown, and half of Vegas was headed out for whatever over-priced foolishness they had planned.

There must have been a couple of hundred people milling around, jammed ass to elbow, waiting for their Ubers or limos. A gaggle of Asian girls in miniskirts and heels damn near as tall as they were giggled and shrieked next to a bunch of former frat boys who, despite their expensive suits, maintained the inability to go three sentences without, "Bro." My temples throbbed and my nose damn near exploded at the cloud of expensive perfume, suntan lotion, and post-pubescent body spray in the air. I rubbed my sleeve across my face to prevent a giant sneeze. Bill would know how to navigate this place.

He'd probably think he'd died and gone to heaven. To me, it was hell without the flames.

That was another thing. Despite the warm night, the AC was cranked so high every nipple, male or female, within view was diamond hard and I was having a hard time not staring. Shaggy sent a nudge to my brain, which sent a quick secondary nudge somewhere further south.

Behave, big guy. He was going to be a serious problem by the end of the weekend.

Check-in was simpler than I expected. I pulled out my credit card and handed it over with my eyes shut. Between the looks of this place and already being on the road for three days, that big three-thousand-dollar limit didn't feel so generous. The stern-looking girl with the slicked back ponytail and the perfectly fitted jacket barely looked up when she asked for my name and ID.

"Thank you, Mr. McPherson. Mr. Cromwell has covered your room, resort fee and incidentals. Oh, and there's a five-hundred-dollar marker for the Casino. Just see guest services. Here's your key; You have a room overlooking the pool. Is there anything else I can do for you?"

"No, I'm good." Somehow, I managed to sound like I did this all the time and checked her name tag. "Vanessa. Thank you very much."

She responded with the "uh-huh" noise people make when they have to say something but are already onto the next customer.

After getting directions to the elevator, which involved more turns than I'd made since leaving Amarillo, I threw my duffel over my shoulder and navigated upstream across the casino. What a shitshow. It seemed everyone was migrating towards me with their head either down at their feet or staring into their phones. I shoulder-rolled my way through, managing not to make eye or body contact with a single living soul.

At the intersection of three identical hallways, I stood like a big boob, trying to decide which way took me to my room. Suddenly, to my right, a Celine Dion slot machine started dinging and flashing and spewing the theme from Titanic at operatic levels. I fled down the aisle marked "Pool," just to escape.

After all the glitz and fake-class downstairs, the room was... just a hotel room. Okay, it was nicer than any I'd ever stayed in, but it was pretty basic, except for something I'd only heard of: a king-sized bed. Snow-white sheets covered a mattress the size of Iowa. It was already turned down and awfully inviting.

I threw my duffel on the bed, pulled a drawer open and put my things away. Everything fit in one drawer except my sports jacket, which went on a wooden hanger in the closet. I wasn't that much of a neatnik, but when I was on the construction crew building Waffle Huts, we slept two or three to a room, and if you didn't stake your claim, drawer and closet space went fast. Old habits die hard. Not that I needed to worry now. I had this great room all to myself, which seemed kind of a shame. That giant bed served as a reminder it would likely be just me for three days, and I wondered how long it would take Francine to put a hurting on those linens.

Further proving Cromwell was wasting his money, a wave of exhaustion nearly knocked me off my feet. Merely sitting and moving your foot on some pedals was tiring as hell. *Who goes to bed at ten o'clock in Las Vegas? This guy.* But first, take care of a little business. I may have been boring as hell, but I was a professional, dammit.

Bill must have been waiting for my text because a split second later, I got

Bill:
Glad you got there. Where are you staying?
Me:
Caesars
Bill:
Sweet!

Okay, if you think so, big guy. I didn't respond, but my boy was not ready to end the conversation.

Me:
Have to meet C's guy tomorrow at 11. Probly just go to bed.

Silence. The lack of response told me everything. He was staring at his phone and cursing me out, I'd bet, trying to come up with a smart-ass remark. Finally, he broke the suspense.

Bill:
Pussy. Talk to Meaghan in the morning. Says she's got the info you asked for.
Whatever the hell that is.

He was still salty that I was having my assistant—who he hired without asking me, by the way—look stuff up for me instead of coming to him so he could bitch about my making him do everything. I wasn't in the mood.

Me:
K

Twelve stories below me, the sounds of splashing and laughter and thumping Techno bullshit told me sleep would not come without a fight. I drew the blackout curtains with way more force than required, stripped and climbed under those unsullied sheets.

Definitely a damn shame to have this all to myself. But that situation was unlikely to change.

Willing the noise from poolside away, I settled in. Tomorrow was my meeting with Lemuel Collins, whoever the hell that was.

CHAPTER 8

Two days before the full moon-waxing gibbous

Pawnshops are pawnshops, and I've seen more than my share of them. When I worked for O'Rourke, I occasionally escorted gamblers to places they could come up with the cash and hand it over before it got "reinvested" in the Cubs versus Milwaukee. Those places are all pretty much alike.

Except in Las Vegas.

In Sin City, hock shops are massive. A few of them are famous from TV and have lines around the block. What do you expect from an entire town built on needing cash in a hurry? Somebody figured out how to make entertainment out of it. God bless America.

Meaghan had texted me overnight to give me as much information as she could. Lemuel Collins was an expert in establishing provenance. He'd been involved in numerous art deals and had never been proved wrong about something. If he said it was a forgery, it was. The guy was the best of the best. That was no surprise. Cromwell, with one glaring exception, always hired top talent.

You wouldn't know it from this place, though. The shop was on East Fremont, a part of town where Downtown Las Vegas turns into the kind of sketchy neighborhood you find around Midway airport back home, except the lawns are all dead and the graffiti's in Spanish. On the corner up ahead, a whitewashed building gleamed in the blinding sunlight, the only business in sight that didn't have a fresh coat of gang signs. Unlike the other shops, this one had a simple, classy-looking sign: 'East Fremont Exchange.' No neon. No flashing bulbs. Amateur hour. The History Channel wouldn't be filming anything here.

This was Cromwell's provenance guy? I expected a classy Sotheby's kind of arrangement, not some neighborhood second-hand store. I pulled the Charger to the curb and checked the time. Unless you were right downtown, there didn't seem to be a lack of street parking. Score one for Sin City.

It was still five minutes to ten, so I cranked up both the AC and the tunes and drummed on the steering wheel. Mom McPherson taught me it just isn't done to show up early. For about the fourth time since waking up in that famous hotel, I wondered what Eileen and Jim would think of me now. A good job with a rich boss. An expense account. Still not in jail. Odds are, she'd be pleasantly surprised. But there was no getting over the lessons she drilled into my head in her attempt to civilize me. Don't show up too early or too late. You basically had a four-minute window in which to meet her approval.

In front of the store, a tall, skinny tweaker paced down the block and back, tugging at his sagging pants every few seconds. With his spiky bleached hair, he looked like one of those inflatable car lot guys with prison tats. Even his belt couldn't make up for his lack of body fat. The meth-head kept leaning out into the street, looking one way then the other, obviously waiting for someone.

I didn't have time to pay him too much attention, because the clock flipped to the top of the hour. I got out, walked past Meth Boy with a nod and an unspoken warning to leave my car alone. I strolled up to the smoked glass door. With one hand on the handle, I took a deep, cleansing breath.

Okay, you're a professional. Introduce yourself, arrange the inspection, get out without looking like an idiot. You can do this. Be cool.

A blast of moist Arctic air bearing traces of disinfectant and metal polish assaulted my senses as I entered the darkened store. Seems it wasn't just the hotels. Everyone in this damned town lived in refrigerators. I blinked twice, adjusting to the relative darkness, and looked around. The outside of the place was deceptive. Once inside, it was maybe the nicest pawn shop I'd ever seen.

Along the window a low shelf displayed electronics, all of them only a few years old except a perfectly preserved turntable in a highly polished wooden cabinet. Three rows of neat shelves offered various items that used to be important to people. Unlike most places, there were no weapons on display. Along the far wall, where most shops either hung guns or had a sign saying they were available, hung a row of musical instruments. Each had been lovingly polished, so that sun beams bounced off the brass of saxophones and the fiberglass and wooden bodies of bass guitars and Stratocasters. I couldn't play a lick, but the Gibson double neck on the last hook was identical to the one Jimmy Page played on Stairway to Heaven. It called to my inner Led Zeppelin-ness. I know I was there on business, but I couldn't help it. I reached out like a star-struck teenager, aching to feel the smooth wood and the thick strings.

"Do you play, young man?" A warm, deep voice asked from the other side of the room.

I turned, a little surprised at being called young. "No, but it's so beautiful. Someone must have hated to let it go."

"Not as much as he hated the ex-partner who gave it to him. What can I do for you today?"

Lemuel Collins leaned with just his fingertips touching a long display case full of jewelry. Earrings, blinged-out bracelets and expensive watches were laid out to tempt the buyer, if they could survive the sticker shock. At the end of the case was a depressingly large number of plain gold wedding bands, priced to move.

I studied the man for a moment. He was African-American, and I don't know why that surprised me. Lemuel Collins looked more like a pastor than a pawnbroker, in a crisp white shirt with a navy blue tie—complete with gold tie clip—and pleated black pants. Thick tortoise-shell frames framed his friendly, narrow eyes.

I strode forward, my hand extended. "I'm Johnny Lupul. Malcolm Cromwell said you were expecting me?"

The corner of his smile twitched a little, and he folded his latex-gloved fingers into themselves and offered me a fist bump.

Great, a germophobe.

His smile was infectious, though. "Nice to meet you, young man. Welcome to my world."

"Thank you, Mister Collins. It's a pleasure." I don't know why he was Mister Collins and not Lem, but it felt right. Eileen would be proud. Respect for your elders and all that crap, although he couldn't have been much over sixty. "Nice place you have here."

"Thank you, kindly." Whatever else he was going to say got interrupted by a loud *ding-ding* from the front door. The tweaker and a second guy, twice as wide and not much smarter, bounced in. The new guy wore a wife beater with pit stains as yellow as his remaining teeth. LOVE was tattooed on the knuckles of his right hand. In the other, which I bet said HATE, was a car stereo with two uncapped wires dangling from the back.

Shaggy immediately perked up inside me and a slow, deep breath kept him at bay. *Easy buddy, not your problem.*

I spared one quick glance out to the street. The Charger sat unmolested. At least it wasn't my stereo. I took a step sideways along the counter.

If Lemuel Collins was bothered, it didn't show. Probably just another day in the life of a business like this. He straightened his spine and his professional demeanor. "Help you gentlemen today?"

The skinny meth head shot his buddy an "I got this" grin. Then he rolled his head on his shoulders. I heard his neck crack.

"Yes, sir. Just wondering what you'd give us for this almost new car stereo." He reached out and took it from his buddy, tucking the loose wire into his fist. A pretty slick move. It marked him as the brains of the operation, as hard as that was to believe.

He offered it for Mr. Collins' inspection, but it was met with a sad headshake. The man behind the counter never even bothered to reach for the outstretched hand. "Gentlemen, you know I don't handle stolen merchandise. You're smarter than this."

Skinny looked over his shoulder to his partner, who grunted and flexed his hands. The big guy's jaw clenched. His eyes went cold as concrete.

I know that look.

So did Shaggy.

I fought down a growl and stepped toward him, but the pawnbroker raised a palm to me and continued engaging with the skinny guy. He must have this conversation twice a day. At least.

"Honest, this is out of my car," the kid said through a weak smile, his voice an octave higher than before. He looked at Collins, but his eyes darted to the right and pleaded with his partner to stay cool. He had this.

"Glad to hear it. If you can show me a receipt, or where it's listed on your insurance, I'll be glad to give you an appraisal."

"A what?"

"Show me proof of ownership and I'll give you a fair price for it."

Muscle Shirt had heard enough. He reached into the back of his belt and pulled out a battered forty-five pistol. "How about I show you this, and you just give us your money, motherfucker?"

Lemuel Collins didn't move. He didn't even sweat. He looked more disappointed than scared.

Tweaker Boy's shoulders slumped. "Oh man, Dicky. What the hell are you doing? You said we weren't going to do that no more."

The hair on my neck stood straight up, and goosebumps rippled like piano keys up and down my arms. A low, wolfish growl bubbled in my throat, and it was a wonder nobody else heard it. Shaggy wanted at this guy, bad.

Just to burn off the energy and keep my worse half under control, I was halfway across the room in a single bound. Getting airborne, I let out a deep growl and clothes-lined the big guy. His thick neck fit perfectly in the crook of my arm and momentum carried us both to the ground. His head struck a shelf bracket, knocking something to the ground. I rolled over him and into a perfect 3-point stance, eyes narrowed and head up, ready for another run at him if I needed one.

I didn't.

Tweaker Boy dropped his head like a five-year-old. "Sorry about Dickie. He just doesn't think sometimes."

Mr. Collins' voice was tense but level. "Take your friend here and get out. Never come back. Understand?"

The big guy rubbed the back of his head. Out of instinct, he scrambled around for his gun, but I found it first. My boot stepped on it and I gave him a visual warning. Judging by his expression, he thought about going for it, anyway. Any other day, against some other mook, he might have. I'm pretty sure he saw Shaggy behind my eyes, because without breaking visual contact, he accepted his partner's outstretched hand and rose shakily to his feet.

I was mostly right, the left knuckles spelled HAT. His tattoo session must have been interrupted. At least I hope that was the reason, I was trying to be charitable.

Unimpressed, the big guy spat out, "Asshole." Whether that was directed at me or his partner, who cared? The wannabe robber checked his scalp for blood. His hand came away streaked red, but he didn't seem worried by the amount. The two idiots staggered out into the blinding light of East Fremont Street, the door closing behind them with a gentle click.

"Are you alright?" Collins and I asked each other at the same time.

The older man chuckled. "I believe I am, Mr. Lupul. Thank you. I prefer to avoid violence whenever possible, but I appreciate the assistance." He paused before adding, "And your restraint."

"Restraint? I coldcocked the guy. I think there's blood on your, uh, display thing here."

His eyes narrowed but he let out a good-natured chuckle, followed by a cough. "Mr. Cromwell told me that was likely to happen if someone provoked you. Given what he said, you handled yourself very well. I appreciate that."

"No problem. Just glad you're okay." *Wait. What?*

The notion that a complete stranger might know my deepest secret was bad enough, but that my employer was just blabbing it to everyone was really aggravating. "He told you about me? What'd he say?" My charming professional mood went *poof-gone* just like that.

"We are in a strange business, son. I like to know who I'm working with. Mr. Cromwell knows if I'm going to do business with anyone in his organization, I have to know about them in advance."

"How long have you been working for him?"

He scrunched up his face. "With him. Not for him. I don't care if he tells you otherwise. But a long time. Probably goes back twenty years or more. Known several of your predecessors."

I had predecessors?

"Like who?" The question came out needier than I intended. *Why does everyone know more about my business than me?*

Mr. Collins shook his head. "I don't tell my client's secrets, and I expect the same, uh, discretion from them, although some of them might talk more than they should. There were a couple of, what does Mr. Cromwell call them? Relocation specialists. Before you. And of course, Miz Francine. She still keeping the old man in line?" He smiled.

"Oh yeah." I was dying to ask exactly what he knew about her—and how well, but there was no way to have that conversation without sounding indiscreet at best, and stupidly jealous at worst. Besides, his focus on discretion meant it would be a short and one-sided discussion.

I still had to know. "Exactly what did he tell you about me?"

"Said you had a tendency to act first and think later, but you were a smart young man."

I'll be damned. "Really?"

"Well, what he actually said was that you were smarter than you looked. I'm paraphrasing. He's right for what it's worth. I appreciate you not busting up my place unnecessarily."

I shrugged way too casually. My head was full of questions. None of them had anything to do with why I was there in the first place. *Focus, you idiot.*

As we talked, he reached down to a small refrigerator under the counter and pulled out a couple of bottles of water and offered one. I didn't realize how thirsty I was.

"Welcome to Las Vegas. Stay hydrated. Best advice I can give you. Probably the only advice you'd listen to, anyway. I remember being your age."

"Thank you, sir." I reached for it and he tilted the bottle out, so I could take it without making contact with his hand. He took the germ thing seriously.

We sipped in silence for a bit, and my eyes drifted around the store, organizing the pinball machine inside my head so I could get back to business. "You have a lot of great stuff here."

"Thank you. They all have their stories, that's for sure."

"Like that guitar I was looking at."

He nodded. "Yup, although that's not unusual. Just a nasty divorce. Some of them, though..." he pointed a perfectly manicured nail to the watch case. "See that Rolex, there? The one with the stones?"

I nodded.

"Guy came in a month ago. Wanted to leave a stack of cash for his wife. Knew there was a contract out on him and wanted to do the right thing by her. Only decent thing he ever did in his life. I overpaid a bit, but it was a good cause. Two days later, they found him out in the desert."

"He told you all that?"

Mr. Collins snorted. "Him? He didn't say diddly squat. The watch told me."

"I'm sorry. The watch told you?" Gramma used to say that about the cards all the time, and I didn't believe her. Didn't *use to* believe her, anyway.

Mr. Collins seemed surprised by my response. He gave me the once over before speaking.

"I would have thought you knew, given how free our friend is with information. What did Mr. Cromwell tell you I do for him?"

"Appraisal. Authentication. Said you knew which of his relic things are real and which are fakes."

"And how did he say I did that?"

He'd never told me. "I guess. What do they call it at museums? Provenance, right? Paperwork, that kind of thing?"

He sat down on a stool with a heavy sigh and drained his water bottle. "Nah, young man. I'm a clairetangentist."

He could tell from my dopey expression I didn't have a clue what that meant. "Means I touch things and they tell me their stories." I blinked at him. "I can tell by touch whether something is I know when something, or someone, is what they claim to be. That's why..." He held up his latex-gloved hands in explanation.

"Oh, come on." It came out ruder than intended.

He didn't seem offended, just surprised. "You work for the great Malcolm Cromwell, and you don't believe in such things? Either you're not telling the truth or you're just not paying attention. Stick around as long as me, son. You'll see stuff will fry your eyeballs. As the Bard said, there are more things than are dreamed of in your philosophy, Horatio. But yes, everything in here has told me its story."

He was a nice enough guy. I played along out of politeness. "Are they all sad stories like that watch?"

"You ever know anyone who went to a pawnshop with good news?"

I toasted him with my plastic bottle. "Good point."

"Our friend asks me to vet some of his purchases. Especially the more oddball items."

"But they're mostly fakes, right?" I already knew the answer. *Some. God knows not all.*

"A good number, maybe most. But then there are others. There are some ugly things in this world." He looked away for a second before replacing the pastoral smile. I suspected if we were drinking something other than spring water, the conversation could get dark as hell.

I wouldn't let it go. "What do you mean?"

"I heard you retrieved something for him a while back. Said it was the real deal, whatever it was. And I don't want to know. Was it a good thing?"

The Anubis Disk? Definitely not a good thing. "It was fucking evil."

He nodded. "Now imagine when you touched it, you could feel every terrible thing it had ever done from the time they made it. That sound like fun?"

It sounded like the suckiest thing ever.

"That's why I make the big bucks. Fortunately, this crystal egg you're picking up is a genuine, one hundred percent forgery. Easy work for a smart young man like you."

A real professional shouldn't feel as much relief as coursed through my body at that statement. A weight I never knew was there disappeared from my shoulders.

"So where is it? When can I pick it up?"

Mr. Collins stood and brushed a drop of water from his perfectly pressed pants. "This is your first time in Las Vegas, isn't it? Ever heard of Karmen Mystère's Spiritual Curiosity Museum?"

He grinned at my ignorance. "Then, young man, you are in for a treat this evening. I'm going to take you to a show."

CHAPTER 9

I stood blinking in the evening sunlight to get my bearings. Karmen Mystère's Spiritual Curiosity Museum and Theatre—extra pretentious points for spelling it with an "re"—wasn't built into some casino or in the middle of a strip mall, like I expected. It was a refurbished wood-sided Victorian mansion that would have looked just as creepy in any town in America. The classic haunted house, if you ignored the round extension that was the showroom, and the parking lot full of rental cars.

Along the wall facing the street were signs that looked like sideshow carnival come-ons. One proclaimed, "See the Most Haunted Doll in the World," followed by a cheesily painted, "If You Dare." Another urged people to brave the world's largest collection of serial killer's implements under one roof, which seemed morbid as hell but not particularly supernatural. What was so scary about duct tape?

Beside the mansion's front parlor door, which doubled as the box office, was a larger poster than the rest. "Limited Engagement: Last chance to see the mysterious Paiute Sky-Egg." The museum had arranged with my boss to have it til the end of the month, which is why I had an extra two days to kill before I could pick it up. Truth be told, I'd have rather just chucked it into the Charger and headed home.

Mr. Collins was there to make the introductions and make sure the egg I got was the one Cromwell actually bought. I couldn't figure out how having the wrong forgery could be a problem, but that was above my pay grade. For some reason, he insisted I see the show while I was here.

"You scrub up well." Lemuel Collins' soft, deep voice came from over my shoulder.

"Oh, hey. Thank you. Trying to look professional, you know?" *That didn't sound particularly professional. What are you, ten?* I resembled a grownup in my sports jacket, open shirt, big boy pants and dress shoes I'd worn maybe half a dozen times.

Mr. Collins, of course, looked like he'd just stepped out of a menswear shop. With a smile, he said, "The boor covers himself, the rich man, and the fool adorns himself, and the elegant man gets dressed."

"Huh?"

"Balzac, Mr. Lupul. Don't worry about it. Shall we go in?"

He ushered me inside. In the lobby, half a dozen tourists stood behind a velvet rope. Sidestepping them, my guide slipped into the VIP line and up to the entrance. The bored Goth-looking girl in the ticket booth eventually bothered to look up from her phone. She recognized my guide because a toothy smile shone past her black-painted lips.

"Mr. Collins, hi. She told me to let her know the minute—"

The girl never got to finish the sentence.

"Lem, good to see you darlin'." The warm southern accent was loud from clear across the lobby. The speaker was a tall woman who looked like a cross between Elvira, Mistress of the Dark, and an old-fashioned pinup girl.

I remembered where I'd heard the name Karmen Mystère, now. She was an illusionist who'd had several TV specials a while back, mostly escapes and bloody stunts. Halloween stuff. Low-def television did not do her justice.

Her hips propelled her forward. She was decked out in a shiny leather dress that looked expensive as hell and clung to her like shrink wrap. Karmen stood damn near six feet in those heels. Everything she wore, including a huge chunky amulet around her neck, was raven-black and showcased her deathly white face. It was a hell of a face.

She looked to be about forty. Most of her did, anyway. Those boobs were newer than the rest of her and not factory issue.

The woman smelled like jasmine and musk and bad intentions of the best kind as she leaned past me to give Collins an air kiss. "Where have you been? I've missed you."

Lemuel squirmed a bit and avoided wiping his face, even though she never touched him. "Looks like you've managed just fine without me, Miss Karmen. The place has grown."

"Hasn't it? Daddy would be so proud of what we've done with it." Then she turned to me. "You must be Johnny Lupul."

I stuck out my hand. "Yeah. I'm..." but she leaned in and wrapped me in a hug of surprising duration and brushed her lips against my cheek. That shut me up in a hurry.

"So good to meet you. I'm glad Cromwell has finally hired some pretty young help. I'm Karmen Mystère. Welcome."

I muttered something close to a greeting, but she was already pulling me by the arm. "There are good seats for the two of you for the performance—not too close up front, of course. Lem's shy, he's always afraid we're going to make him part of the show. Take a wander around the museum until then. Have you ever been here? As soon as we're done, I'll meet up with you and we'll make the arrangements." The woman must breathe through her ears. She talked so quickly it left no space for a response. It was clear very few people got a word in edge-wise, and she didn't care much what they had to say when they did.

Shaggy didn't seem charmed, and in fact his hackles were up. I chalked it up to the approaching full moon and his usual mistrust of strangers.

A woman's thin arm, covered in rose tattoos, waved frantically through the slit in a curtain. Karmen noticed as well, because she patted my arm in farewell. "Enjoy the show, gentlemen." Then she and her tempting smell vanished into the crowd.

Mr. Collins sucked on his bottom lip, fighting a grin and waiting for me to say something. Anything. It took longer than he expected.

I finally cracked. "Okay, that was interesting."

"Yep. Miss Karmen's, uh, an interesting woman, sure enough."

I looked around at the crowd of tourists oohing and whispering to each other as the star of the show passed through the throng. The parlor of the old mansion served as a lobby, but the main museum was through a pair of velvet curtains. A huge guy with multiple piercings in his face stood, letting a few people through at a time, then holding the others back with a look that could freeze vodka. He looked up and waved us forward.

"Go right on ahead, Mister Collins."

"Thank you, Dan. Give my best to your mother."

"Yes, sir." *Is there anyone this guy doesn't know?*

The older gentleman held the curtain and gave a mock bow, waving me through first. After the shockingly bright sunlight in the lobby, I found myself in what looked like it might have been the ballroom at one time. It was dark, the only light from shadow boxes and shelf lighting. Shelves lined the walls, crowded with assorted crap, each with little placards and descriptions.

One item, a shrunken head according to the sign, attracted my attention. Mr. Collins stood dead center in the room and shrugged. "Go ahead. I'm good here. I've seen it."

After inspecting several of the items and not being terribly impressed, I joined him in the center of the room. I kept my voice low. "What percentage of these are fakes?"

He took his time before answering. "Oh, about two-thirds."

He pointed to the 'actual shrunken head from the wilds of Borneo.' "That's papier mâché, and not even very well done. The Boston Strangler's scarf is from JC Penney."

We laughed and shuffled along with the sunburnt tourists into the next chamber. This one held larger items. One, in particular, caught my eye. A full-size guillotine stood in the corner in a triangle of LED lights. The sign read "The only guillotine execution north of Haiti took place in 1889 on the island of St Pierre..." along with a bunch of other details. I turned to my guide.

"That's a fake, right?"

The older man stood near the door with his arms folded and shook his head. "Nope. That one's real as sin on a Saturday night. Can we, uh, move on?"

"Yeah, sure."

The surrounding crowd was a heady mix of believers and skeptics. The loudest ones were likely believers pretending to be skeptics. People who had seen the television specials were more likely to be impressed than the folks who were just killing time between shifts at the video poker machines.

A trio of pretty young girls in black t-shirts and too much eyeliner mingled through the thong. I watched as one of them leaned in to eavesdrop on the conversation of a family from Kansas. She jotted something in a notebook and moved on. I'd have been good at that job, since my ears picked up everything from across the room. Her co-worker did the same thing when an old man being pushed around in his wheelchair mumbled something to his caretaker.

What are they up to? I didn't worry about it too much. There was enough to look at, and I was trying not to sneeze. My nose itched like crazy at the dust, tourist smells and over-cooled air.

There were four more major display rooms, each of which contained items supposed to be haunted, cursed, hexed or just belonging to someone objectively evil. The third room Lemuel wouldn't enter at all, never offering an explanation. His upper lip was damp with perspiration even though, like everything else in this crazy town, someone set the air conditioning too high.

If there were any evil emanations, or "psychic debris" as the museum handout claimed, I never picked up on it. My stomach was in a bit of a knot by the time we reached the "World's Most Haunted Doll," and I confess I got a little queasy in the room with "the Devil's Hope Chest," but I chalked that up to the overwhelming dust, formaldehyde, and sunscreen, rather than malignant forces.

The last chamber was completely dark, with only one item on display. Mr. Collins whispered, "Here's what you came to see."

Four lights shone on a pedestal. Under a glass case was a crystal object, identified as "The Paiute Sky-Egg." It appeared pretty much, well, like a giant egg, except the narrow end looked like someone had broken it off. It was topped with jagged shards.

I circled the pedestal, obeying the written order not to touch. *What's so special that Cromwell would go to all this trouble?*

Mr. Collins stood right at my shoulder, with no apparent reservations about getting close to this relic. He removed his glasses and polished them with his tie. "I'll let Karmen tell you the story after the show. She tells it better than I do."

A creaking noise in the far corner of the room caught my ear and a wall panel slid to the right. In the dim light I couldn't really see her, but a woman in what looked like a dominatrix outfit with torn black fishnets and Doc Martin boots stepped through. In the voice of a cheerleader she chirped, "Hiya, Mr. Collins. I need to take this out to the showroom. It's the star of the show, you know."

As she entered the lit area, I saw she was about my age. Spiky red hair crowned a pale prettyish face that was way out of sync with the dungeon wear. Complicated tattoo patterns ran along her collarbone, while green and red sleeve tats covered both arms. It was too dark to make them out. She wasn't fat, or even heavy, but those thighs looked like she could leg press a truck. This girl worked out.

"Excuse me." She had one slightly crooked tooth in a perfectly white smile. I moved out of the way as she placed a hand truck under the pedestal and tilted it back.

"Do you need a hand with that?" I moved to help her, but she gave me the old stiff arm.

"I have it. Thanks." Without even a grunt, she wheeled the pedestal towards the opening in the wall. "See you boys inside."

"That you will, Cree. Break a leg," Collins' deep voice answered.

I raised an eyebrow. "Cree?"

"Lucrezia Jensen. Nice kid."

Yeah, if you like being spanked and called a naughty puppy. "Do you know everyone in this town?"

He never got the chance to answer. A sultry feminine voice interrupted us from the speakers overhead. "Please make your way to the showroom for tonight's performance of 'Karmen Mystère's World of Occult and Magick.' We ask that you turn your phones off and don't take any pictures in the showroom so as not to disrupt the spirits."

Mr. Collins chuckled. "Those darned spirits are notoriously camera-shy. Ready?"

It was showtime.

JOHNNY LYCAN & THE VEGAS BERSERKER

CHAPTER 10

I knew it was going to be a long night when the cover of the program read: "Karmen Mystère's World of the Occult and Magick."

Ugh. Good thing the seats were comfy.

The only thing I hate more than magic is "Magick." One is an entertainment based on making you look stupid. I live with that feeling pretty much every day—there's no need for someone to pull a giraffe out of my ear to emphasize the point, but at least it's an upfront hustle. The second is usually practiced by women who drink too much tea, sport Celtic tattoos, and spend half their time together lighting candles. It's just as fake but supposed to be ancient and empowering. And real. Like Gramma's crystal ball act without the sense of humor.

The minute Karmen walked onto the stage, it was clear I was in the minority. The place went nuts. Like bat shit crazy. Some were thrilled to see a celebrity. A few of the husbands were entranced by her obvious non-occult charms, but a surprising number were just enthralled. There were an awful lot of black-clad, mascaraed young people. Most of them were female. I remembered the "No Coupons," notice in the box office. These folks had paid full freight. They were true believers.

She stood for a moment, letting the adoration wash over her. Karmen's eyes swung back and forth, then raised her arms in welcome. In a voice as Southern and sticky and sweet as honey on biscuits, she welcomed us.

"Well, good evening y'all. Welcome to our show. This isn't the usual Vegas glitz and glamor. Tonight, you're going to see a more serious look at the darker side of the spirit world. Now some of you might know what you're in for from our TV specials—" the crowd cheered and stomped. All except for me and Mr. Collins, who sat stone-faced, his arms folded, and pretending not to check my reaction out of his peripheral vision.

As Karmen prattled on, I took in the crowd who were a mix of curious, horny, and adoring. The guy in the wheelchair sat in the aisle, one row down from me with his wife nattering in his ear the whole time Karmen lectured, patting his arm.

"But first, let me introduce you to two important women. They're members of my coven and my lovely assistants for the evening. First, our badass warrior bitch Boudica." A tall blond with a single braid half-way down her back and wrapped in black leather (of course) stalked in like a Siamese cat. A sleeve of black roses covered insanely toned arms. A belt of knives circled her bare, six-pack abs as she strode onto the stage. The woman struck a cross-armed pose, her face immobile.

Without a word, the blond reached into her belt, took two knives in each hand, and before anyone knew what was happening, threw them across the stage in opposite directions. The *thunk-thunk* on the right-hand side came just a half-second before the *thunk-thunk* on the left. All four knives were sunk dead center in plywood targets.

Dang, nice work. Boudica accepted the thunderous adoration of the crowd as her due and bowed low. If she was pleased with her impressive performance, she forgot to tell her face, which remained absolutely expressionless. After a moment she offered a polite, even deferential, nod to Karmen, performed a perfect pirouette ending up in a hands-on-hips-full-on Xena Warrior Princess pose stage left.

Karmen continued, pointing offstage in the other direction. "And our newest coven initiate. The namesake of the mother of poisoners, our Mistress of Potions. Give it up for Lucrezia."

To more rapturous applause, my furniture-moving buddy appeared from stage right. She'd exchanged her Doc Martins for slightly more graceful footwear, but looked as if she did it under protest. Offering that crooked-toothed smile with visibly false bravado, her eyes dropped to the stage and her lips silently counted the steps until she found her spot. Once in place, she raised her head, plastered on a grin, and lifted those toned guns of hers in triumph. She received less applause than her partner got, except for Lemuel Collins and yours truly. I never could resist an underdog.

The stage went black except for a single spotlight on the star of the show. Head lowered, she remained silent until the crowd hushed, expecting something, even if they didn't know what. Slowly, that white face lifted up until it faced the far upper reaches of the showroom.

"Before we begin the fun, the spirit world is restless tonight. I am receiving so many messages I have to clear the air, or they won't leave me be. Beginning with Emma... Emma... Ella?"

Seriously, she's doing this corny crap? I'd watched Gramma do her séance tricks often enough I could probably do just as good a job.

If I wasn't taking the bait, neither was anyone else. At least at first. Karmen frowned, shot a dirty look offstage, then repeated, "Does the name Ella mean anything to anyone?"

"Yes. Yes. Over here" A woman two rows over waved her hand. A very relieved Karmen stalked to the stage apron and looked beyond the lights. Conveniently, the woman and her husband—it was the guy in the wheelchair—were close enough to be heard without a microphone.

Well, that explains the teenaged minions circulating around the museum.

The woman, a silver-haired woman in a Slots-a-Fun t-shirt and tight Capri pants, bounced excitedly in her seat. "It's his mother," she said. Then she added, quieter, "Was. His mother, I mean."

Karmen bent at the waist, hands on her knees. Even with my Shaggy-powered ears the silence was oppressive. The woman on stage said nothing. She simply kept her eyes trained on the poor bastard, who avoided her gaze as best he could. He had his face in his hands and if anything could have cured him and made him run from the room, having a couple of hundred eyes trained on him would have done it. He shook his head at his wife, but she got caught in the headlights of Karmen's eyes and wouldn't, or couldn't, shut her trap.

"Tell her, Ivan." More concerned about offending Karmen than her husband, she shrugged. "He doesn't talk about it much."

Karmen raised a palm to cut her off and focused on him. "Ivan? Ella is your mama?"

After about a month of uncomfortable silence. He nodded. "She was."

"She still is hon. She has a message for you."

The growl building in my throat wasn't as quiet as I thought it was because Mr. Collins hissed out of the corner of his mouth, "Shush, son."

I glared at him. *You think this is okay? This bitch is torturing the poor bastard.*

He pressed a finger to his lips. For no reason I can name, I obeyed, clenched my butt cheeks and leaned back to watch the oncoming car wreck.

Karmen was now off the stage and halfway up the aisle. A spotlight no more than a foot wide focused on her face, and her eyes glittered like sequins. The magician stopped in front of Ivan and gently took his hands in hers. Against his will, he lifted his head to look at her. A frog caught in the snake's enchanting gaze.

"It's really important that you hear this, Ivan. You think she's angry, don't you?"

His wife nudged him, but he remained silent. "Tell her," She prodded, as if he was intentionally embarrassing her in front of everyone. "Honey, please."

Karmen ignored the harpy. Her voice remained smooth and calm, all her focus on the man in the wheelchair. "She needs you to hear this. Ivan, look at me." He raised his head, tears in his eyes. It was all I could do not to groan in sympathy.

"It wasn't your fault. She wants you to know that. She needs you to believe that, Ivan. It wasn't your fault."

The hiss came from the pit of his stomach. My ears picked it up clearly, but I'm sure most of the audience couldn't hear. "Stop it."

Undeterred, that sickly sweet voice kept slithering out of her black-painted mouth. "She doesn't hurt anymore, Vannie. She called you Vannie, didn't she?"

His head snapped up. This time, everyone heard the quivering voice. "Shut up You don't know."

"No, I don't. But she does. Your pain hurts her, Ivan. Something awful. Ella needs you to stop hurting yourself. She says it's not your fault."

His wife's hand stroked his heaving shoulders. "See, baby?"

"But it was. It was." He was holding back an ocean of tears and snot. So was most of the audience, by this time. They couldn't tear their gaze from the poor fly, getting his wings torn off. Even my seatmate let out an audible sniff.

A single perfect tear left a snail trail down Karmen's pasty-white cheek. "No, Vannie. Mama needs you to know she doesn't need to forgive you. There's nothing to forgive. She wants to move on, but she can't until... you forgive yourself."

I tore my eyes away from the scene. Onstage, the two "coven members" watched quietly. Boudica may as well have been one of those statues at Caesars: unemotional and even impatient. She had more knives to throw and wanted to get on with it. Lucrezia—Cree— was a different matter. She wiped the back of her hand across her eyes. Her lips quivered, and she looked like she wanted to crawl into a ball.

So did Ivan. He sat in that foldable, cheap metal wheelchair. His lips quivered and his eyes shone in the reflected spotlight until he let out a groan of such pain it woke Shaggy deep inside me. He dropped his head into his hands and wept, his body wracked with spasms of spiritual pain.

Karmen said nothing. She eased the wife's hands away and wrapped the brutalized man in her arms, pulling his head to her chest. His head rested there while those long fingers stroked his hair, *shush-shushing* him until the microphone headset, purely by coincidence of course, picked up his soft. "Thank you."

The room burst into cheers and applause. Karmen let the wife take over consolation duty and stood erect in the spotlight for the perfect amount of time, gently dabbed a tear away and turned back to the stage, approaching it in silence.

I turned to Mr. Collins. "Was that supposed to be entertaining?"

He calmly replied, "They seemed to think so, didn't they?"

My anger overcame any deference to his age. "Is there some reason you wanted me to see that?"

He nodded and looked into my eyes for a moment before answering. "A man should always know who he's doing business with." It seemed like good advice to me.

CHAPTER 11

After way too long in silence, Karmen raised her head. Then she lifted her arms, and the recorded music kicked in. That ten thousand-watt smile reappeared, and she strode back to her rightful place; center stage and smack dab in the spotlight.

The mood and pace of the show picked up the energy, as if she hadn't just left poor Ivan's guts all over the floor. The audience certainly appreciated the shift of mood. There was a lot of strutting and posing met with rapturous applause, and at least 3 quick-changes, each outfit more colorful and revealing. That may have been the most impressive trick of all, given what the Mistress of Magick wore when the curtain went up.

All the while, her "coven" mates played their parts. Whenever the star vanished backstage for a costume change or to prep the next trick, Boudica performed some kind of cool-yet-terrifying sharp-shooter thing. Proficient as she was with knives, apparently the cross-bow was her favorite toy. I confess it was an impressive over-the-shoulder-behind-her shot that blasted an apple right out of Cree's hand. There were also a couple of cool axe stunts so perfectly performed the ice queen damn near cracked a smile, even if it never reached those stone-cold killer eyes.

I found myself applauding, despite the boo-boo face I wore through most of the show. Magick my ass. That was pure talent. Give the bad-ass her due.

It was hard to tell which was more impressive, that shot or the way Cree—who I just couldn't think of as a "Lucrezia,"—had more faith in her partner's shooting than her own ability to navigate high heels. As the arrows plucked the fruit from her hand and splattered against the wall, she kept that adorable, crooked smile in place. It was trying to maneuver across the stage that took concentration. A natural performer, she was not.

Watching closely, it became obvious her real value lay in stage-managing the stage tricks. Such humongous illusions took some serious wrangling.

The show's set-piece was "Salem's Revenge." Basically, it was three elaborate escapes based on the idea that the Salem witch trials were grade A, old, cis-het white-guy bullshit. Which they were, but it still seemed a bit over the top.

In her best Southern school-marm voice, Karmen began the lesson with the basics; Puritans, slave girls, patriarchy, blah blah blah. Then things took a more intriguing turn. "We all know, kiddies, that if those poor girls really were witches..." She paused long enough to tee the crowd up. "... they'd have kicked some ass."

The goth-girl mob hooted and stomped while the curtain rose, revealing three impressive stage props; a water tank, a crane with a stack of bricks, and what looked like a good witch-burning stake, complete with highly flammable bonfire material.

Ms. Mystère gestured to the water tank. "Back in the day, there were basically three ways to prove witchcraft. The first was to dunk the suspect. If she floated to the surface, then obviously she was a witch. I guess they never counted on these flotation devices." Karmen winked and shook her store-bought tatas at the crowd. This time, the guys responded with the same enthusiasm as the women. *Boob jokes, the great equalizer.*

She continued. "Of course, if they didn't float, they would probably die, but at least they weren't witches, so... yay? The system obviously needed a little work. But let's put their little theory to the test, shall we?"

What followed was the same water-tank trick illusionists have been doing since Houdini, only with a Lynyrd Skynyrd-esque soundtrack and an unharmed but dripping-wet Karmen Mystère. The show offered fun for the whole family.

After another exhibition of why nobody will ever break into Boudica's apartment (this time involving flying ninja stars) Karmen reappeared to take her place in front of the crane. Another lecture followed.

"Another persuasive little tool the bastards used was pressing. This is where they laid a barn door on top of the suspect and kept piling on rocks until the person either confessed- which was a little hard to do with a collapsed lung—or they died. Innocent, but flat as a pancake. Now doing that stone by stone could take a while, and we don't have that kind of time, so we've devised this little demonstration instead."

The stage went dark, except for a raised dais bathed in blue light. Boudica helped Karmen lay on her back while the narration continued. "it usually took ten or twelve twenty pound stones—four hundred pounds sometimes—to reach the desired effect. Cree, honey, let's just make it an even five hundred, shall we?"

Cree nodded, smiled, and grabbed a very realistic, and damned heavy, boulder. Lifting with her legs like any good gym-trained weightlifter, she hoisted it onto the pile of brick and stone. Whoever her trainer was had earned their money. I had the fleeting, and not politically correct, notion that those thighs could crush my skull like a walnut, and it would be worth it. Even Shaggy—who'd been pretty much hibernating since the Museum—gave me a quick nudge of *what-the-hell-dude* and I shook it off.

Heedless of my lecherous thoughts, Cree closed a thick net around the rockpile and locked it. Then, with a few tottery steps approached the crane, took a deep breath, and pulled the lever. Amid more

Skynyrd and the grinding of gears, the whole pile lifted until it was near the stage lights. Concentrating hard, the redhead pushed and pulled until the whole cargo swung out over the audience.

There was a lot of nervous laughter and some squirming in seats until Karmen spoke up.

"Nervous, y'all? How do you think I feel? Okay, Lucrezia, honey, let's do this."

Boudica placed a black sheet over Karmen, hiding her from sight but leaving a very distinctive shape under the material. There was no hiding it was the Mistress of Magick under there. She even stuck a perfectly manicured hand from underneath the sheet to offer the crowd a wave.

The net full of rocks swung back into place, looming dangerously over the magician.

Karmen's voice whispered through the sound system. "Ready, Lucrezia? One. Two..."

Before she could say "three," Cree pushed a comically large button on the crane's console and the whole shebang dropped like, well, a ton of bricks, completely demolishing the platform.

For a moment, there was dead silence. Then from the back of the theater a familiar voice said, "Hey, this is the part where y'all go crazy." The spotlight swung to the very back entrance. Amid cheering so loud it was damned near a mob, stood Karmen Mystère. Hip thrust, arm lifted, in yet another outfit, and certainly un-squished.

I hate magic—and feeling stupid—to the point I've spent way too much time on YouTube studying how magic tricks are done. I had a pretty good sense of what was involved; trap doors, a tunnel, but damn, had to give her props. The woman was *fast* as well as good.

The last set piece was the bonfire, and there was no mystery what mayhem was about to occur. As the star of the show strutted to deep, wailing, blues chords, every eye in the joint was locked on the bonfire and whispers rippled through the audience.

Mr. Collins, who'd been stone-silent up to this point, leaned over. "The lady is awfully good. Have to hand it to her. Look at those faces

I automatically obeyed. A couple of hundred adoring gazes locked on one woman, their eyes wide, expressions ranging from worship to awe to slack jawed trance. If this woman had been a politician, they'd have invaded Poland for her without a question.

His voice was so low I wouldn't have heard him without my wolf-ears, as he continued. "That, my boy, is why we keep our secret, um, talents to ourselves. These folks know this is all nonsense and they still can't look away. Thirteenth century, twenty-first, doesn't matter. People are people. God bless'em." The way he said it, I was pretty sure bless wasn't the word he wanted to use.

The fire effect was amazing, even if it was basically the same mechanics as the rock drop, only flashier. Boudica and Cree "lashed" her to the post while Karmen droned on about men burning annoying women. She gave a number of women burned at the stake that was so high it couldn't possibly be true, but sounded impressive. As her boss spoke, Cree bent to brush something away. Probably unclogging a fuel jet, if my guess was right. Then the unsmiling Amazon used a flaming arrow to ignite the fuel.

A wall of flame shot straight up, obscuring Karmen from sight, which was the whole idea. There was a blood-curdling scream from beyond the inferno. It sounded like the illusionist, but she should have been below the stage and halfway to the exit by now. My nose twitched as I picked up the scent of butane- a pretty good choice since it burns fast and bright but not very hot. They masked it well, and I'm betting nobody else in the theater detected anything.

Of course, the flames suddenly died out. The post was empty, and our heroine emerged from the wings unscathed. The crowd noise reached a level I'd never heard indoors before. Whatever was higher than "ape-shit," it was that enthusiastic.

Karmen took all the adoration as her due; grinning, nodding and holding her arms over her head in triumph. Just when the noise was settling, she stepped forward.

"Now, we've had a lot of fun with three of the basic elements of Magick—water, earth, fire. But while fire can destroy, it also gives light. Which brings us to our last demonstration of special elemental power. Light and air...."

Cree had Mr. Cromwell's Paiute Sky Egg on a wheeled platform and pushed it to a place of honor beside Karmen, gave a polite nod, and backed away. Ms. Mystère reached out a hand and stroked the crystal object affectionately.

Inside my chest, Shaggy was stirring. He hadn't responded to the egg when we were in the display room, but now he wasn't happy. *What the hell is his problem?*

The show continued despite my Lycan misgivings. "This is the last time we'll be doing this illusion, as the egg has been purchased by a... private collector and will no longer be on public display." A chorus of boos came up from the Goth contingent. Any chance to heckle the patriarchy, I guess. Karmen offered a gracious smile.

"I know, but hey, a girl's gotta eat." That defused tensions a bit, and she continued. "This object has a long history going back to the Paiute people who belonged to this land long before white settlers arrived."

She circled the egg, never removing her hand. "The tale is told that in the Before Time, two huge, handsome lizards who walked like men visited the Earth Mother. She loved them, and they taught her much." She paused and lifted a hand to her mouth as if whispering, "I'll just bet she did. I hear Earth Mother was a bit of a pistol."

The usual laughter at a dirty joke turned to something else as a different murmur bubbled through the crowd. Scattered people leaned over and whispered to their partners. My pea brain couldn't figure out what was causing the commotion. I turned to my seatmate, who sat like a sphinx, not acknowledging my confusion and certainly not offering an explanation.

The woman on stage smirked. "I see some of you are locals. For the uninitiated, here so close to Area 51 and such, we know there are three kinds of visitors from outer space. There are the Little Green Men, there are the Greys, and there are the Reptilians, or Lizard people. Now, I'm not saying Earth Mother's reptilian friends were aliens..." The crowd chuckled uncomfortably while she seemed to ponder that statement.

"Okay, it was totally aliens." She soaked in the laughter and applause that followed.

Her demeanor changed a little, and she got that "magick is serious business," look again. "Before mysteriously disappearing, they left her this gift..." She stroked the egg thoughtfully. "... To offer light to her people when needed most. Now these seem like some awfully dark times to me. What say we see what kind of light we can conjure up?"

Her statement met with the predictable cheers and mayhem. "Now, if any of you are bothered by intense lights, I urge you to put on the souvenir sunglasses in the pocket of your seats there. This is going to get a little bright."

I should have listened.

As the music swelled and a guitar let out a chord Jimmy Page would have killed to play, a single beam of white light shot from the broken tip of the egg like it was trying to blast through the ceiling. I squinted against the light and felt Shaggy wake up inside me. He hated concentrated light more than I did. *Easy big fella, it's just pretend.*

Much as I love a good power chord more than most people my age, there was something in the music that didn't sit right. While normal people would hear only loud, bluesy licks, there was a second set of sounds slithering underneath. This subterranean sound was more guttural, droning and just a bit off the note. The longer I listened, the more it bothered me, and the thing living inside my gut.

Onstage, Karmen solemnly lifted the egg and held it out in front of her. With no warning, beams of illumination shot from the damned thing in sixteen different directions at once. I barely had time to wonder how she did that, detached from a power source as she was, when the pain laser-drilled into my skull.

The light strobed all over the theater, and each time it came my way was an icepick to the inside of my cranium. Hundreds of arena rock shows had exposed me to every kind of laser there was, and as a rule, they didn't bother me much, long as I wore sunglasses. This was different. It was whiter, colder, with an energy to it I could feel in my core.

I covered my eyes with one hand and fumbled for the souvenir shades they thoughtfully provided. Plainly it was too slow for the hairy, freaked-out, rage-machine inside me.

Shaggy wanted out of there.

Now.

With a groan just short of a full-fledged howl, I grabbed my head in both hands and leaned forward, cowering between my knees. Under my flesh, the drumbeat of my pulse grew louder and louder, the hair on my arms bristled. It took all I had not to let the fur sprout wild.

"Are you alright, Johnny?" Mr. Collins' voice was full of sincere concern, but he'd slipped his hands under his ass to eliminate any chance of touching me, even accidentally. He was no longer a neutral observer. Lemuel Collins was freaking out, whether out of concern for me—or about being so close to me—not that it made a difference. Didn't really matter. I needed to get the hell out of there before Shaggy caused a real scene.

Fortunately, those around us were transfixed as the light danced in time to music and Karmen passed across the stage, holding it out for their admiration.

The last thing I saw while staggering up the aisle to the exit was a concerned usherette in black. She asked, "Are you okay, sir?"

I barked out a Shaggy-empowered, "Do I look like I'm fucking okay?" and pushed past her into the safety of the dark, blissfully quiet hallway. The poor kid nearly burst into tears and slammed the door behind me. Protocol might have been to follow the customer and make sure he was okay, but she was no idiot, and to be fair, I was being a total dick.

Down the darkened corridor, bouncing off the walls, I saw an opening. A black hole to the side of the creepy hallway offered sanctuary. I staggered in before recognizing it as the room that had housed the Paiute Egg. It was quiet, empty, and blessedly free of light except for the single pot light on where the display case had stood.

Finding a far corner, I sank to the floor, hugging my knees, rocking back and forth and panting ragged breaths..

Calm down big guy, it was just lights.

Cold lights. Meaghan's warning scratched at the back of my mind. *Breathe goddamn it. Breathe. One... two...*

It was so close to the full moon I wasn't confident I could wrestle Shaggy to a stalemate, but after too many panicky minutes, I felt him backing off. He had a thousand questions, and my brain provided precious few answers.

Years of training and muscle memory took over. Deep breaths expanded my chest and pushed Shaggy deeper. In. Out.

Every time I breathed out, it left a vacuum in my chest and brought a bit of the panic back. Another deep inhale tamped it down. Then again. My fingernails had thickened and turned dark to prepare for a change, now they gradually returned to their normal chewed-jagged pink selves. The skin on my arms stopped itching, and I was soon back to my hairy, but human self.

From the showroom, the roar of rapturous applause soaked through the walls. The show was over. *Thank god.*

A dry cough caught my attention. "Just stay here, young man. We'll meet with Ms. Karmen after the show. Take care of some business and you never have to come back." Mr. Collins stood in the doorway, close enough to offer comfort, but not anywhere near enough to risk physical contact. I couldn't blame him. I wouldn't want to touch me like this either.

That sounded appealing, if not convincing. "Yeah, I'm good."

He frowned. "If you say so."

"That light. I've never felt anything like it."

"It's just a show, son. Mr. Cromwell's egg is a fake. Take it and go." His furrowed brow showed he was just as confused as I was, but for reasons of his own. There wasn't enough energy left in me to ask.

I banged my head a couple of times against the cool wall just to clear my head.

Then what in the actual, ever-loving, fuckety-fuck was that?

CHAPTER 12

At first, I thought the buzzing against my leg was just the aftershocks of that light show from hell. It was my phone. Normally, I'd ignore it, but a cell phone was something normal I knew how to deal with. I answered without checking who it was.

"Hello?"

"How's Vegas?" It was Francine. Thank God, someone mostly normal to talk to.

I lied my ass off. "It's good."

"Doing anything fun?"

Oh yeah. Having the time of my fricking life. "I went to a magic show tonight."

I heard her snarky snort from two thousand miles away. "Whew, big time. It's Las Vegas, Johnny. If you come back here without at least one story you're deeply ashamed of, I will be very, very disappointed. I know you're at Caesar's. How's the bed?"

A slight grin fought its way to my face. "Like Soldier Field with pillows."

"You need to find someone to bear down with then." She could even make a stupid football team's slogan sound dirty. God love her.

"Gimme a break, I'm here on business—"

Her voice shifted into Nurse Ball mode. "About that. *Officially*, I'm calling because Mr. Cromwell wants an update and you haven't exactly been Captain Communication. How's Lemuel?"

I looked over at Mr. Collins, who raised an eyebrow. I covered the mic and said, "It's Nurse Ball."

His teeth glowed white in the dark room. "Tell Miss Francine I send my best."

After passing on the greeting, I struggled to my feet, nodding to Lemuel that I was alright, which I was. Mostly. Shaggy was hibernating again, and the timbales in my head took a break.

"Look, I'm making the final arrangements tonight. Tomorrow I pick it up, put it in the car and head for home. I don't think I'm a Vegas kind of guy."

There was a pause before her tone changed. "Kiddo, I don't think you know what kind of guy you are. I'll let the boss know you're on schedule, and for Chrissake, live a little, will ya?"

Mr. Collins stepped into the room to escape the thundering herd of adoring Mysterians (Yes, Karmen's groupies had a name. Many of them now had the t-shirts to prove it) leaving the auditorium. I stepped further into the dark to escape prying eyes.

I turned to my companion. "Can we get this done and get out of here?"

"She'll be here soon as she can. Best straighten yourself up a bit."

He wasn't wrong. I shrugged some of the creases out of my jacket and tugged my cuffs into the right position. Remembering Karmen's statement earlier, I buttoned my pit-stained shirt as high as I could manage without being throttled. There would be less pelt showing for Karmen to run her creepy fingers through.

"How do I look?"

He frowned. "Well, it's more like three miles of bad road instead of ten, so better." Then, without touching my flesh, he reached out and straightened my shirt collar inside my jacket like I was a five-year-old. *Real professional, Johnny. Nice work.*

Light appeared around the wall panel and I scrunched my eyes against it. They were still sensitive, so at first I wasn't sure who was coming through. Then I saw the dolly and the stand the Egg perched on. It was Cree.

She stopped when she saw me, tilting the dolly against one leg. "You okay? You took off in a hurry."

Crap, she'd seen it. "Yeah, I'm just a little light sensitive. You saw that?"

She grunted, dropped the stand with the egg in place, and wiped her hands on fishnet-covered thighs. "Un huh, looked like you were really uncomfortable." Her forehead wrinkled. "Are you epileptic? Sometimes the light can cause—"

"Something like that, yeah. Here, let me help you." She was trying to jiggle the dais into place on top of a pressure plate—probably part of the alarm system. I remembered at least some of my manners and helped her wrestle it into position.

Running a hand through her hair, she said, "Thanks. That sucker's heavy."

"You looked like you were managing."

"It's a heck of a lot easier in these." She stuck out her leg, showing off her boots.

Somewhere down near my liver, Shaggy sniffed and grunted approval. *Down, boy. Jesus. We're on the clock.*

Out in the hall, the last stragglers made their way out, studying their phones and chattering like magpies. Cree gave me a smile. "Want some water? Karmen will be out in a minute. She always stays and does selfies til everyone's gone. Social media for the museum and all. She loves that crap."

The way she answered made me think she didn't. "No thanks. I'm good. Do you like it? Being up there in front of all those people?"

"Not really. But I need to be there because I engineer all the illusions and run safety. Bo—I mean Boudica..." She said the blonde's full name like it struck a filling, "Loves it, but she actually has skills. I just stand there and make the 'ta-da' pose."

She demonstrated a game show model move with those toned arms over her head, and a leg stuck out show-girl style. *Not a damned thing wrong with a good ta-da pose.* Before I could say something to prove I had no game whatsoever, two figures appeared silhouetted in the doorway.

The blond Amazon came through first, her eyes peeled for assassins or something. A second curvier figure followed, eyes aiming right at me.

Her fingers grazed my coat sleeve. "Are you alright? I'm sorry if the lights bothered you." Before I could say anything, she switched topics. "My, wasn't that a lovely crowd tonight? They really seemed to enjoy my... I mean the show. What did you think, Johnny?"

What did I think? She'd cut open some guy's private pain and put it on display for the world, then almost laser-surgeried the eyes out of my head. "Yeah. It was great."

Karmen nodded like there was no other plausible answer.

"Lemuel, darling. I assume you have assured our friend this is the egg I promised to deliver. Do you need to do your thing?" she wiggled her fingers in some sort of vague spooky magic way. "Just to prove it is what he bought?"

Mister Collins was already tugging the latex gloves off his hands. "Oh, I'm sure it's fine, but if you insist." With a wink at me, he pressed his palm to the egg and... nothing. His brow furrowed for just a moment, but then he nodded and put his gloves back on.

I realized I'd been holding my breath, but the old man smiled as he said, "This is the same object as was purchased. All right as rain."

Everyone looked at me. It was probably the right time for me to say something professional. "Uh, okay. So, can I pick it up tomorrow?"

A brief cloud passed over Karmen's face, but she put her smile returned quickly. "Yes, but let's say one pm. A girl needs her beauty sleep. I am going to miss the Egg as the finale. We're breaking in a new last illusion next week. I wanted the old man to hold off for a few more weeks, but he was most insistent we do it at the end of the month, and that nobody could pick it up but you."

I don't know what surprised me more—that Cromwell had left such explicit instructions not to entrust anyone else with this chore, or that she talked about him that way. I don't think anyone had called him anything other than Mister Cromwell since he was in the fifth grade.

One o'clock. The plan was to be on the road by sunrise and halfway to New Mexico by noon, but it was what it was. "That'll be fine. I have the papers back at the hotel, so I'll bring them by at one. It was nice meeting you." I held out my hand and Karmen took it in both of hers, stroking the hair on my wrists gently.

It took a bit of work to wrench my hand free from her grip. "Well, goodnight, then."

Cree blurted out a bit too quickly, "Do you have big plans for your last night in Vegas?"

There was a second of stupid silence while I tried to figure out if that was just a polite question, or maybe she was hinting at something else.

Your luck doesn't run that good. Quit while you're ahead.

It didn't matter at all, because before I could say anything dumb, the walls and floor shook. There was what might have been a small explosion and definitely men yelling. Then another far scarier noise.

Crap. Those are gunshots.

CHAPTER 13

"The rest of you head that way. We got this." A male voice barked orders from the far end of the building.

Boudica, armed with a belt-full of blades strapped to her waist, ran from the Egg Room. I was right on her heels, equipped only with Shaggy and a lack of common sense. Cree and Karmen were somewhere behind us. I had no clue where Mr. Collins was, but I wasn't counting on the older gentleman for backup if we needed it.

Backup would have been good. Definitely.

Rounding the corner to the corridor that led back to the first gallery and the lobby. Three big guys cradled weapons in their arms. Actually, two big guys and a human oak tree. One of them had to be a good half a foot taller than me, and twice as wide across the chest. All wore camo and black balaclavas in case we missed the subtle message the military style-rifles sent.

Shaggy was on red alert inside me as my skin prickled and hair stood on end. He was literally itching to get out and tackle these guys, but there were too many witnesses, and I had no clue what the hell was even happening.

"What do you think you're doing?" Karmen stomped forward like she wanted to talk to his manager. Now.

The guy in the middle, skinnier than the rest and holding his gun just a little tighter, took two steps forward. "Where is it?"

"Where's what?" I didn't believe for a moment that Karmen had no clue what he was talking about. For sure, the leader didn't, because he shot a look to his teammates like "watch this," and backhanded the woman across the face. Karmen banged off the wall and slumped to the floor in shock, touching her cheek and cursing a blue streak.

A whoosh of air passed inches from my head. There was a 'thunk,' and the handle of a throwing knife vibrated right where the guy's heart should be. He laughed hysterically and pulled it out, calling Boudica a whole list of filthy names. His normal-sized partner lifted his weapon and hit the blonde right on the nose with the butt. Blood gushed everywhere, and she crumpled, clutching her face.

The guy pointed his finger at Karmen. "Don't be a fucking idiot. You shouldn't have sold it to that old bastard in Chicago. Now where is it?"

Chicago was full of old bastards, but I knew who he meant, and what they'd come for. *They want the egg.* That would have been my first priority if I were any kind of professional. I was more pissed that they were hitting girls.

It's not easy to punch someone as hard as you can while keeping your inner wolf contained, but I managed. Fueled by pure anger, my fist connected with the guy who'd hit Boudica. He might have had a bullet-proof vest, but that mask wasn't fist-resistant. There was a satisfying *crack-thunk* as his head took my shot and bounced off the wall. He dropped to a knee.

My usual work boots would have been better to kick him with, but my dress shoes got the job done. I let fly and put him on his back, then stomped once into his solar plexus, hearing the air leave his lungs. Love that sound.

Whoever these guys were, they were an old-fashioned command-and-control outfit. Nobody made a move without the boss, so he received my undivided attention. Our eyes met. My nostrils flared, filling with a strong whiff of his confusion and fear. *Perfect.*

Snarling, not caring how much Shaggy he heard, I shouted, "Not expecting anyone but girls, asshole?" My body coiled to jump at him, all my concentration locked onto my target. Total laser focus.

Bad plan.

In my peripheral vision I saw a shadow and then my world exploded into stars, comets and multiple shiny blips across my eyesight. The huge guy had stepped between me and my target, jolting me with a haymaker that might have killed someone else. I staggered back into the wall, glaring at him, assessing my enemy, trying to pick my shot. Shaggy wanted a go at him, but it still wasn't right. Not that I wouldn't have appreciated the help. The conditions were wrong.

Before this moment, I'd never wished for a bazooka. I'd have gladly settled for my Ruger, but I'd safely tucked away it under the seat of the Charger. Since this guy likely wouldn't let me run out to the car, I did the next best thing. I bum-rushed the giant. Lowering my shoulder, I aimed for that gut and hoped my weight and momentum would get the job done. A guy that size, it was likely his most vulnerable area. Hell, it had worked on the redneck in Amarillo. The classics never go out of style.

If that was his weak spot, I was screwed. It was like running into a cinderblock wall. I know he felt me crash into him, because he made a little, "huh" grunt as I ricocheted back about three feet. While I wobbled, shaking my head and attempting to focus, he looked at me through his ski mask. His eyes were watery but sparkling and damned if he wasn't grinning. He was enjoying this.

A bap-bap-bap burst of gunfire into the ceiling and a shower of dust and broken tiles made everyone freeze where they were. "Enough screwing around. Bring me the Egg, woman." The leader regathered most of his mojo and was back to giving orders, albeit saltier than ever.

My brain heard my mouth say, "I can't let you do that."

He let out something that was supposed to be a laugh as he took stock of me with his shifty eyes. "You work for Cromwell."

"That's right. Who's pulling your strings, dipshit?"

He gestured with his head to Karmen, who had pulled herself together enough to regain her feet and most of her attitude. "Ask her. She knows. If she'd done right the first time, none of this would have been necessary. Would it, sweetie?"

Her top lip almost curled up on itself upon hearing him say that. "Bowden. And don't call me sweetie. Your daddy put you up to this?"

"Didn't have to. We won't be disrespected in our own backyard. You oughta know that. Now give me the damned egg and we can get out of here."

Now some of this was making sense. Bowden was the guy my boss outbid for the egg. Why they were going through all this for a fake was above my paygrade. What I knew for certain, it was my job to keep the egg for Mr. Cromwell. "No chance."

Leader-boy gave his head a fake-sympathy shake. "And exactly what are you going to do about it? There are three of us. With guns. You've got what? You, three dumb whores and an old man, who's about as useless as a screen door on a submarine." He chin-nodded at Mr. Collins, hanging back in the shadows, willing himself invisible.

Now soldier-boy was just being a dick. He wasn't wrong, but it was still a crappy thing to say, and he was enjoying himself way too much. Bullies always pissed me off. Shaggy didn't like him either. I growled at him. My hands flexed and unflexed in an effort to be ready for a fight, while keeping the change under control.

My attention was on the leader while scoping out the big guy who had no name yet, if his mother survived his birth long enough to give him one. I'd forgotten about the guy I'd sucker-punched earlier. He was still around.

The guy came at me, trying to put me in a headlock. Ducking low, I moved to my right and hit him with a left jab that stunned him for a moment. I had every intention of hitting him again, but there was a loud "WHAH" from my left. With a flash of a Doc Martin boot, the guy disappeared from view.

Cree caught him with a perfect round-house kick and knocked him the hell out. It wasn't clear who was more surprised, her or the bonehead laying on the floor. She regained her composure and struck a ready pose, fists up, backhanding a strand of red hair from her face. Instinctively, I put my arm in front of her and tried to push her back behind me.

She swatted my arm away and hissed, "Really?"

Boudica stood behind her, her face a little puffy but with a blade in each hand. If she didn't look like an Amazon before, she sure as hell did now. The woman had guts, even if she literally brought knives to a gunfight. We weren't exactly the Avengers.

Bowden took the guy on the floor by the collar and shook him. "Get up, you useless piece of crap. Got your ass kicked by a woman. Get the hell out of the way." The guy started crawling away, but too slow for his boss's taste. Bowden unleashed a kick in the seat of his pants, and the poor bastard crashed into the wall and stayed on the floor, safely out of the action.

"You know I can't let you have that egg, right?" If my ass was getting kicked over a forged piece of glass, I would at least pretend it was a noble cause. I was also going to need more space than the corridor provided. Motioning for the women to stay put, I slowly circled to my left until I stood in the opening of the first gallery. If nothing else, we'd be able to come at them from different directions and divide their attention.

Bowden pointed his weapon at the women, his sneer visible through the mouth hole in his mask. "Alright, this is going to be more fun than I hoped. I'll make sure Cromwell picks up your hospital bills, since he's responsible for all of this." He turned to Goliath at his side. "Bust this place up. Starting with him."

Crap.

The ogre threw his weapon aside and clenched one fist while the other reached up and ripped the ski mask from his head and he flexed his neck. I guess he wasn't too worried about witnesses, which probably meant he didn't plan to leave any behind. Not good news.

The guy was a few years older than me and a whole lot uglier. Above a thick beard that hung to his Adam's Apple were two jagged scars running up his right cheek, and another across his forehead. His face was red, capped by a snow-white buzz-cut. A tattoo snaked out from beneath his shirt and up by his ears, but that neck was so thick the ink wrapped around the back of his head, and I couldn't make out what it was supposed to be. If intimidation was the idea, it worked.

I was going to require all the help Shaggy could give me without crossing the line. I'd also need space to maneuver. Remembering the gallery had displays all along the walls but plenty of room in the center, I backed up. The big guy matched me step-for-step, smiling the whole time. My heart sank. While I enjoyed a good scrap, this guy lived for it.

Step one was to wipe that grin off his face and get him to take me seriously. Looking up at him, I tried to distract him while my hand got a little hairier, bigger, and stronger. It's near impossible to be a smartass and rein a werewolf in at the same time. It was only a couple of days til the moon and I was concentrating so hard my temples pounded. Maintaining eye contact as I took off my jacket, I opted for psychological warfare and blew him a kiss. "Hi sailor, come here often?"

His momentary confusion was the break I needed to launch a right hand. It caught him flush on the chin, and would have knocked anyone, including me, out cold. Instead, the big bastard took two steps back, shook his head, blinked twice, and let out a yell that was more of an animal roar. He lifted his arms over his head, screamed again, and brought his fist down on the display case.

The display shattered. A dozen or more of Karmen's oddities hit the ground amid broken glass and splintered wood. She let out an outraged scream and Bowden's voice dripped with sarcasm. "Sorry honey. He gets a little destructive when he's in a bad mood."

I studied my opponent, who seemed to care less about me than causing mayhem. He roared a third time and destroyed another case. In a frenzy, he picked up handfuls of haunted memorabilia and scattered it wildly across the room. Those eyes blazed with pure yellow hatred, and he completely ignored the shards of glass embedded in his forearm.

His attention came back to me when I drove my fist as hard into his gut as I could. I was pretty heavy-handed to begin with, and with Lycan assistance, that punch should have at least slowed him down. It didn't. I settled for grabbing his shirt and using my move of last resort. I drove my forehead right into his nose.

Done right, a good headbutt can knock a guy out. Done badly, that guy is you and you've crippled yourself. I executed the move perfectly, and it didn't seem to matter at all. He staggered for a second and shook his head. Rubbing his nose, his fingers came away covered in blood. The big guy examined them for a minute, then raised them to his face and sniffed deeply. Staring right at me, he smiled and slowly licked them clean, one by one. This guy was big and freaky.

He let out a shout in some language I couldn't make out—German or Scandinavian, maybe—and it echoed through the room. My werewolf's ears were sensitive as hell, but this was ridiculous. Nobody should be able to yell that loud, no matter how big they are.

I let out a roar of my own and charged. The ogre rushed to meet me, and we collided amid all the rubble. He was so much bigger than me that I got knocked off my feet. He kept coming, slamming me backwards into a display of haunted objects and shattering what was left of it. His chest pinned me to the wall. Yellow eyes were bright but his anger had him almost blind. He was throwing fists and stomping at anything in his way, alive or dead.

Then he stopped and tilted his head in apparent confusion. Instead of tearing me apart, he took several deep breaths and studied me. The giant sniffed slightly at first, then pulled me close to him and inhaled deeply, like he was trying to suck me up his nose. His eyebrows shot up and he shoved me back against the wall. Whatever he smelled on me pissed him off, because he grimaced, showing off his big, square white teeth. Then he said something in that other language.

"Ulfhednar?" He said it the first time, like it was a question. The second time, he threw his head back and screamed. "Ulf-ed-nar!"

What the holy hell's an ulfdar? With the blood pounding in my ears, I couldn't make it out. All I could figure was, whatever it was, didn't meet his approval.

It was then his scent reached my brain. Shaggy damn near burst out of me. My skin rippled, burning to change as the funky odor set my senses on fire. The guy stunk like a bear.

I don't mean he was just as funky, sweaty, and hairy as me. I mean he smelled like an honest-to-God, shits-in -the-woods, grizzly bear. The scent was all too familiar.

When I was in Middle School, before I really understood what I was, my school went on a field trip to Brookfield Zoo. Everything was fine until we got to the bear enclosure. Then big ADD-weirdo Johnny McPherson felt something explode in his brain. I burst into tears, whining about the smell making me sick and wanting to go home, and wound up waiting in an empty school bus, sniffling and shaking until the rest of the class returned.

So, yeah. I knew bears. I hated them. More accurately, the monster inside me did. But what this guy was and why he reeked wasn't my immediate concern. Trying to survive those huge paws wrapped around my throat was. I felt my windpipe being more and more constricted. The bear-guy roared and attempted to choke the life from me. Only by wiggling like a fish on a line and driving a solid kick to his balls was it possible to get away. I dropped to the floor and somersaulted away, gasping for air, flailing around to get my bearings.

The guy was enormous. He was vicious. He was also out of his damned mind. It was as if he couldn't decide whether to finish me off or just cause as much damage as possible to everything around him. He smashed, kicked, clawed at everything around him like a blond, pissed-off cyclone. One minute the monster would stomp on one of Karmen's exhibits, then take a blind, wild swing at me before picking up some shelving and smashing it against the wall. He was a thing possessed, intent on destroying something. Anything.

It was Bowden who saved my life. Above the noises of battle, I heard him yelling at the goon. "Okay, enough." Both Jumbo and I turned to see him standing in the doorway, rifle across his chest.

The light in my playmate's eyes changed, and he looked more human, if not saner. His body language changed, and his shoulders slumped a little.

Bowden snapped his fingers twice at him. "We got it. Come on."

Goddamn it, they got the egg. Johnny, you had one fucking job.

Since the boss now had the big guy's attention, I scrambled to my feet and took an inventory of my bodily components. Everything was present and functional, although I was going to be bruised as hell in the morning. I wiped my sleeve across my nose. Sore but not broken.

A gruff male voice shouted from somewhere in the distance. "Let's go. Move it."

Bowden nodded and shouted to the big bear-guy. "Leave him, or we leave you. Let's go."

Like shaking off a bad dream, the big man shivered head to toe, then took a last, quick look around. From where I stood, he seemed maybe a little embarrassed by what he'd done, but not surprised. With a grunt, he trotted out of the gallery, picked up his gun and rumbled out with the others. That left Karmen, Cree, and Mr. Collins in the hallway. I shot past them and ran back to the room where the Paiute Sky Egg should have been.

It was there. The crystal object sat undisturbed on its perch atop the dais in the spotlight right where Cree and I had left it. I breathed a sigh of relief.

The others arrived a few seconds behind me. Karmen Mystère, with all sense of control shot to hell, was weeping into her hands and shrieking about her museum. Cree wrapped an arm around her, hugging her tight and telling her it would be fine. Mr. Collins shook his head at the surrounding madness.

I bent over to catch my breath, one hand on the stand holding the egg. *Well, at least they didn't get it.* I was already imagining myself telling Cromwell how we—okay, I—had held off armed intruders to save his merchandise when Boudica ran into the room.

"They took it. They took the egg."

Karmen, Cree and Lemuel Collins said nothing. Karmen broke into tears while Cree and Mister Collins exchanged glances that meant something to them but just confused the snot out of me.

"What are you talking about? It's right here."

Boudica had no time for my ignorance. "No, genius. They took the Egg from the vault. They got the real one."

Wait. What?

CHAPTER 14

I paced back and forth in Karmen's office. Cree, Boudica, Mr. Collins slumped in chairs or on the sofa and the magician sat at her giant antique desk. She held her head in her hands, trying desperately not to let tears fall. Whether the waterworks were legit or for my benefit remained to be seen, but she was plenty upset about her busted-up museum, so maybe.

I was too wired by Shaggy, the moon, and excess adrenaline to do anything but pace back and forth, running my hand through my hair and muttering to myself.

I was desperate to make some kind of sense of all this crazy. I wished Bill was there to talk it out. Instead, I carried on the discussion by myself. "There were two eggs?"

Cree suddenly found whatever was outside in the dark more interesting than our conversation and looked away. *Guilt. She might have been part of this, but it wasn't her idea.* For some reason, I found that reassuring.

Karmen took a deep breath to steady herself, then looked up. "Yes. The egg on display, the one Malcolm Cromwell bought, is still there."

"And it's a fake."

She nodded. I turned to Mr. Collins. "Did you know it was a forgery?"

He stiffened. "I told you it was."

That was true. "Did you know there was another egg?" I watched his face. He thought about it a moment too long, then his shoulders slumped. "Not until tonight. When I told Mr. Cromwell about it, that was the egg I tested. But I had my suspicions."

"So, you found out when I did?" I was making this up as I went along, but there were enough nods around the room to confirm my theory so far.

He shook his head. "More or less. When I touched it in the room, there."

Karmen's brow furrowed, at least as much as Botox allowed. "How did you know?"

Mr. Collins shrugged. "It told me it wasn't the one I wanted. Well, I knew something wasn't right. Not sure what, exactly."

My head began pounding again. "Wait. The one you used on stage. The one with the lights. Which one was that?"

Cree's voice drifted over my shoulder. "The other one. The real one."

The "huh," must have been clear all over my face, because she continued. "We've been using the fake as a decoy. The real one emits that light when exposed to certain radio frequencies. No idea why, but it looks cool as shit, so we started using it. We bury the sound in the stage music. It mimics the frequency of a high-pitched electric guitar."

That's why the guitar riffs were off. I was the only one who could hear them.

Wait a minute.

"You mean you were spraying those lights on an audience and don't know what they are?"

Cree straightened her spine to challenge me. "We ran dozens of tests and used it in front of hundreds of people. You're the only one who ever reacted negatively." She stopped and her eyes looked up at the ceiling, her lips forming words with no sound as if doing algebra problems in her head. "Is there something special about you?"

"What do you mean, special?" Okay, it was a tad defensive, but I'd been called "special" often enough I didn't take that word as a compliment.

"Jeez, sorry. I just mean epilepsy or migraines or something." She was over-apologizing now. And looked sincere, which made me feel worse.

Nice going Johnny. She was just trying to help. "No, nothing like that. Sorry. I snapped. Long night."

"That's okay. And no shit." She gave me an apologetic smile, but it was clear she was still doing some kind of mental calculus.

I stood for a moment connecting dots, again wishing my buddy was there to play the Sherlock game, but I had to go this alone.

Dot one. "That Bowden guy. He knew this object was a fake?"

Nods all around. Dot two. "Did you have the other one when you sold it to him?"

Karmen slumped in her chair. "Yes, fine. Word got out among the serious collectors I'd bought the real one, so I had this one created and spread the rumor it was a fake after all. Even had Lem—Lemuel, sorry—test it so they'd believe. His word carries weight in this community. They all thought, 'Oh, Crazy Karmen got taken again. Another exhibit for her phony museum.' So they backed off. All except Bowen and the old man." She was pissed off, which meant I was more likely to get honest answers out of her. Hard to carry a grudge and fake anything else. Good.

Dot three. "They both thought they were still bidding on the real thing, or at least the only one there was. Why did Cromwell pay so much if he knew it was just a piece of glass?"

The woman at the desk was done playing nice. "Because he had to show his dick was bigger than the other guy's of course. I guess even Clive Bowden doesn't have as much money as everyone says."

Bowden. The whole situation was becoming slightly clearer. An idea drifted through my brain, buzzing and circling like a fly on a turd. There it was. Dot four. "Unless he had no intention of paying for it in the first place. Figured it was easier to just take it. Maybe send a couple of messages at the same time."

Boudica muttered something that sounded like "macho bullshit," while Cree and Karmen both nodded.

"Bowden's always had it in for my collection. If he can't have it, no one can blah blah blah. What the hell am I supposed to do now?"

Work with bookies and loan sharks, and you become familiar with minor larceny. I asked her, "Are you insured?"

She sneered. "Not without a police report. What am I supposed to say? I was committing fraud and the richest asshole in Nevada complained?"

She had a point. Still, I felt bad for her. There had to be a way to help, which there was, but it was shadier than an old oak tree. "What if you didn't know who did it?"

"What do you mean?"

"You're a high-profile person. Do you ever get nasty emails? Threats?"

"About three a week." Cree was catching on to where I was going with this line of questioning. "Mostly religious nuts. Playing with the forces of evil, thou-shall-not-suffer-a-witch-to-live BS."

God botherers. Perfect. "Great. Find two or three of the weirdest messages and give them to the cops. You never got a look at the perps. They were busting stuff up when you arrived and took off. Cree, Boudica and I ran them off." I looked at a deflated Mister Collins, looking like he'd aged overnight. "This would be a great time for you to call it a night, sir."

Lemuel nodded. He wasn't upset to escape the madness, but needed to save face. "You're right, I probably won't be much use while all that's going on. If you need my help putting it all back together, Miz Karmen, you let me know. And let Mister Cromwell know I'm always at his service." With that he gave a quick nod and slipped out of the room.

I nodded to him, but paid no mind as he made his escape. I had another problem. *Cromwell, crap. I have to tell the old man.* There was a list of several things I'd rather do, including do-it-yourself vasectomy, but I was on the clock. Johnny Lupul was nothing if not a by-God professional.

Karmen's voice interrupted my inner argument. "How am I supposed to get my egg back? Can you help me?"

I wanted to. First, because I owed Junior Bowen a world-class ass-kicking. I also needed to know more about Bear Guy. But first, there was an unpleasant conversation ahead of me.

"You'd better call the cops on your mysterious witch hunters. I have a call of my own to make. Oh, and lose the surveillance recording. They'll ask for it for sure."

***

The original plan was to step out into the hall and leave a voicemail for Cromwell. That way, I could take time to answer questions from the cops, spin some horseshit story, and give my employer just enough information to keep my job. Even with the time difference, it was barely five in the morning in Chicago, so I never expected the cranky old guy to answer the phone. I forgot old people don't sleep worth a damn.

Worse, they use technology less ably than I do. He insisted on a video call so he could look me in the eye, which is how I found myself talking to a giant liver spot on the top of his bald head because he had no clue where the camera was. He was looking at my picture at the bottom of the screen while the camera scanned Mount Baldy.

The great Malcolm Cromwell was having what my mom used to call a conniption. After explaining the situation for the third time, I let him splutter himself out enough to rationally discuss next steps.

"I want that Egg. I paid for it, and I want it." *That sounds reasonable enough.*

"Well, it's here. I can throw it in the car and head out in the morning..."

"No, the real Egg. I want the real thing." *And reason just left town.*

"But we don't have it. Bowden does."

"Then get it. Find it. Bring me the real Paiute Sky Egg. And Johnny, there is no subtlety required here. Clive Bowden has chosen to act outside the rules of the game. He gets what he gets. Do what you need to do. And a bit more, if you get my drift."

The drift was gotten, and the Shaggy-driven part of me was glad. Payback might be a bitch, but it was underrated as a source of amusement. And it was almost the full moon, so I was as ready as I was going to be.

There was the small matter of finding out where Bowden and the egg were, but I had a feeling Karmen knew more about the cowboys than she'd let on. *Karmen. Crap.*

"I'm happy to go after it, if that's what you want, sir. But you know technically, you bought the fake one..."

The brownish gray, Greenland-shaped spot shook violently as he shouted, "That's another thing. Put that woman on the phone."

I stepped back into the room and held the phone out like it was a rattlesnake. "He wants to talk to you."

Karmen took a deep breath. "Girls, why don't you go out front and wait for the cops? I'll be with you in a minute."

Cree and Boudica both nodded and, bleary-eyed, shuffled out of the room. I may technically have creeped on Cree's muscular butt as they passed by.

In her best smiling Southern voice, Karmen pried open my fingers, taking the phone from my hand.

"Malcolm, my darling. I'm so sorry to cause you trouble..."

Shaggy gave me a nudge that made the heat rise in my cheeks and my lip twitch. He was leery as hell, and so was I. Karmen wasn't sorry at all. And she wasn't done making my life complicated.

There was another mystery. *What's an Ulfen-thingy?*

CHAPTER 15

After B.S.ing the cops for an hour, I was wrung out and needed sleep. Cree and Boudica had long left, and Karmen needed alone time. I desperately needed to speak to someone sane, so I texted Bill.

Me:
Dude you up?

As much of an early bird as he is, 3:30 in Vegas is still 5:30 in Chicago. My friend was sleeping the sleep of the righteous. I figured he'd answer by the time I got back to the hotel, and we could have an actual conversation. Or, maybe, it could wait awhile. That huge empty bed at Caesar's suddenly seemed like the most inviting place in the world.

My dress jacket was a smelly mess, and the blood drops on the lapel would need work. My pants looked like I'd mugged a homeless clown for his clothes. Fortunately, the hotel could take care of that for me. It was a pretty safe bet that Nevada dry cleaners had plenty of experience getting body fluids out of clothing. *Meaghan's right, I can't have nice things.*

Meaghan had been right about a lot of things. Cold light at the top of the list. And the women. I had no idea what to make of Karmen's coven. Cree seemed okay. Maybe.

Cool, pleasant air greeted me as I stumbled out of the Museum into the real world. No humidity, a cloudless sky, a moon not full but big enough to cause havoc—maybe this wasn't such a bad place after all. Karmen's theater was far enough off the Strip that the air smelled fairly clean for a big city. The wind blowing in from the north had something to do with that. I took a deep breath, rolling my shoulders. I'd have to stretch before bed or my whole body would really feel tonight's adventure.

My faithful Charger sat waiting for me in the dim glow of the parking lot light. So did Cree—one hip resting on the hood, arms folded, tapping her foot. She'd been waiting, what, an hour or so?

"Took you long enough. I was about to give up and go home." She wasn't in any better mood than I was.

"Covering your boss's ass took longer than I expected. The cops don't really believe her, but... What are you doing here?"

"We need to talk about something." *Crap.* I may not have a lot of experience with women, but I know nothing good starts with 'we need to talk'.

"I'd love to, Cree. But is there any chance we can do it in the morning? I'm exhausted."

"I know, me too. But if I don't talk about this with someone, it's going to drive me crazy. Please? Just for a minute."

She bit her bottom lip as she waited for a response. A crazy thought manifested in my brain. *Maybe she's really into me.*

I nodded and pulled out my keys. My car was old enough it didn't have remote locks, and the door opened old school; with a key the way God intended. Jingling my key chain, I moved towards her side of the car. Cree took one quick step back, like she was afraid I'd brush against her.

Okay. Not into me, then.

I opened the car door and waved her inside. "I'm guessing you don't want the entire world to hear our conversation. Need a ride home?"

Whatever she needed to say was important enough that getting into a stranger's car was worth it. Mind you, the girl could handle herself. She nodded, but before getting in she threw the Mickey D's bag off the seat onto the floor, and slid in.

My exhaustion outweighed my manners. "I wasn't expecting company."

"That stuff'll kill you, you know." *Great, probably a vegan on top of everything.* But of course she'd hate junk food. Her body was a temple. Mine was more like a dollar store in a terrible neighborhood.

"Yeah, like that's what'll finally get me." My mood was darkening and the frustration of trying to figure out what the redhead was up to only made it worse.

"Thank you. For earlier. What you did for Karmen and... just thanks."

She just wanted to express her gratitude, and I was being a jerk. "You're welcome. I mean, I couldn't just stand there, could I?"

"We weren't just helpless girls, you know... but we couldn't have done it without you. You can really handle yourself."

Yeah, like you handled yourself real well when he threw you across the room. Big hero. "Thanks. So can you. That was a hell of a kick. You study MMA or something?"

The question fell on deaf ears. She stared straight ahead, like she was figuring out what to ask next. "He called you an Ulfhednar. That big guy."

"I get called a lot of things. And I was a little busy. I don't even know what it means."

Now she turned to study my face. "You really don't?"

"Don't even know what language it was. I was a little more concerned about the fact he was throwing me around like a rag doll. What's an Ulfdorner?"

"Ulfhednar." She said it again, drawing it out, so it sounded more like *ool-fen-thar,* like it would mean more to me the second time, with a lot of emphasis on the first syllable. I wasn't any smarter. "It means wolf warrior."

It was a good thing I wasn't driving yet because a chill ran the length of my spine. "In what language?" My voice sounded remarkably calm for all the panic rising inside me.

Cree's expression changed as she turned towards me. Her face had that same look Meaghan got when she had to explain something to the dumb, hairy guy. "Old Norse. The Ulfhednar were one of the main warrior cults. The wolf warriors. There were others—"

"Wait. So what, the big guy is some kind of Viking?" Exhaustion added to my cluelessness. She was geeking out on this stuff though, clearly enjoying herself.

"I think he was a *berserker.*" Pronouncing the word like it was the answer to everything didn't make it any clearer. She needed to bail me out. "Look how destructive he was, like all he wanted to do was smash things up and didn't care who or what. Berserkers would go mad in battle. They couldn't be stopped and wouldn't calm down until they slaughtered all their enemies. See if the Ulfhednar are wolves, the berserkers are—"

"Bears." That funk was still in my nose as I said it.

"Bears. Exactly. You knew that, right?"

I avoided her gaze while I contemplated the existence of such a thing. *What do you even call it? A were-bear?*

"Am I taking you somewhere?"

"In a second. Why does he think you're a wolf warrior?"

Because his nose works as well as mine does. "Could be he's just crazy. You saw him in there. Berserk is a good word. He would've probably killed me—all of us—if Bowden hadn't called him off."

"Boudica and I can handle ourselves." Saying it didn't make it true, but believing it made her feel better, so I let it slide. "You're not just hired muscle from Chicago, are you?"

"It's kind of hard to explain."

"Try me."

"Nope." I turned the key and gunned the engine just to hear the Charger roar. "Look, I don't want to be rude but it's really late. I just got my ass kicked, and I have to figure out how to get that goddamn egg back or I'm out of a job. Am I taking you someplace, or..."

"Take me home. There's something there I want you to see." Under other circumstances, that would be a great offer.

The way things stood, it was my best chance to escape this conversation, which was plenty. Cree was already in the car, and Bill hadn't called yet. Leaving her alone in a lonely parking lot after the night's chaos didn't seem safe. Plus, she was cute even if a culinary snob. I slammed the car into gear and pulled out of the parking lot. "Where am I going?"

"Oh my god, I love The Who." She leaned over and turned up my radio to blast "Baba O'Riley." This was the unbreakable first commandment of being a passenger—thou shalt not mess with the driver's music. I let her slide under the circumstances. Besides, who didn't love Roger Daltrey?

She directed me East on Charleston. She must have thought she'd won the first round, because Cree bounced in her seat like she had a secret she was bursting to tell. I split my concentration between not killing us—there was a lot of traffic for this time of the morning—and wondering what the hell she thought she knew about me.

The inquisition began. How did I like Chicago? How long have I been working with *arcana*? That was the word she used. Arcana. Classier than creepy old shit, I suppose. It was obvious she could not only kick my ass if she wanted, but was twice as smart as I'd ever be. She seemed to know a bit about everything.

Way out of your league, Johnny. Just get her home and you can go nighty-night.

"Have you lived in Chicago your whole life?"

If this were a date, I'd already be planning how to avoid a second one. Talking about myself was never the best way to showcase my good qualities and the interrogation never seemed to stop. I adopted blind date rule number seven: give them enough information to seem boring and they'll drop the subject. "No, I'm adopted. But I've lived there ever since. What about you?"

JOHNNY LYCAN & THE VEGAS BERSERKER

"I'm from no place you ever heard of, trust me. So where were you born, then?"

"I don't know. I was really young at the time." Her laugh was more girlish than I'd expected. Likely, she'd take that as an insult, given the whole badass Goth/Wicca thing she had going on. In truth, it was adorable, and I wondered what else I could say to hear more of it. Tomorrow.

"Here. On the left. Come on, where were you born? Did they ever tell you?"

Dodging traffic and most of her questions, we pulled into an apartment complex in a neighborhood full of sand-colored units. A thin line of blue light creased the sky to the East, and the moon hung low and huge. She directed me to a visitor's parking space.

I put the Charger in Park and leaned back against the seat, wishing I could fall asleep right there. "Rumania. It was a thing in the eighties to adopt Romanian orphans."

Cree slapped her hand on the dashboard. "I knew it."

Knew what? I had gone from bone-tired to totally confused.

She unbuckled her seat belt and hopped out. "You coming? You're definitely gonna want to see this."

For a second, I visualized just slamming the car in reverse and getting out of there. I snuck a peek at my phone. If there was a God in heaven, Bill would have answered me and I could use that as an excuse.

The Almighty was off duty.

Exhausted and worn down, I nodded and stepped out. I'd never been less excited to be asked up to a woman's apartment.

CHAPTER 16

I followed her up the outside stairs to a second-floor sand-colored apartment with a slightly more beige-y door in keeping with Vegas' "everything is the color of dirt" decorating scheme. Apparently, they like to save all the bright colors for the Strip. A small deck with a table and a couple of folding chairs took up most of the landing. Cree grabbed something off the table, fumbled in her purse for a lighter and set the bundle smoking. Then she waved it all over herself, starting at her head and working down.

"Sage." She said by way of explanation. "It gets rid of all the creepy, evil vibes of that place. I need to do this every day. I'm not bringing that shit inside with me. Especially when those cases broke open." I detected a small shiver. It was plain she wasn't joking, so I didn't laugh. Besides, I remembered the sick feeling in my stomach at some of those nasty doodads.

My nose twitched long before the smoking bundle got anywhere near me. Shaggy smelled it too, and he didn't care for it one bit. While he growled and whimpered in my head, I squirmed like a five-year-old whose mother is trying to wash his face with spit and Kleenex.

"Oh, for God's sake, stand still. It won't kill you." Probably, but it was making me throw up in my mouth a bit and Shaggy was protesting so much I was afraid she'd hear him growl. At least it was nowhere near as awful as Gramma's herbal werewolf repellent. I sucked it up, closed my eyes, held my breath and stiffened until the trial by smoke ended. Then she waved me into her apartment.

Whatever I was expecting, the joint didn't look like the den of a badass, MMA-practicing witch. It was... a kitchen. Happy yellow plates sat on open shelves, a vase of supermarket flowers brightened up the countertop, and a Georgia O'Keeffe print hung over the sofa. I know nothing about art, but a flower that looks that much like—well, it was definitely Georgia O'Keeffe.

The only unpleasantness in the place was the angry hissing of a cat—black, of course—perched high up on the armoire, making his displeasure known. Hair stood straight up on its neck, and the hate rolled off it in waves. The only creatures that loathe me more than dogs are cats. It was mutual, too. Nasty creatures. Shaggy desperately wanted to eat him, but murdering someone's pet in their home is considered rude in most cultures.

Cree tsk-tsked at the critter. "Pooky, knock it off."

"Your cat's name is Pooky?" I'd have bet on Lilith, or Medea or something Wiccan-ish. Pooky sounded almost normal. My muscles relaxed a bit, and I wondered if maybe this was a social visit after all.

"Uh-huh. He's usually much better with company. Come on down and say hello, baby." She held her arms out, but the cat swatted at her, yowling again.

Cree seemed embarrassed by the critter's bad manners and gave me an apologetic shrug.

Letting her off the hook, I said, "I get that a lot. Don't worry about it."

"Can I get you anything? Tea, or..."

"No. Thanks. You said you had something you wanted to show me?" Sunlight was already oozing through the plastic blinds. *Let's do what we have to and get out of here.*

My phone vibrated in my pocket—probably Bill answering my text. Tempted to answer it, I opted for just finishing business and getting the hell out of there. I could check in on my way back to the hotel.

Cree hesitated a moment, took a deep breath, and let it out slowly. "Okay. The grand tour. Kitchen, obviously. Living room. Bathroom's over there if you need it." She moved to a hallway to her left. My room's the big one on the end." Her hand reached for a wooden knob to a second bedroom. "What I want to show you is in here."

I expected a home office or a storage room. Something as normal as the rest of the house.

I wasn't ready for a full-blown chemistry lab complete with distilling bottles and Bunsen burners hooked up to propane tanks. It had to violate her lease, although judging from the neighborhood, it wasn't the only chemical lab in the vicinity. The workbench took up the full length of one wall. Next to it were wooden bookshelves turned into storage. The top two rows held jars of dried plants, beneath that, books and pamphlets, neatly arranged but by what filing system I couldn't fathom. If Martha Stewart ran a meth lab, this is what it would look like.

I stepped closer to examine it. Some of those plants looked a lot like Gramma's tea ingredients. "Is this why Karmen called you the Mistress of Potions?" *She's so smart, she can't really believe all this crap, can she?*

"I suppose. As you can imagine, she tends to exaggerate. I'm just a hedge witch with a chemistry degree. Here's what I really want you to see."

Something in dark wood hung on the opposite wall. It looked like a spice rack, or the cross section of a birdhouse. There were two shelves containing a variety of little items. On the top shelf sat two large candles, one black, one white. They bracketed a metal bowl.

That, I recognized. "Is that a scrying bowl?"

She smiled and shrugged. "It's supposed to be. I suck at it. Have you used one?"

My head wagged. "No, but I've seen them." It seemed like a bad time to tell her my only experience with such a thing resulted in it exploding all over the place and that I had the same effect on magical instruments as coffee on a keyboard.

So, this was her altar. I'd known enough pseudo-goth chicks to understand the basics. The idea was to hold items for religious purposes as well as magical tools and things of spiritual importance to the user. The candles made sense, so did the scrying bowl. There were other souvenirs on the altar—a dried rose, a pentagram on a silver chain, but none of them drew my attention like the item dead center on the lower shelf. It was ebony-black and hook-shaped. It came to a lethal-looking point on one end and was jagged where it had been broken off on the other.

A Lycan's claw.

What the actual flaming fuck? I wanted to bolt, but my feet were cemented to the floor and I couldn't stop staring. Shaggy let out a whine and churned my guts to butter. Creatures like me don't just drop their fingernails on the ground. It was a damned good bet whatever she took that from was dead. *Had she killed a Lycan? Was she going to kill me?*

Cree's voice penetrated the brain fog. "Yeah, that's what I wanted to show you."

I couldn't even pretend not to know what it was. "Where did you get it?"

Cree's voice was soft, and I detected a quick catch of emotion before she spoke. "My brother. Tomas."

I stood silent, guessing she'd have to build up to the explanation. That was fine. I needed to gear up just to hear it. She walked to the altar and picked the talon up, stroking it with a finger. "He was a couple of years older than I was. Adopted." Her eyes turned my way. "From Romania."

. "Where is he now?" It was a lame question, but the only one to ask under the circumstances.

"He died. Four years ago."

"I'm sorry."

"Are you—like him?"

Jesus, how's a guy supposed to answer that? Pretending ignorance was my go-to defense. The smart thing to do would be lie my ass off.

"Yeah, I guess I am."

"That's why that guy called you an Ulfhednar. Because you're like Tomas."

"I should go. You don't—"

She reached her arm out and touched my elbow. "I was helping him control it. The change, I mean."

With great restraint, I let her hand rest on my arm and didn't just chew it off. "What do you mean, control it? How?"

"We came up with a... natural suppressant, I suppose you'd call it. It helped him maintain control at the full moon. When he took it, that is."

Too many questions rattled around in my head. *What happened? Did it really work? Did he go off his meds? How do I get out of here without looking like a moron, coward or flaming asshole?*

A vibration ran up my leg again. Cree noticed it and her eyes asked if I was going to answer. Bill was being his persistent self. That seemed like a superb time to make my exit.

I waved my phone at her as an excuse. "I need to take this, and we all need some sleep. We'll talk about this later, okay?"

"Tomorrow?" She would not let this go. I needed time to process everything that had happened, plus her little bombshell.

And tomorrow was already today. The sun was peeping over the hills so notions of last night, today, tomorrow were relative. She reached her hand out again, then thought better of it and yanked it back, crossing her arms across her chest.. "I think I can help you."

The only thing that could actually help was a shit-ton of sleep.

"Yeah, um. We'll see."

CHAPTER 17

As the Charger peeled out of Cree's parking lot, I called Bill.

"Dude, what's going on? What are you doing up so early? Or are you just going to bed? I hope." He was way too chipper for the circumstances.

"Heading for bed, but not that way. Everything's gone sideways."

His voice dropped an octave and butched way up. "Tell me." There was the solid, logical Bill I needed.

It felt good to vent, and I told him at least most of it: Lemuel Collins, Karmen, and the egg being stolen. Bowden and the wannabe soldier boys—minus the little detail about the Bear Guy. I wasn't ready to have that discussion. Cromwell being on the warpath. The rest—Cree, her brother, the magical werewolf suppression potion—were sideshows I didn't have time or patience to deal with yet.

I navigated directly west into the rising sun while babbling to my friend. It wasn't easy—the early morning traffic was ugly, and my eyeballs felt like they'd combust any second. I slapped around on the passenger side for my sunglasses, but they had vanished into the dark world under the seat. *Frickin' perfect.* Somewhere between the Museum and Cree's place they'd vanished along with my well-thought-out plan for being out of town by noon.

Navigating local Vegas traffic, even in their lame excuse for a rush hour, took more patience than I possessed. It felt like everyone on the road was either driving head-on into the fireball of a sun with their eyes closed, still drunk, or hungover enough to be impaired. Plus, legal weed. That probably explained why every second billboard in Vegas was for an injury attorney. People here drove like they lived—with a high risk tolerance.

Tonight was the full moon, and Shaggy hadn't been let out to run in over a month. With every honked horn and illegal U-turn from the middle lane, he was itching for a good road rage dustup. Twice I pounded on the steering wheel and screamed at the top of my lungs.

Bill's "Johnny-take-a-breath," voice crackled from the speaker. "You know, she's probably a very nice person."

"Who?"

"The one you just called the C word."

"You should have seen the move she just made!" *Baby on board my furry ass.*

"Dude, when are you coming home?"

Excellent question. Maybe never if this goes any worse than it already has. "Sorry, yeah. At least a week. I need to get that stupid fricking egg back."

"How?"

"That, Watson, is the question. I'm going to grab some zees, then figure it out."

He was silent so long I was afraid the call had dropped. At least it gave me enough time to pull into the back garage at Caesar's before he finally spoke. "Take care of yourself. Gramma says hey. Meaghan says I'm supposed to remind you to stay away from cold light, whatever the hell that means."

The shiver up my back distracted me enough I nearly plowed into the car ahead of me at the gate. *Did freaky laser shows from outer space qualify?* "It means she needs to do something besides flip those damned Tarot cards all day. But thanks. Say hi to everyone."

Everyone. All three people in the world who gave a crap about me. Four, if you counted Francine. Not that it mattered. None of them were in Las Vegas at the moment. It was just me and Shaggy against a bunch of paramilitary wackos. Maybe Cree could help—though I was probably kidding myself. Who knew what side Karmen was on? Or Lemuel Collins.

Answers could wait. Sleep first. I staggered through the casino, intent on that welcoming enormous bed. This time of the day my Lycan-powered nose revolted at all the Axe body spray polluting the environment. Frat boys never sleep, apparently.

But I did. On top of the covers with my clothes on, shoes included.

Four blessed hours. Not enough, but when I'm in a high-cycle frenzy and facing certain catastrophe, it was more than I expected. Or deserved.

CHAPTER 18

Day of the Full Moon.

At eleven that morning, I stood in Karmen's office trying to figure out how not to get killed. Each of my ideas began with me going to Bowden's ranch, finding the Sky Egg, stealing it back from a bunch of Call of Duty fanboys, and getting it back to Chicago. Ideally with both it and me in one piece. Beyond that, the possibilities were endless. Getting shot as soon as I stepped on the property was the least ugly of the bunch.

It was going to be even harder to think clearly because, as tired and snarly as I was, Shaggy was worse. He was doing backflips and growling inside my head every time the Mistress of Magick spoke. He distrusted Karmen more than I did, which was saying something.

After my second or third lame suggestion, she muttered, "Jesus, where did Cromwell find you?"

The only other people in the room, Boudica and Cree, watched in silence. Whenever Karmen said something nasty, the Amazon smirked. Cree flinched, but kept quiet. I didn't blame her for not standing up to her boss. She didn't really know me from Adam, and good jobs in the mistress-of-potions business were probably scarce.

A large map covered Karmen's desk. She tapped one of her pointed gel-tip nails on a building in the center of the map. "It's at the ranch. He wouldn't trust it anyplace else and even the Feds won't go near it. But the house alone is nine thousand square feet, not including the barns and garages. It's two miles in from the main road. Are you just going to walk into a heavily armed compound across open desert, on your own two legs, snoop around, find the egg, steal it and run away with it?"

"Well, yeah. Pretty much." She made it sound worse than it was. I wouldn't be on two legs. And a mile or two wouldn't be a hindrance in my Lycan form. Other than that, she nailed it. Not such a sound battle plan, when said out loud, but nobody'd offered anything better. I was making shit up as I went along.

"I can get in there, alright. I just need to know where they're keeping the egg. Then I swap out the fake for the real one and hightail it out of there."

Boudica, dressed in a black crop top with dark jeans and boots, crossed her arms. "You'll never get to the house. And for sure you'll never get out. They have at least ten cowboy assholes with guns."

With a flourish, I reached into my belt and pulled out my Ruger. "I have a gun." In my head, it looked cool as hell.

Boudica snort-laughed. "Seriously? That amateur shit might work in Chicago, but this is the Wild West errand boy."

She stomped to an framed antique poster in German of a woman magician named "Minerva, The Queen of Mystery." Behind it was an immense wall safe. Four beeps later, the gray door swung open to reveal three semi-automatic rifles and half a dozen big-ass handguns, all of which could eat my little automatic and not even burp.

She waved her arm in an ironic "ta-da." "And this is just the stuff we keep handy."

Cree bit her lip and avoided my gaze. Karmen slapped the tabletop. "Will you two stop comparing dick size?" She managed a slight grin and looked me in the eye. "You'd probably lose, by the way. Focus."

I needed to reestablish some alpha male cred. "They said they were taking it to their evil super-villain lair, right? We know where that is. Get me in there, and I'll find it." Assuming Shaggy could sniff it out, which was likely.

Pale and a tad shaky, Karmen slumped in her leather chair, face in her palms, her black hair obscuring part of the map. "Let's assume you get in. We know where it is. But we don't know *where it is.*"

Cree raised her hand, hesitating to jump into the conversation. "What if we figured out what room he was keeping it in? That would help, right?"

"Yeah, at least I'd know where to look." I felt a weird need to be supportive, even though I couldn't tell where she was going with this.

"We can do that. Well, Karmen can. Right?" She looked past me to her boss. "Scry in."

Karmen ran a tongue over her bottom lip. "We could narrow it down for sure. But you know scrying isn't my actual gift..."

"Okay, a tracking spell, then. You're frigging amazing at that."

"That type of magick works better on people than things. It wouldn't exactly locate the egg, but they wouldn't be very far apart. I'd need something from the person we're looking for. Something with their essence."

Cree reached into the right pocket of her shorts and pulled out a plastic baggie. Inside was a tattered piece of cloth, stained a rusty brown. "This came off the big guy's camo when Johnny was fighting him. It was snagged on a broken display case. Where he is, Bowden is, and where Bowden is, you'll find the egg. He's not going to let it out of his sight, right?"

Shaggy perked up, and I wondered if he could smell the blood through the bag. It wasn't the worst idea I'd heard, so I went along for the ride. "Great, so you can do whatever voodoo you need to do and just tell me where to find it when you're done. Perfect."

Karmen reached out a hand for the bloody scrap. Cree passed it over and stepped back beside me, offering a look out the corner of her eye, along with the tiniest hint of a smile.

The magician—I was not prepared to call her a witch, at least in that sense—studied the item, turning it over and over. "I'll need you to be part of this. You need to see it for yourself or there's no point."

Crap. "Yeah, no. That won't work."

Using her fingers, she brushed her hair back, part of pulling herself together. "You don't believe, I gather."

I thought about Gramma's crystal ball, and Cromwell's scrying bowl, and how my presence was like pouring sugar in the psychic gas tank. "It's not that you can't do it, it's just that if I get too close, it won't work."

Boudica muttered something behind me. I tried to explain. "Seriously, any kind of psychic activity? I'm not saying you're not legit. But if I'm there... it's..."

"Like static electricity. It messes up the signals." Cree finished my thought. All three of us turned to look at her. "What? My brother, Tomas, was like that."

Her brother. The Lycan. Did they know about him? Hell, do they know about me?

Boudica shrugged. "What, so testosterone fucks up magic? Figures."

It took a lot not to go full Shaggy on her, but I gritted my teeth and stayed mum.

"It won't work if you can't be part of the ceremony." Karmen said quietly. I could tell from her face she was trying to puzzle out what her assistant knew that she didn't. That lovely pale forehead scrunched and wrinkles formed at her eyes, but before she could put two and two together, Cree jumped in.

"I think I know how to get around that. Uh, Johnny, can I talk to you for a minute? Out there?" Her head jerked to the office door.

"Yeah. Sure. I mean, I guess." I held a finger up to Karmen. "Give us a moment."

What the hell?

I followed Cree from the sun-drenched office into the dark hallway as Boudica and Karmen's suspicious glares burned holes in my back.

Soon as the door closed, Cree held a hand up to shush me. "I'm sorry, but I didn't want to say too much in there. They don't know what you... well, they know there's something funky about you because you work for Cromwell, and everyone who works for him is sketchy as hell. But they don't know what it is."

"So?"

She took a moment, searching for the right words. "Tomas had the same thing as you, okay? Couldn't be around real magic because of his... you know."

I always suspected it was a werewolf thing, that it wasn't just me. "Then you know I can't do what she's asking. It won't work."

"It might. If you let me help."

Shaggy scratched down near my spleen. "How?"

"Remember? I said I had something to control that thing in Tomas?"

I kept quiet, which she took as permission to keep going. Her words rattled on like a boulder rolling downhill, picking up speed.

"What if we tried it?"

Before I could say the magic words, "Fuck no," she jumped in.

"Not a lot, just enough to, I don't know, dampen your power a bit. Call it a test. If it can limit the negative energy even a little, you can take part in the tracking spell. What do you have to lose?"

My life was at the top of that list. Shaggy was becoming agitated, and I barked at her, "I said no," with more force than necessary. I wasn't trying to be an asshole, but arguing with her and Shaggy at the same time was exhausting and made my head ache.

Cree took it like a champ. Not too many people could withstand that kind of negativity blasted in their faces, but then she was a werewolf's little sister. Her body stiffened, but she never flinched.

There was no way I'd be able to find the egg if I didn't get some help, and Shaggy was making it clear this idea really sucked. I couldn't believe I was going to ask, but here it was. "Did it work?"

"I wouldn't suggest it if I didn't. I mean, you're bigger than he was, so we'd have to play with the dosage a bit to do a full suppression, but—"

"I'm not your goddamned lab rat. And I'm not taking enough to... Just to get through this little puppet show." After a moment, I found

113

myself asking, "What's the least it would take to get through the tracking spell?"

I hadn't even noticed she'd been gripping my arm until I felt her relax. From yet another zippered pocket in her shorts, she pulled out a plastic squirt bottle full of a sludge-brown liquid.

"That's it?"

Cree displayed it proudly. "There's enough here to prevent two months of, well, activity. For him, maybe less for you. What do you weigh?"

"Two hundred."

She chuckled. "Okay, so two hundred and fifteen pounds." She held the bottle up, running calculations in her head.

"Hey."

"Do you want to risk an overdose?" She ignored my whiny answer. When satisfied, she nodded. "This is a ten percent solution. It should mellow you out enough to sit with Karmen."

"I don't know..." Truer words were never spoken.

"Do you trust me?"

Shaggy sure as hell didn't. I was a little less skeptical, but not sure it was worth my life to find out. Then again, if it worked, I'd be running into an armed camp with just a fur coat for protection.

And what if this stuff did the job? What if it really allowed me to control Shaggy for good?

There was too much to think about. Losing focus could get me killed. And the stuff probably didn't work anyway, right?

Screw the odds. Vegas, baby.

CHAPTER 19

I'm really going to do this, aren't I?
Cree slapped the plastic bottle into my outstretched hand.

"What's in it?" I pulled the cap off and gave it a small whiff. The stench was like an arrow to my brain and Shaggy tried to exit through my belly button. "Holy crap, that's wolfsbane. Are you trying to kill me?" While nowhere near as potent as Gramma Mostoy's werewolf repellent powder, it was enough to put my system on red alert. My guts flip-flopped with just one nose-full.

"Don't be such a baby," she said, snatching it back. "There's a couple of milligrams of Aconitine as a catalyst. It's not like I'm making you drink the whole thing. A few drops. And it'll be offset by..."

Wolfsbane, monkshood, whatever the hell you call it, Aconitum's various chemicals are deadly to anyone, but especially someone like me. I knew little about drugs, but I'd done a pretty thorough Google search of stuff that can kill Lycans. A man with any sense would have already been halfway to Chicago, but I was still there. Did I really believe her, or did I just want to? And why? That wasn't a question I could solve right then. First things first. "You said Tomas took this crap?"

Whatever killed him, her brother would have been at least partly in Lycan form when he died for her to have that claw. *Had he stopped taking his meds, or did it stop working?*

"For almost a year. The problem was he didn't take it before he..." She shook her head and then focused on me, speaking slowly and calm. "We're only going to use enough to jumpstart your system. Then it's offset with all kinds of extracts. Mostly it's a couple of different distillations of benzodiazepine. And a little cannabis oil to help you chill."

Hash oil, I knew, it's the other one that worried me. "What's benzowhatever?"

"Valerian root, mostly. Some other grain derivatives. Widow's Rye..."

This began as a bad idea. Now it seemed suicidal. But I didn't want her to think I was chickening out. "No eye of newt?"

"It's not vegan." With my system in an uproar, it took me a minute to figure out if she was busting my chops. That damned smile gave her away. "A few drops in water should be enough to relax your defenses against magick. That's all. Promise."

She crisscrossed her heart, and it was so damned adorable I felt my resistance crack.

"Just enough to do Karmen's tracking thingy, right?"

"Yes." She actually bounced up and down. "Come on."

She grabbed my hand and pulled me towards a small maintenance and storage room. Among the mops and cleaning products were bottles of water on a pallet and a utility sink against the wall.

She eagerly twisted the cap off a bottle, then ran a thin stream of water into the sink. With her werewolf tranquilizer in one hand, she eyeballed the measurements. Despite her excitement, she must have seen how worried I looked. "Come on, Johnny. I wouldn't hurt you. Plus, if this doesn't work, you don't get Karmen's egg back, and I need this gig."

I nodded, falling into her green eyes. This wasn't the stupidest thing I'd ever done to impress a woman. Top five, maybe, but not the worst.

"Yeah. Me too. Let's do it."

Like a mad scientist in some old movie, she took some tap water, added a drop to her potion, swirled it around, and added another drop. Then a second and third.

"Four, five... shit!" She pulled the vial away from the water, sending brown droplets splattering onto the floor.

"Shit? What's shit?" I asked, impressed by how calm I sounded. Inside, I was freaking out. Did I really want it to work? What if it did? Hell, what if it didn't?

Cree shook her head. "No, it's good. Just squeezed too hard there." She looked from the water to me, back to the bottle, doing calculations in her head. Finally, she bit her lip and held it out to me. "We're good."

Reaching to take it from her, my fingers softly brushed hers and she didn't yank her hand away. *Shake it off, Johnny. If you survive this, maybe you can ask her to the prom.*

I lifted it to my mouth.

"Shake it up first. Make sure it's mixed well."

I gave a Neanderthal grunt and shook it a couple of times. "Good?"

She nodded. "You have to drink all of it in one chug."

It was an awful lot of nasty-looking liquid to chug down. "What's it taste like?"

"Like ass soup. Chug it all down before your tastebuds know what hit them."

Charming. I tilted my head back and took a deep swallow. For three heartbeats, I felt nothing.

Then the world went crazy.

Shaggy knew what was coming before I did and immediately lost his mind.

The last day or so it had been hard to keep him under control. Now he was already too close to the surface. Hair thickened on my arms, and my face ached as my teeth shifted in my mouth. "*No, goddamit, get it together, Johnny. Shaggy, NO.*"

Giving it every part of my brain, I willed myself to stop the change. The beast part of me ricocheted back and forth, dropping me to my knees. After a few terrifying seconds, I felt my human will take over. There was still half a bottle left, and I wasn't sure I could make it before Shaggy put in an appearance.

Cree pressed herself against the wall, her eyes wide as dinner plates. To my Lycan ears, the pounding of her heart was nearly as loud as her gasps, but I couldn't smell panic on her. She'd likely seen this behavior before. Even still, watching a werewolf battle himself is a lot for anyone to process. I offered a weak smile and toasted her with the bottle, tilted my head back and chugged the rest of it.

That didn't go well.

The change began anew. This time my muscles twitched, skin rippling under my clothes. I let out a full-blown Shaggy growl, pounding my fists on the floor and rolling on the ground.

Focusing so hard on keeping Shaggy contained, I didn't realize my stomach was in open revolt until I felt a seismic rumble in my gut. I croaked out, "crap," and then spun and projectile-vomited in what I hoped was the direction of the sink.

Everything I'd eaten since arriving in Vegas returned with a vengeance. My gut spasmed, my muscles burned, and my head felt like it was going full pinata. When the retching stopped, I heard Cree call my name, but there was no possible way to answer. I was too busy maintaining the last finger hold on my sanity.

My body burned with the white-hot sensation that accompanies the change and my next thought was, "Keep Cree safe," and then...

Nothing.

My head stopped pounding. My stomach rumbled harmlessly but stopped trying to expel all my other organs. Most importantly, Shaggy was quiet. No, not quiet. He wasn't there.

At all.

I couldn't feel Shaggy anywhere.

He's gone. Holy shit, he's gone. The idea that he wasn't there should have made me happy, but it freaked me the hell out. It was too quiet. My body felt hollow and ungainly. I staggered to my feet, using the sink for leverage, and wobbled in place. *Where the hell are you? What have I done? Are you crying, you pussy?*

Cree offered me some water, and I swatted her hand away, but she insisted. "It's just water. You'll need it."

I took a tentative sip, then three big gulps. "Thank you." I looked around me at the mess I created and tried not to breathe the puke-fumes too deeply. "Oh jeez. I'm sorry."

Cree was a champ. Breathing shallowly through her mouth, she took my elbow. "How are you doing?"

"Good, I think."

Cree used the same voice you use when you think someone's crazy. "And your—what's he up to?"

"I can't feel him. Oh shit, I can't—it's like he's gone." Panic washed over me. I didn't know what to do with all that echoing emptiness inside. It had been twenty years or more since I felt alone inside my own skin.

She couldn't hide the triumph in her eyes. "Told you." Her smirk turned to concern when I reached out with shaking hands, waving them like a blind man looking for his coat..

"Where is he? I can't feel... fuck, this is so weird. I can't-"

"No. Don't worry, he'll be back. This is only temporary. We need to get back in there before it wears off."

"You're sure?" That smile again. This time with a confident nod.

"Yeah. Give me your hand. Ick, watch your step. Okay, let's go see Karmen." She took my hand in hers and led me to the door. I followed like a puppy. The emptiness threw my whole body out of whack, like I wasn't sure how to hold my arms, and my legs were wonky. I had to think *left- foot-right-foot* to make progress.

"Cree?" I halted with one hand on the wall for balance.

"What's wrong?"

She was wrong about one thing. Ass soup would have been ten times better than whatever was in my mouth. "Have you got a breath mint?"

CHAPTER 20

"You ready?" Cree had one hand on the door handle to Karmen's office, the other on my arm.

Hell no. Not even close. A melon baller scooped my soul out of my body and I'm dizzy and I'm pretty sure there's puke on my shoes. "Yeah. Course I am."

She nodded and squeezed my arm as she ushered me in with a little sing-song in her voice. "Okay, we're ready."

Karmen and Boudica's heads popped up like meerkats when we blew in. Who knew what they were saying, but dollars to doughnuts it was about me. The blonde Amazon stepped back, giving me room to collapse into the chair across the desk from her boss.

Karmen wrinkled her nose at me and directed the question to Cree. "What did you do to him?"

"Just cleaned the pipes out a bit. So he can interact with the magick. Told you I could do it." Cree set both hands on my shoulders, giving me a little mini-massage like a fighter between rounds. I damn near purred as the contact grounded me and kept me from floating away. Maybe I could do this after all.

Not that there was much of a choice.

Karmen didn't seem convinced. "He's okay, though? We can only do it once." I hated that they talked about me like I wasn't there, but couldn't do much about it. My tongue was five sizes too big for my mouth and the distance between my brain and mouth felt like a mile. Thoughts were taking far too long to reach the exit. I nodded and leaned back with a cocky grin. That might have been easier if my elbow didn't slide off the arm of the chair, sending me rag-dolling to the side before I caught myself. "Lesh do thish."

While we were out, Karmen had prepared her desk for the tracking spell. It looked like a lot more trouble than a good old-fashioned scrying. Instead of a bowl full of water, a tablecloth with embroidered runes along the hem covered the desk blotter. A white candle and a black candle took up opposite corners. A porcelain bowl, its innards covered in a thin coat of ash and that baggie with the bloodstained khaki took center stage.

"Hey." Karmen snapped her fingers in front of me. "Y'all focus. We only get one shot at this, so I need you to pay attention. Once it begins, you need to maintain physical contact with me until we're done. Pay attention to everything you see and hear and try to remember as specifically as you can. Think you can do that?"

Karmen's condescension aside, this was too important to let a bruised ego mess things up. It was also true I wanted to find the Egg worse than she did, plus deliver some serious payback to Bear Boy. Worth putting up with her crap. I'd heard worse.

Seeing double added to the stress, so I focused on the blank spot between the two Karmens, straightened in my chair and held out both hands. "Hit me."

Cree's reassuring hand left my shoulder, and it took everything I had not to reach for it. I heard a soft, "You got this."

Gramma Mostoy with her crystal ball, and old man Cromwell and his scrying bowl did their thing without a lot of hoopla. Focus, ask their question, get the answer. Not surprisingly, Karmen was adding drama to the scene.

Ordinarily, I'd study every move to see how she was faking it, but damned if I didn't actually want—no need—this to work, so I shut my yap and let her do her hoodoo.

Maybe it was Cree's juju juice working. Then again, it might have been wishful thinking. I'd seen enough weird shit lately to take it in stride.

With a wooden match, Karmen lit first the white candle, circled the match head over it, then repeated the maneuver over the black, calling on the spirits for their aid. I don't know if all the theatrics helped or not. Maybe the spirits are more impressed than me.

At last, she took the material from the baggie and held it over the bowl with both hands, like an offering. "We seek you, in the four corners of this world and all others. Reveal yourself. We know nothing is hidden from the spirits who aid our righteous cause..."

I tensed with anticipation. By this time, Shaggy would have been going crazy and all hell breaking loose, but there was just a numb, blank emptiness. A dank, icy breeze blew through my guts and all I felt was mild impatience and a need to pee.

Karmen's eyes were narrow slits, focusing on muttering the spell, now in a language I didn't recognize, but still with a southern accent, which felt wrong somehow. Giggling wouldn't help, so I bit my bottom lip. She pulled one hand away from me to take the scrap in her hand and dip one corner in the white candle's flame, then the opposite corner in the black. She dropped the burning remnant into the bowl and her ice-cold fingers intertwined with mine once more. "We beg the aid of magick light and dark to come to our aid. Find the one we seek and show us..."

The natural debunker in me looked for tells. Whether it was a crystal ball, water in a bowl, or this production, it all worked the same: focus on the object, seek help, shut up. Karmen just made more of a show about it. I don't know if this would be more effective, or the Mistress of Magick just couldn't help herself.

There was more, but I stopped paying attention and tended to the task at hand. Remembering how the scrying bowl worked, I focused expectantly on the burning cloth. A thin spiral of smoke rose, and the fringes burned red then black as the cloth became ashes.

WAYNE TURMEL

My breathing was faster than Karmen's. We probably should be synchronized if we were going to do this as a team. I didn't believe in magic, but that didn't mean I should actively block it. *Play along to get along.* I inhaled slower, deeper, until my respiration matched hers. She rewarded my efforts with a gentle squeeze on my fingertips.

I still saw nothing psychic or magick-y as the scrap of rag was reduced to atoms. *When does the show start?*

After several long seconds, Karmen gripped my fingers harder. Softly, she whispered, "We must."

Who must, what? And who's she talking to?

Without Shaggy to amplify sound, my hearing was normal. When the soft murmur came from somewhere behind me, a shiver knotted my guts. A female voice responded off to my left, "He's not welcome."

Karmen pleaded. "We must. I need him. He has to accompany me." *You tell her, Karmen.*

"No." Another voice, ancient and angry, spat into my ear, making me jump in my seat. "Not him. Not ever."

Who were they and what the hell had I ever done to them? *Don't say anything. Keep your stupid mouth shut.* It took all I had to stay focused on the smoking bowl.

The quiet voice seemed far away, but clearer now. It was kinder than the crone in my ear, but her tone was dead serious. "You know what we'll ask of you?"

Karmen's grip tightened on mine for a second. Finally, in a voice low and deadly serious, she said, "You'll have it. What I seek is worth your price."

Cold, moldy air blew into my face as the crone shouted, "Never." By then, I was prepared to agree with her. This was a spectacularly awful idea.

A stiff breeze blew one way across my body, then the other, each gust accompanied by voices I couldn't make out, but then they weren't talking to me. It was some sort of argument.

Somewhere behind me, as if in another room, I heard Cree's voice. "Is that them? Are they here?"

Then Boudica shushed her. "Shut up, idiot."

I wanted to defend Cree, but that wasn't where my head needed to be. I kept my eyes forward, the expectation damn near killing me.

After way too long, the ghost that didn't completely hate me spoke. She must have won the argument, but wasn't thrilled. Like a mother giving in to a tantrum, she emitted a heavy, sad sigh. "The deal is struck, then, daughter. As you wish."

There was one last gust of frigid air, and Karmen and I were alone again. My lungs sucked in a deep gasp of air and I held it. Time seemed to stand still. Nothing happened.

Nada.

Not a frigging thing.

One eye cracked open, only to meet Karmen's gaze. She stared at me, but not at *me,* just at something in my direction. *Should I say something? What do I do? This is such bullshit.*

I squeezed my eyes shut again and concentrated. I would not mess this up. If this failed, it wouldn't be because of me. *Come on, spirit world, do your thing.*

Suddenly, Karmen let out a ragged gasp of fear.

Screw focus. "What is it? What—" Before my brain even formed the question, something huge grabbed my shirt. As if I'd slammed the brakes on my car going ninety, something yanked me from my seat. There was a sensation of flying followed by black, sickening silence. Mentally, I braced for impact.

Heat flushed my skin, and I opened my eyes to bright sunshine. I had to blink a few times to see anything. Dust-devils swirled at my feet and my peripheral vision shimmered like heat waves in a circle around me. Us. Karmen was there, too. Her hand now clasped mine like we were welded together.

Wherever we were, it wasn't her office.

CHAPTER 21

Karmen's voice was calm and low. "Whatever you do, don't let go." She didn't have to worry. I gripped harder, feeling nothing but a vague, cool pressure. My eyes had to confirm we were still connected.

"Where are we?" I asked, matching her calm tone despite freaking the hell out.

In answer, she pointed behind me to the biggest house I've ever seen in person. It was Spanish style, as expected, with two wings rising three stories high. A huge American flag flew over one corner, a "Don't tread on me," flag flapped in the breeze over the other. In between was a long, low room with sliding doors that opened onto a concrete path.

"Bowden's main house," Karmen answered without her lips moving. Her voice echoed inside my skull.

The crunch of boots on gravel to our left drew my attention. There was my buddy Bear Boy. He held four sizeable pieces of firewood in his arms and whistled as he headed for the house.

I wanted to charge him, but Karmen's hand squeezed into a death grip on mine. Although I couldn't feel her, it was more like I just knew she was doing it. "Say nothing. Do nothing. Just watch and try to remember everything you can." I heard her in my head, rather than through my ears. *Was she just thinking at me?*

"Yeah. Okay," I thought back. *Damn, it worked.*

The big Viking balanced the wood in his arms and slid the door open. He passed inside, leaving the doors open. Hand in hand, we followed behind him into the creepiest place I've ever seen.

Golden sunlight streamed into the room. The clean sand-colored paint couldn't make up for the rest of the room's vibe. Every available inch of the walls was covered with hunting trophies. Even a city boy like me recognized four types of deer, which actually made my mouth water, along with a moose, and three mountain goats. Whoever was the great hunter had butchered half of Africa as well, judging by the lion, leopard, and antelopes with funky horns staring at me.

In the far corner, a ticked-off grizzly bear reared up in a full, eternally silent roar. The only things in the place that weren't dead and unhappy about it were the leather L-shaped sofa and arena-sized flat screen hanging over the fireplace.

Karmen's voice drifted into my ear. "Bowden's primary trophy room."

"Primary? You mean there's more?"

"He has one for his special treasures. That's where the Egg will be."

The egg. Right. Stick to the mission, big guy.

The Berserker, who looked more like a farmhand, dumped the firewood into a bin beside the hearth and grunted. I felt a minor victory when he rotated his shoulder slowly, rubbing it with his free hand. *Good, I hope it hurts like hell.* Then I remembered Shaggy wasn't there, and hot panic flushed through my system. What chance would I have if I never got him back? This asshole nearly killed me, even with my Lycan skills.

We followed five or six steps behind into a hallway. Our feet made no noise on the tile floor, unlike the giant, size-one-hundred boots on the big man. It was an eerie sensation. We weren't floating exactly, but it was clear we were invisible and didn't make any noise.

He froze as a walkie-talkie squawked. The big guy puffed out his cheeks and lifted the military-style device from his belt to his face. "Ja."

"Torson, get your ass in here!" An old man's voice barked through the speakers. I almost laughed at the way the scary oaf rolled his eyes. No matter how much of an ogre you are, you can still think your boss is a dick. Almost made me feel sorry for the guy. Almost.

Further down, the berserker turned to another door, with us hot on his heels. He stopped in the doorway for a moment and looked around quickly, as if sensing or smelling something that shouldn't be there. Karmen and I froze, but he shook it off. Huge fingers punched in a code: one, seven, seven, six. Seventeen seventy-six, because of course it was. What else would this overly patriotic dickwad use? We followed him into the room.

They'd painted this trophy room midnight-blue. In the center of the space was a padded bench like I'd seen at the Art Institute. Against the far wall was a glass case with the Paiute Sky Egg proudly on display. The younger Bowden and an older guy in a cowboy hat and desert camo straightened as the bear guy—Torson—entered. The old man leaned on a wooden cane, hand carved from tip to handle with symbols, probably Native American to go with the whole Southwest vibe. He looked up when we entered the room.

The old man grunted. "Took you long enough, Torson." It was a little weird knowing the behemoth had a name. I was pretty happy just thinking of him as Bear Guy. But his name might be important. I wish I'd brought a notepad. Seventeen seventy-six. Torson. I repeated it over and over, hoping it stuck.

The older guy, who could only have been Clive Bowden Senior, looked right where we were and squinted. After a moment, he shook his head and turned to his son. "Okay, make sure the guards know what's up tonight. Extras on the North side especially. Road's better from that direction and it's what he'll go for. Only an idiot would try the southern road. If we're not going to be here, we need to make sure Cromwell's guy doesn't try something stupid. You're ready, right?"

Torson nodded, but my mind was busy. *Cromwell's guy was in trouble. Oh, that's me. They know I'm coming for it. That's bad. But they won't be home. That's good. Guards on the north side. That mattered. The south road sucks, but that's what we'll have to use. Seventeen seventy-six to get in. Towson—no, Torson. Crap.* The list was getting too long to memorize.

The younger Bowden shook his head. "No one's that frickin' dumb. And he's just one guy with no backup except those chicks and the old man. And for what? We don't even know how to work this stupid thing. Might be a lot of trouble for nothing."

The old man smacked his palm against the wall so hard the room shook. "It's not for nothing. This one is the real deal. And even if it's not, we've taught that Chicago asshole who he's fucking with."

I studied the egg in its trophy case on the far wall, then around the rest of the long, narrow room. There were fewer animal heads hanging from the walls, for sure, but the ones there were creepy as hell. One looked like a wolf, but without fur. Its bottom jaw was lined with fangs that jutted upwards.

I leaned forward for a closer look, but Karmen pulled on my hand. "Pay attention. I don't know how much longer we have."

"Yeah, sorry. But what is that thing?"

She looked and shrugged. "It's a Chupacabra."

"But aren't they- " I swallowed the sentence. I was a werewolf standing in a room ninety miles from his body, holding hands with a witch. The "those-aren't-real" ship had sailed. But to have one on his wall meant the old man probably killed it himself. I pictured Shaggy's head on a hardwood plaque and shivered until Karmen gave my hand a ghostly squeeze.

I wanted to zero in on the conversation, but the conversation was getting more muffled, as if we were standing further away even though we hadn't moved at all.

The old man was losing patience with his offspring. "She swears it's the real deal, and she's going to show us how to activate it. She knows better than to double cross us if she wants what we promised."

Karmen's hand tugged on mine, and her voice echoed in my head. "Johnny, we have to go."

"Wait, they said she. Who..."?

I know I formed the question but couldn't tell if she heard me or not. Karmen's face was blurry, just a halo of raven-black hair framing a white oval. The room spun around me. Something was definitely wrong, but damned if I knew what it was.

"We have to go. We're out of time." Karmen's now-distant voice sounded disappointed, and I tried to pull away, needing more time.

Despite the need for silence, I felt myself shout. "This is bullshit. Who are they talking about?" Then it dawned on me why my head was spinning, my guts were on fire, and the spell was falling apart.

Shaggy was back. And he was pissed.

My stomach clenched, my whole body tensed. Suddenly, I smelled Torson's ursine odor, and a growl built in my throat. *Not now. Crap.*

Shaggy pounded on the walls of my brain with hairy fists. My fingers were soaked with sweat, even in Karmen's cool hand. The grip loosened, and I tried to clasp her fingers, but I scratched her with my lengthening nails and her eyes widened.

It was already too late. The tour was over.

Whatever grabbed me and flung me into this vision now yanked just as hard on the back of my neck and tossed me backwards into the chilly, dark abyss.

CHAPTER 22

Whether it was my soul or my spirit, whatever part of me had been at Bowden's place, slammed back into my body with the thud of an unlucky skydiver. No sooner did I recognize my surroundings than I rolled out of my chair and onto the ground, clutching at my face. Shaggy was annoyed at being evicted and had returned home with a vengeance.

My skin rippled and swelled with the first twitches of the change. The last thing I wanted was to go full wolf in front of the women, so I tuck-and-rolled across the floor to a corner.

Through cracks between my fingers I saw Cree bending over me, yelling about Christ only knew what. My grunts and moans drowned her out. Boudica held wicked blades in both hands, crouching low and glaring at me. I knew if I let Shaggy take control, she'd gladly gut me like a salmon to protect her boss.

She was looking for an excuse already. Damned if I'd give it to her.

Sunlight doesn't necessarily prevent a change when it's that time of the month, it can help keep it under control. Fortunately, I laid in a bright patch of yellow on the floor, putting all my effort into calming Shaggy. The sunbeams beat down on my face, and that's where I concentrated my efforts, feeling the ultraviolet rays wrap around me.

My lungs sucked in deep, raspy breaths. *No, you don't. Just stay Johnny. Shaggy will get to play tonight, I promise.*

The jury was out on whether I'd regain control. Finally, my body spasmed one last time as Shaggy retreated to a neutral corner of my brain, with the unmistakable message he wasn't happy about it. It felt right to have him back. It was certainly more natural knowing he was there than AWOL, but his timing sucked. There'd be no controlling him tonight, but that was hours away. If I was chasing that egg, I'd need him to be his Shaggiest.

Cree's voice cut through the fog. "Johnny. Johnny, talk to me."

Obliging her, I croaked out, "Guess that shit works, huh?"

She wrapped her arms around my waist and hugged me. Something wet ran down my cheek and checked to see if it was me. Cree wiped an arm across her red, bloodshot eyes. I lay there, allowing her one more good squeeze, and then put a hand on her shoulder. Using her for support, I struggled to my feet and stumbled to the chair by Karmen's desk.

My brain tried to form words, but Cree just looked confused and shook her head. My hand mimed writing. I whispered, "Paper. Pen."

Karmen slapped a piece of paper on her desk and shoved it across to me. Then she reached for one of her gold pens, changed her mind and grabbed a cheap plastic one. She rolled it across the paper to me. "Here, while you can still remember everything. Get it all down."

Taking the pen in my fist like a three-year-old, I scribbled down everything I could think of. Words appeared randomly; half the time I didn't know what I was writing until it was on the page. Some of it made sense.

Torson. *That's Bear Guy's name. Good.*

Seventeen seventy-six. *The hell is that? Oh yeah, the door code. Right.*

Guards north side. *Self-explanatory, probably important if you don't want to get your ass shot up.*

That's what the ink smears were supposed to say if someone could translate my chicken scratch. Penmanship isn't a priority when you're trying to keep a werewolf under control. Still, I'd done a decent job. There were eight or ten items, some of which made zero sense to my rational brain but sounded right, so I left them there. The last thing I wrote was "SHE?" I couldn't even remember what that meant, but it felt like it mattered. I added it as an afterthought.

At last, shaking and sweating, I threw the pen down and looked across the desk at Karmen. I had to ask. "Seriously. That was a Chupacabra, right?"

"Yeah. it was."

"He killed and stuffed something that doesn't really exist?"

Karmen gave an exhausted shrug. "That's one way to look at it."

I didn't have time to ponder the other view. "And those voices?"

Boudica snorted. "Oh, you met them? I'll bet they loved you."

They sure as hell didn't want me along for the ride. Whoever they were.

Cree stepped forward, a weird look on her face. "What voices? He heard the Mothers? You heard the Mothers? What were they like?"

Boudica offered her a malicious grin. "Oh, that's right, you've never met them, have you, Lucrezia?" Her tone left no doubt it was a total Mean-Girl move. Shaggy created an image of ripping the blond's throat out. Couldn't blame him, I wanted to leap to Cree's defense, pointy objects be damned.

Karmen jumped in to bring us all back to the task at hand. "They're my—I suppose you'd say spirit guides. Past leaders of this coven now moved on. I can call on them when it's really important."

That sounded reasonable, although it raised the question of their price. She'd agreed to something, and it seemed she'd paid above retail for it. *What did that little parlor trick cost you, lady?*

The world became increasingly normal again. I'd stopped sweating, although you could wring about a gallon of saltwater from my shirt. Oxygen flowed in and out of my lungs comfortably and with Shaggy back, my center of gravity had returned. I was oriented enough to know up from down, at least.

"You okay?" A hand softly rubbed between my shoulder blades.

I hated that Cree was so worried about me. Kind of liked it too.

"Never better." I offered the redhead a reassuring smile, then turned my attention across the desk. "Anything you remember I should know?"

The Mistress of Magic was worn out. Her hair hung limply and small creases around her eyes defied her normally perfect makeup. She turned the paper towards her, pursed her lips as she scanned it and turned it back to me. "I don't think so. What's your plan?"

Karmen leaned back and drummed her fingers on the desk. Boudica's over-buff arms were flexing across her chest. She was prepared to hate whatever I came up with. Cree ran fingers through her short spikes while offering an encouraging nod.

"I go in tonight and get the damned egg." They expected more, which was a shame since that was as far as I'd thought it out. I improvised, hoping it would all make some kind of sense. "They're watching the North road, so I'll come in from the other direction. We have the code to the room, so once I'm in the house, I'll swap the fake egg for the real one and get my ass out of there."

It sounded so simple when I just blurted out like that. Easy-peasy. Except it would involve the one thing I swore I'd never do, which was risk going to jail. I'd done a lot of shady crap in my life, but felony B&E wasn't on the list. Not that I'd do time. It was either get the egg or Shaggy's head winds up on Bowden's wall next to the Mexican devil dog.

No jury would convict Bowden for shooting me. Robbery was a crime in Nevada. I wasn't sure about attempted suicide. They might let me skate on that one, assuming I survived.

I wished Bill was there to help me walk through this, but I was completely alone. Well, aside from Shaggy, who would be in charge once I got to the ranch. "I'll drive out and come in somewhere on the Southwest side. I can cover a couple of miles easy." *Shaggy can, whatever. He needs the exercise.*

The rest of the scheme just spilled out of my face. Get to the house, bust in—no time for subtlety and picking locks would take precious time—take the shortest direct route to the trophy room, seventeen-seventy-six the hell out of the door, swap eggs and high-tail it out with my hide intact.

Karmen squinted at me. "Alone? You'll need backup. Boudica, you go along and—"

Oh, hell no. "Nope. None of you can be involved. It'll be faster to work alone, and I don't want any of this blowing back on you or Mr. Cromwell." I didn't trust the Amazon to watch my back under the best of conditions. The current circumstances were far from ideal. *And I for sure don't want any of you having to deal with Shaggy's chaos.* I couldn't guarantee anyone's safety, and the last thing I needed if I wound up in hell was a permanently soiled conscience.

"I'll go with him." Cree clenched her jaw and her eyes shone. Clearly, she wasn't just being polite. Boudica gave a derisive snort and Karmen shook her head, but Cree's voice was low and determined.

Unh-uh. "No, I—"

She never gave me a chance to finish. "You can't go alone. You'll need someone to navigate for you and keep an eye out. And when you get back, you'll be in no shape to drive. You know it's true."

Cree was right, but that didn't mean her idea sucked any less.

"You need someone who knows your... methods." We both knew what she meant by that, even if Karmen and Boudica didn't. The boss gave her a suspicious eyebrow raise. The blond just glared.

They didn't get a vote, though. Cree was one of the few people I'd ever met who had non-lethal contact with a Lycan. She'd been close to her brother and knew the drill. At the very least, she wouldn't scream and pass the hell out when I changed.

"It's not safe." It was the second weakest warning I could give. The lamest, of course, was "you'll put your eye out." Either way, I knew she'd ignore me. Cree'd already proven she was plenty stubborn and knew how to get her way. Plus, I really didn't want to go alone.

"Somebody needs to be at the extraction point to get you and the Egg home." The word extraction point reminded me of Francine and her goon squad of ex-marines. What I wouldn't give to have Justin the Human Doorstop as backup now. But they weren't here, and calling

Cromwell for resources would only let the old bastard know I wasn't up to the job. *Double fuck him. I can do this.*

I think.

I relented. "Yeah, fine."

Her eyes lit up as if we were heading to Disneyland instead of an armed compound full of lunatics. "Alright, there are some things we'll need. We have to stop by my apartment." For more alchemical potion-y ammunition, I guessed. There were things we'd need of a more practical, earthly nature, too.

We had four hours til sundown and some shopping to do.

CHAPTER 23

Night of the full moon.

Mike Tyson once said, "Everyone has a fight plan until they get punched in the nose." Something like that. His point was valid. You need a plan even if you know there's a one-hundred percent chance it will turn to crap as soon as you start. With a plan, either you'll be surprised when it works, or badly disappointed, but you can think about contingencies. Without one, you're just screwed from the get-go.

Cree and I sat in the Charger in a Walmart parking lot off Charleston. Styx blared, despite Cree's obvious distaste. *Screw it, a condemned man gets a last meal, right?* I was writing a supplies list in a small notebook., After scribbling two three-one-two area code numbers, I ripped the page out and handed it to Cree. "If anything happens to me, tell these folks what happened. You can tell them everything. Don't look at me like that. I mean everything." Bill and Nurse Ball. They had a right to know. Francine could break the news to the old man.

Bill would have been a huge help right now, but he'd gone radio silent. At first, I thought it was just a time zone problem. Then it got worrying. He never goes twenty minutes, let alone three hours, without checking his messages. I heard nothing from Chicago. Nada.

After three texts and a voicemail that sounded more chipper than the situation warranted, I let it go and focused on the task at hand.

Bill went to the top of my "worry about it if you live" list. I'd already ruled out calling in Francine and her cleanup squad. Meaghan and Gramma were better off not knowing anything.

Mostly it was ego. Also, trying to text out an explanation on my phone was more than my clumsy thumbs could manage. Autocorrect would have burst into flames. And what the hell would I say?

Cree smiled assurance at me. God, she had just the slightest Liv Tyler overbite. It was cute as hell. Her eyes gave her away as she said, "Nothing's going to happen."

"Yeah, it will, we just don't know how bad it'll get. Believe me, I really hope you won't have to make those calls."

She looked out the windshield instead of at me. "Okay, we should break this down so we don't forget anything. Transportation, logistics, and defense."

"We have transportation." I affectionately patted the steering wheel of my trusty Charger.

"Seriously? You're going to drive a black and orange muscle car across the desert to sneak up on a bunch of cowboys who know you're coming?"

I'd kind of imagined a "fast and furious" approach, complete with guitars wailing. In my mental movie, it was cool as hell. Her point was valid, though. *Crap. Why couldn't I be cool just once?* "I s'pose not."

Cree nodded and drew a big check mark on the page. "I can get the maintenance truck from the Museum, so transportation. Check. Next?"

"Wow. You're good at this."

She smiled. "Thanks. It's the chemical engineer in me. Boudica and Karmen think I worry too much, but if you don't plan everything out, things go boom."

"I know what you mean." Boom was the natural order of things in my world.

"That's why you've got me, right?"

Is it? Do I?

She avoided my eyes and gently took the notebook from my hand. "Just in case another human being needs to read this. Now, how are we going to get the Eggs in and out?"

That began a whole back-and-forth trying to turn this suicidal idea into proper plan I could survive.

It slowly came together. I'd need my phone and GPS to get out there. Once I turned, it would be useless to me, though.

"It doesn't matter. I can use it to track and find you. Afterwards. You have a 'track my phone' app. Right?"

"Yeah. Bill insisted after the third time I lost it." She picked up my cell, put it on her lap next to hers, and let her fingers fly. Whatever hoodoo she was doing there, Cree was far less judge-y about it than Meaghan would be.

"There. Now I'll be able to track you any time."

Always going for the joke, I said, "That's a little stalkerish, don't you think?"

"Why?" she asked. "Are you going somewhere you don't want me to know about? What's her name?"

She was kidding, but for a moment, I flashed on Francine's face and a couple of inappropriate images. "There's nobody."

"You are straight, though, right?"

I managed not to sound indignant. "Course I am. You?"

"Yes, as a matter of fact." She grinned and leaned against the car door, arms crossed. "Surprised?"

"No. I mean, yeah. A little. The hair and... most Wiccans I know are pissed off at men generally." *Smooth, Johnny. Silky freaking smooth.*

She ran her hand through her short orange spikes. "Nah, just got tired of it getting in my eyes at the gym. And yeah, I dabbled a bit just to piss off the patriarchy. Okay, my dad, but it didn't stick. Can't help it. I like boys."

Duly noted.

After a few excruciating seconds of silence, she said, "Well, you could have said 'Yay,' or something."

I actually thought, yay, but said nothing. I was getting better at the whole staying-focused thing.

After letting me squirm a second, Cree spoke. "Okay, back to business. How are you going to carry the Eggs?"

I needed to be in Lycan form to get to the compound, but those hands were useless for carrying anything delicate. A case of some kind wouldn't help. I looked up through the sunroof for inspiration.

Cree leaned forward. Whatever brainstorm had struck had her bouncing in her seat. "How much do you grow when you... you know, change?"

"A bit. It's more, what would you call it, redistributing muscles."

"Could you carry a backpack?"

I had an image of a big, hairy werewolf heading off to middle school. "If the straps were long enough, and it was light, yeah." *Oh, Shaggy would LOVE that.*

That settled it. Twenty minutes later, we had a good water bottle, some industrial grade bubble wrap for the Egg, a box of shells for my Ruger, and a Las Vegas Raiders backpack that offended my Chicago sensibilities. At least it was big enough to do the job. I took a hard pass on Mutant Ninja Turtles or Hello Kitty. I didn't want to be literally caught dead wearing cartoon characters, despite Cree's belief it would be ironically hilarious.

Then it was back to her place. There were long silent spaces between our chatter. It was only a couple of hours until the full moon, and we both felt the clock ticking down. I pulled my car into her carport, got out, and followed her up the stairs.

As she clicked the lighter two or three times to get the sage smoking, I asked, "What do we need to get here? Do you have some kind of potion or something that'll help?"

She took a deep breath, then tilted her face to mine. "I made a protection charm. For you to take."

"Wow. I mean, that's nice, but you know that psychic energy and me..."

"I know. Tomas was the same way. This worked for him." *Tomas. Her dead brother. Worked like a dream, apparently.*

She must have seen my skepticism, because she took a deep breath before saying, "He wasn't wearing it when he died."

I had to ask. "What happened?"

Cree shook her head. "I'll tell you the complete story sometime. I promise. Stand still."

Shaggy squirmed at the stench of the sage. It took all my concentration not to swipe Cree's head off as my Lycan protested the smoky odor and whatever it did to his energy. The badass witch had enough sense not to push the issue and finished with a weak flourish of her sage bundle and a mutter of something that sounded German.

When the door opened, there was a scream. A flash of black shot across the room to the back of the apartment. Pooky the Familiar wanted nothing to do with me on the verge of turning. It amazed me Cree did. Hell, I didn't want to be with me when the moon was full.

After making sure her kitty hadn't had heart failure, Cree emerged from the back room holding something in her hand. "This was Tomas's. I want you to have it."

I held out my hand, and she dropped a cheap metal chain with a strange locket attached. It looked like silver but wasn't, fortunately. The locket was actually a heart, made of some clear plastic, about half full of a blue liquid that sloshed back and forth. There was some form of energy trapped inside, because my palm tingled where it lay, but there wasn't enough juice to upset Shaggy.

Then she gave that excited little bounce on the balls of her feet. "Oh, one more thing." She went to her freezer, opened the door, and pulled out a bag of frozen meat.

"What's that?"

"In case you run into dogs. I brewed up a tranquilizer for them. Totally harmless, but it will save you from getting a chunk taken out of your butt. I hope."

I looked down at the charm in my fist. My hand was a little warm, but not uncomfortable. Whatever this was, it was more symbolic than helpful.

"It's pretty weak, I know. I suck at real magic. Potions are the best I can do, 'cause they're basic chemistry. But I think it will help."

"No. I can feel it's buzzing. This is great. I don't know how to thank you."

"Buy me dinner when you get back."

"Really? I mean, you want to have dinner with me?"

She let out a genuine laugh. "Obviously." She grabbed a hoodie off the couch. "You're a smart guy. Why do you always play dumb?"

There was no real suitable answer to that, so we left her place while I still had her fooled.

CHAPTER 24

We bounced down an unpaved Forest Service road somewhere in the desert. We passed a lot of nothing before seeing a pair of double-wide trailers with a gigantic neon sign hidden behind a hill.

"It's a brothel," Cree explained.

"That's a long way from Vegas. If it's legal, why don't they put them in town?"

"Has to be outside Clark County lines. Prostitution isn't legal in Vegas proper. You have to get your jollies the old-fashioned way. At least until you get to Pahrump."

Another illusion shattered.

I envisioned going into battle in my cool-as hell-Charger, rolling up in a cloud of dust with the music blaring. Instead, I was riding shotgun in a Ninety-Four GMC pickup of indeterminate color with 'Museum Staff' flaking off the side. There was no decent sound system, and the radio picked up crackly country music or Jesus, so we moved in silence. I wasn't even driving. Cree had the wheel. It was the only way the Maintenance manager would loan her the truck. She didn't want some "maniac" driving it. Obviously, no one had seen Cree drive.

Like the farm girl she was, she wasn't afraid of potholes or chipped windshields. She just pulled onto the gravel sideroad at the same speed she'd been tearing up the pavement. I didn't think the "fearing for my life" part of the program would begin quite so early in the evening.

The sky glowed orange in the West, and although I couldn't see it behind the mountains, I felt the moon's pull on my nervous system. Talking helped keep me calm, as long as the topic wasn't me.

"So what's Boudica's deal?" I asked her.

Cree's mouth tightened. "What do you mean?"

"She doesn't like you much. Me, I get. But who wouldn't like you?"

Cree let out a little "ha" but gave the matter some thought while swerving around a jagged rock in the middle of the road. "She doesn't think I'm worthy of being in the coven. And the fact Karmen has clumsy old me on stage makes her crazy."

"Aren't you chief potion brewer or something? That's a big deal."

"Boudica certainly doesn't think so. Not only is she hot, and way too proficient with all those weapons, she actually has really potent magic. Like, off the charts strong. She bows to Karmen because that's how things work, and probably has a crush on her. But she respects the hierarchy, more or less. Some of the coven members agree. A couple at least."

"But not you."

She ignored the question. "From what I hear, Bo's tight with the Mothers, too. My actual magical abilities are pretty lame. I'm the weakest link. A fact she's only too happy to remind me of. "

I shuddered at the memory of the crones. "I take it she's seen the Mothers."

Cree nodded. "They're on a first name basis. Karmen's tried to connect me with them several times, but I'm too weak. She says I can do it, and I love her for trying. She's been good to me. But it's no use. The Mothers can't be bothered with anyone who doesn't have the right mojo. I think the only reason Boss Lady keeps me around is I upgraded all of her illusions and I really know my shit when it comes to herbs and potions. Plus, I'm pretty good in a fight, in case you haven't noticed."

I'd noticed. It was kind of hot watching her put a boot upside the younger Bowden's face. "I'll bet you're a hell of a cage fighter."

Cree shrugged. "Probably could be if I wasn't such a pussy. I don't like hurting people. Lack that killer instinct, I'm told."

"There are worse problems than not wanting to hurt somebody." *Like constantly wanting to hurt them, for example, but why ruin a pleasant night with that kind of talk?*

She checked her phone for the millionth time. "How far out do you want to start?" We were about 3 miles from the compound and the sky was turning purple. She was good at this being-in-charge stuff. I was glad to have her there.

"They're probably patrolling the north road by now, about a mile out. Let's make it 2 miles to be safe."

"That's a long walk."

I paused. "Not for him."

Her brow scrunched adorably. "Him, who?" I just looked at her until the light dawned. "Oh, right. Tomas used to refer to his... other side... in the third person, too. Why is that?"

Because it's easier than owning some of the crap he's... I've... done. Rather than discuss it, I just shrugged.

Cree checked the GPS, squinted through the dusty windshield, and pulled over to a relatively flat, bare spot beside the road. "Two-point-one miles. This okay?"

"Perfect." Without another word, I snatched up the backpack and began an inspection. This bag might be the wrong team, but it had super-long straps and Velcro pockets instead of zippers. Being able to reach for anything with Shaggy-hands would be impossible, but ripping something open would be easy.

In one pouch was my pistol and an extra clip of shells, for all the good they'd do me. I couldn't shoot anything once I changed, and the other side had a full arsenal. The other pocket would hold my phone when I unplugged it from the charger. I kept it tethered until the last minute, because it sucked power. Cree could track me the whole time.

Two items lay in the big central compartment. First was the bag of rapidly thawing meat. I could already smell it through the thick plastic and my stomach growled, a reminder that I really needed to get going before I couldn't control the change—or Shaggy's appetite—any longer. The most important item was the fake Sky Egg, nestled snugly in a triple layer of bubble wrap. It was surprisingly light and harmless-looking.

In and out.

Don't look for trouble.

There were still things I needed to do before zero hour. For one thing, I hadn't stretched in a couple of days, and my muscles were letting me know it. I needed every advantage my Lycan form offered. For another, I needed to calm my mind and get my bearings.

Staring out the window, my eyesight was already changing. The bright sunset was behind us, but it lit up every rock and gray-green plant. A flutter of red caught my eye. I thought it was a bird or something, but it was just a piece of plastic on a wire stand.

Cree held her phone up to me. "Okay, Bowden's place is two-point-one miles. Uh, that way." She pointed vaguely northwest. I took her wrist and moved it a couple of inches to point further north.

"Actually, it's exactly that way."

Her eyes widened, and she did that little jump-up-and-down in her seat thing. "How do you know? Can you smell it or something? Ooh, maybe you orient by the stars. A lot of animals—"

I hated to burst her bubble. "Survey flags. See that red thing flapping? There's another one fifty yards up. When the gas company put in the line to the compound, they didn't bother pulling the flags up. I just follow them." Those years of working construction in the sticks were good for something, at least. It would have been way cooler to let her think I had a superpower.

The truck door groaned as I opened it and shifted my weight. Then I popped my phone off the cord and slipped it into the backpack's left-hand pocket.

145

"What are you doing? The moon's not up yet." Cree looked pale and was white-knuckling the steering wheel.

"There are a couple of things I need to do before then." There was a follow-up question in her eyes. "Fine. I have to stretch out. Otherwise the... change... hurts like a bitch."

"So, stretch. I'll stand guard. Hell, I could use a good stretch. I'll do it with you."

How do I explain this one? "I kind of need to do it naked."

Her laugh filled the cab of the truck and then some. "Okay. Stretch naked. Do what you gotta do. What are you, shy?"

And that's how I wound up standing in a hot sandy patch by the side of the road at dusk in just my boxer briefs. Bill had watched me stretch plenty of times, but never just before a change, and it felt oddly pleasant to share the moment with someone. I started with a slow slide into a lunge, feeling the burn in my quads while Cree had her foot on the hood of the truck and bent her head to her kneecap. Had to hand it to her. The girl was bendy for someone so buff.

Stripping down had been mortifying, and I watched her watch me undress, looking for signs of disappointment or revulsion, but she watched with a cheeky grin, enjoying my embarrassment. The only thing she'd said about my body was, "jeez, that must get warm" when she saw my hairy chest and belly.

It could get toasty, but the spring night had a cool breeze, and the temperature was dropping fast. Probably wouldn't be this nice in a couple of months. It was a safe bet any Lycans in Vegas migrated north for the summer.

"Nice panties. I thought you were getting naked." I couldn't tell if she was curious or just enjoying my embarrassment.

"All in good time."

As I squatted low and let the muscles work out, I watched her stretch. She had a light sheen of sweat on her forehead, pasting a couple of orange hairs to her brow. Since she was wearing just a sports bra and shorts, I managed to scope out more of her tattoos. A couple of Celtic rune-looking things decorated each arm; standard Wicca-issue ink. The part that fascinated me was the small, precise tats right along her collarbone.

In a perfect semi-circle around her throat, Cree had high-quality images of a Celtic cross, an ankh, a star of David, a crescent, a black raven's feather and that black and white yin-yang circle, whatever it's called. This was a woman who wasn't taking any chances. She covered all her bases. Must be the engineer in her.

She caught me looking and grinned.

"Take a picture. It'll last longer."

"That's a good idea." I grabbed my phone and fumbled around until I got the camera going. She smiled and kept the position until I snapped a pic. Cree insisted on getting one of me, but I negotiated a selfie of the two of us leaning against the truck. She stuck her tongue out at the last second and we both laughed at the goofiness. A nice normal moment. Maybe the last one for a long time.

In the picture you could see the amulet she gave me. It was hanging from that inexpensive chain, and for sure wouldn't survive the change. Plus, Shaggy wouldn't like it, even as weak as it was. I removed it from around my neck and put it in my hand. Looking around, I placed it in the pack, same pocket as my phone. At least I was taking it with me. Cree watched as I velcroed it into place, but said nothing.

Finally, warm and limber as I was going to get, I took a deep breath and studied the moon. Three quarters of his white face already peered over the mountains and Shaggy shivered and deep within me.

It was time.

"You're going to want to get in the truck," I said.

"No. Let me—"

"No," I yelled, gruffer than necessary. This wasn't negotiable. I didn't want her within reach when Shaggy took over. He was going to be a problem to control and there couldn't be any chance of something—me—harming her.

"Okay, fine." She picked up her phone and studied it. "Okay, it's tracking your phone."

Without another word, she picked up the backpack and loosened the straps as much as they'd go. Then she held it up to me. "Alright, big guy."

I turned my back to her, dropped my boxers, and threw them on the pile with the rest of my clothes. I asked over my shoulder, "You are going to give those back to me when this is over, right?"

"Probably." The pack slipped over my arms and hung almost to the crack of my ass. When Shaggy took over, it would shift.

Her cool hand rested on my shoulder. "You're sure about this?"

I couldn't look at her. "Nope, but we're doing it, anyway. Get back in the truck. I'd rather you didn't watch, but I know you will. Just stay in there where it's safe. Please."

She placed a friendly kiss on my shoulder. "Okay. Yeah." A second later, I heard the truck door slam shut.

Show time.

CHANNEL 25

I tried blocking Cree from my thoughts. Honestly, I felt her eyes on me and wanted nothing more than to turn around and stare back. Instead, I focused on the moon's pull on my guts, the vibrations under my skin, and on the scary rush that came with Shaggy waking up and bursting loose.

It had been months since he'd really had a chance to run free anywhere other than a forest preserve, and my body vibrated with his rage and frustration. After having banished him with Cree's mixture, even temporarily, I remembered now how truly alive I was when he was in control. Tempted to surrender immediately, I held tight to a small part of my—our—brain. My rational side needed to maintain enough control to get the job done while letting him vent. This was going to be a royal bitch, but there was nothing else for it now. One long deep yoga breath, and I surrendered control.

White-hot pain exploded from deep in my chest and radiated out to my fingertips, my toes, and the top of my head. Even as warmed up and stretched as I was, the world echoed with the cracking of ligaments and my own screams, but it was over quickly, and I opened my eyes to an entirely new world.

The desert smelled alive. All that sand and dust and half-dead plant life suddenly reeked of vitality, and energy, and a kind of buzzing music. There were unfamiliar smells. Strange scents. Never having spent time in the desert before, I always thought it was dead and boring. Shaggy knew better.

His ears picked up the drone of insects, the rustling of a soft, cool breeze through the Joshua trees. In the distance, a rabbit skittered, and a coyote barked at something new and terrible and unknown in its territory. The sensations were magnificent, and I threw my head back and howled with pure joy.

He wasn't happy about the weight on his back. The pack was heavy against his spine and rubbed against the pelt. Shaggy spun and clawed at it in an attempt to rid himself of the annoyance, and it took a lot of cooing and whispering for him to accept it.

Being a beast of burden left him angry and confused, but everything else brought pure joy. Shaggy's eyes and ears sought every novel sensation. I soaked it all in with his eyes when that laser-gaze focused on the truck, and the warm, living, shrieking thing inside it.

Cree had held it together until now. I felt Shaggy's need for prey and sent all the mental focus I could to his control center. *No, she's a friend. Friend.*

The monster resisted, trying to push me out of his head, but I held on.

The bear. You want the bear. My thoughts centered on the moldy, rotten-meat caged-grizzly smell, hoping that would do the job. Shaggy paused for a second, then let out another howl, this time one of rage and bloodlust. He wanted that big freak worse than the tasty morsel in the truck.

With a little extra concentration, I got the Lycan to raise his claw to her in a half-assed wave goodbye. With a trembling hand, Cree lifted hers and waved back. All I wanted to do was to stay, but Shaggy needed to run, and there was work to do.

Find the bear, and the men who hurt us. With a little effort, I created an image of Torson. The bear-scent filled my brain, and I felt those thick hands on my body, the sight and smell of my own blood. It triggered all the right kinds of anger.

The snap of that red flag in the breeze caught my attention. It was bigger and redder through Lycan eyes, and I sent the message. *Follow the flags, find the Bear.*

Shaggy began running. At first on two legs, then on four, faster and faster until the world was a blur of odors and tones. My blood boiled with both a wild freedom and an animal urge for revenge. Rocks, plants, animals hidden from Johnny's senses watched this new, horrible creature run past them, a black thunderbolt.

My stomach ached with the force of Shaggy's hunger. Much as it pained me, it had to be killing him. It was nearly impossible to reach him when he was like this. Control was going to be an illusion until he took the edge off. This wasn't like the teeming forests back home. What was there to eat in this god-forsaken desert?

Whatever doubts I had, Shaggy didn't share them. He lifted his head, his radar nose seeking something to eat. No, to kill. Eating would be the icing on a bloody cake. Then he smelled it, prey. Different from the brazen, stupid animals I hunted at home. This one was bigger, different, but prey nonetheless.

I gave Shaggy full control. When he was satisfied and calm, I'd run the show. For the moment, it was all him. He felt me shake loose of him and let out a blood-curdling howl, then followed the scent. Faster, lower to the ground, a bullet aimed at whatever he was chasing. The sheer joy of the hunt radiated through us both, and I shared his exhilaration. Screw Cromwell and everyone else. To stay like this forever would be the most amazing feeling in the world. It was like my heart was going to explode with joy.

Minutes later, it was over. The young mountain goat, brave instead of smart, stood his ground a moment too long, and Shaggy struck teeth first. If I were just Johnny, I'd have been horrified at the blood and gore and ripping sounds of claw and tooth into raw flesh, but I wasn't in charge, and the glow of satisfaction after being denied so long was like a warm bath I was happy to soak in. For a while, at least.

Jesus, buddy. You were hungry. How frustrated and furious had he been? Could I really have controlled him if he'd turned on Cree or someone else? I didn't want to think about it.

Once the meal was over, Shaggy paused and relaxed, long enough for me to exert control again. *You're strong now. Find the bear.*

Another howl, and he followed the flapping plastic further north and west. The wind cooled the blood and chunks of meat against our face. It was glorious.

Some time later, I spied a yellow glow ahead. Bowden's compound. Shaggy stopped and sniffed. Desert smells, the reek of gasoline from small engines—someone had been riding ATVs or dirt bikes through the area not long ago. Probably guards.

The meat in the backpack was fully thawed, and the blood tantalized my nose, making my snout water. Thank God he'd eaten a while back, because Shaggy spun around to reach it, making me a little dizzy and requiring me to wrench back a little more control.

NO. That's for the dogs.

Except I couldn't smell dogs. Someone as paranoid and just plain vicious as Bowden should have big-ass Rottweilers or Rhodesian Ridgebacks or rabid German Shepherds, but there was no sign of canine life.

Or any other kind, for that matter.

The house was exactly as it had appeared to Karmen and me. The main building was partially lit, while the towers sat dark, but there were lights in the kitchen and the trophy room. Bowden said they were going out and no one would be home, but he couldn't have meant literally no one. Staff, security, they knew I was coming. Where the hell were the palace guards?

Shaggy shared my confusion. Frozen in place, he sniffed, snorted, and turned in a slow circle, taking everything in. Quiet. Boring. The Lycan in me wanted to charge the door. Just like we'd planned, but something was wrong. Obviously a trap, but where? I nudged Shaggy to the French doors leading to the trophy room.

Go slow. Bad men.

Shaggy's eyes were adept at finding the red lights that indicated alarm systems and motion detectors. This close to the house, we should have noticed them, or at least heard the electric buzz through the wires. Nothing.

Screw it. We'd come this far.

The oversized handles on the French doors posed no obstacle to my claws. The talons rested on the fake brass for a second, then with a grunt and a yank he reefed on the handle. With a crack that could be heard back in Vegas, the panel came off the top hinge.

I held us back, waiting for the wail of a siren or the shout from one of the guards that should have been on duty. The only noise was the creaking of the hinge as it fought to keep the door from hitting the ground.

Either the guards were completely stupid, or they weren't where they were supposed to be.

Shaggy's brain registered the slightest scent of Bear Guy. It was residual, hours old, but it was enough to get him fired up. Rather than sit and wait to get shot, I directed him to the trophy room.

He paused, confused at the sight of all the dead animals, or what was left of them, mounted on the walls. I'd seldom seen Shaggy afraid, but there was no doubt he hated this place as much as anywhere he'd ever been. He hadn't been this freaked out since the debacle in South Dakota four years ago. What did he know I didn't?

It took a serious mental shove to get across the door open to the corridor, then two giant steps down, we found our target. The odor of the bear and other humans was stronger here, but still faint. And still no cavalry.

It took some time and painful effort, but I got one of Shaggy's claws to retract enough for me to open the digital lock. Seventeen seventy-six.

Shit, that's a five. Try again.

The second time, it worked. The door popped open, and I relaxed, giving Shaggy his other claw back.

Okay. Go in, get the egg, get the hell out.

153

Bowden's treasure room was completely dark except for the display light in the egg's case. It was still there, just waiting for us. Just like the plan.

That should have been my first clue that something was seriously funky.

I heard the gentle click of a light switch. The room exploded in bright light, setting Shaggy's eyes on fire. He backed into the door, momentarily blinded.

"What in God's name is that?" It was the younger Bowden. He was ghost-white and looked—and smelled—like he was about to pee his pants. There were two other figures with him.

Next to him stood his father, a smug look on his face and something in his hand. Torson was on the other side of the display case, stripped to the waist and already growling.

A spitting noise filled the room, and a sharp pain struck my chest. Bright yellow feathers stuck out of my hide. Shaggy couldn't make any sense of it. Somewhere in my head, my brain took the reins. *I know what that is.*

Then my second thought. *Crap. That's a tranquilizer dart.* That was my last coherent thought before everything went black.

CHAPTER 26

The change ripped through my body with all the pain and unpleasantness that came with it. Muscles spasmed, teeth gnashed, claws ripped at cloth, but what it was 1 didn't know. My muscles screamed. One second, 1 was myself, the next Shaggy ran the show, then back. 1 needed to figure out where the holy hell 1 was, so after a couple of attempts, 1 wrestled back control for good, waited for the muscle twitches and mental spikes to ebb, then opened my eyes.

It didn't help orient me because 1 had no damned idea where "here" was. 1 laid on a small camping cot, a sweaty, partially shredded blanket that smelled like a wet dog in a heap on the floor. A faint line of blue-white LED lights ran where the wall and ceiling met around the perimeter, offering just enough light to see shadows, but not enough to identify anything.

The electric whir of a closed-circuit camera drew my eyes skyward. The telltale red dot told me 1 was being watched.

Whoever it was caught me looking at them. A voice crackled through a speaker. "You weren't out near as long as 1 expected. You're a tough bastard, aren't ya?"

I know that voice. Sounds like a bad comic imitating a movie cowboy.

Old man Bowden.

"Why don't you come in here and find out?" Good offense is the best defense, blah blah blah. I was in no mood to play games.

"Actually, I'd like to do just that. I want to talk to you, Lupul. McPherson, whatever. Agree to be civil and we can do that."

"Or?" I knew he wasn't offering an alternative, but it was worth a shot. After a second or two of bluffing, I uttered a weak, "Yeah, fine. Come on in."

Immediately, the clicking electronic lock drew my eyes to the door. Light poured in like a firehose and spiked my eyeballs, driving me against the wall. I shaded my eyes, but didn't cover them. *Not going to let him see me hurt. Screw him.* A shadow stood in the doorway, the black figure leaning on a cane with one hand.

In the other was a handgun the size of a howitzer. No surprise. He probably took a Glock into the bathroom when he took a dump. Gun nuts are like that.

I turned to let my legs dangle off the cot. With all the dignity I could muster while naked and a prisoner, I forced a grin. "Clive Bowden, I'm guessing."

"You know god-damn good and well who I am, kid. Just like I know who you are. And what you are. Where did that old sumbitch Cromwell find you?"

"At the pound. I was a rescue." There was more truth there than I wanted to admit.

"Well, you're mine now. Along with his egg. Finders keepers, like they say. He's losing this game rather badly."

Disregarding the crack about who belonged to whom, I leveled my eyes with his. "Funny, he said the same thing about you not too long ago."

The old bugger shrugged. "Momentum changes. At the moment, I'm on a bit of a hot streak. You, on the other hand, are shit out of luck."

"Sorry, I messed up your plans."

He coughed up a loogie and spit on the floor, with a wet nasty cough for emphasis. "No, you're not, but that's okay. This is just business. I don't take it personally."

Great. I'm dealing with a freaking Bond villain.

"Course, mine aren't the only plans you messed with, and our associate isn't at all happy. She'd like you to disappear permanently."

Crap.

"Don't suppose you could tell me who she is?" My money was still on Karmen, but didn't have enough to go on.

"If you haven't figured that out, you're not as smart as I think you are. Let's just say you're mucking up some long-standing plans." *There they go overestimating me again.*

"Is this the part where you take me out and shoot me?"

"Nah. If I wanted to do that, you'd already be dead. Legal too. Caught you breaking into my house. Now, Junior here, he'd like to put a bullet in your head and be done with you, but he has no sense of sportsmanship. No, I have something way more interesting in mind."

He was dying for me to ask him. But the hell with what he wanted. I crossed my legs to maintain a little dignity. I just glowered at him.

He carried on as if I'd actually responded. "I'm sure you remember Odin Torson. He'd like another crack at you. Especially in your, um, other form. I have a few very select friends who enjoy that kind of sport. It'll be quite a show. Long as it lasts.

Definitely a Bond Villain. The only things missing were the laser beams.

"You want me and your pet bear to have a... what? A dogfight?" Cockfight was probably more appropriate but given my current nudity, it seemed a little too on the nose.

"You could call it that. Lose and your head goes in my special collection. I have a new plaque already picked out and everything."

Is he seriously talking about putting my head on a wall?

"Just for giggles. What if I win?"

Bowden laughed. "I like your attitude. Lupul. Won't happen, but keep that spirit. It'll make for a hell of a show."

"That's what this is? A show? Some kind of sick comedy?"

"Oh, it's no joke. We're going to livestream this sumbitch. A lot of sick fuckers out there who'll pay good money to see someone—like you—in action. I'll send Cromwell the link for free so he can watch what happens to anyone who crosses me."

"When is this big production supposed to happen?"

"In about an hour. My understanding of such things is you need the moon to be at the top of your powers, that still gives you some time before sunrise. Want to keep things above board, fair and square."

With no windows in the room, I'd lost sense of time. "It's still Tuesday? How long was I out?"

"Only about ninety minutes. We thought we had enough to put you to sleep for hours. Like I said, you're a tough one."

He dropped his gun hand and turned to the door. Then he turned back. "I don't suppose you'd consider changing employers? I could use a good man with your skills." That didn't deserve an answer. Bowden bit his lip and tipped his cowboy hat. "Probably just as well. Torson's enough of a pain in the ass without having two of you to manage. Alright then. We'll come get you in about thirty minutes. Make your peace. Or whatever."

Then Clive Bowden was gone, and the door slammed clicked shut. That left me alone with my thoughts, which were never good company.

Fuck. Fuckity-fuck-fuck mcfuckface.

Shaggy sensed my distress and tried taking over. That wouldn't solve anything, and I needed to keep a calm head. I did allow him one good, throat scraping, wall-shaking howl. With any luck, it scared the hell out of whoever was watching.

A lot of pacing and useless scheming later, the door opened again. Both Bowdens, Junior and Senior, stood back-lit by the bright lights in the hallway.

The old man had his gun out but pointing towards the floor. The younger version held an impressive assault weapon against his chest, with his finger uncomfortably close to the trigger. Poor gun safety. Someone could get hurt like that.

Senior held some zip ties in his other hand. "Are we going to need these, or are you going to just come along?"

The look in the younger one's eyes told me I'd be shot to pieces before I changed, and without Shaggy's help, there was no way to get out of this pickle. I nodded.

Sonny Boy sniffed. "Told you he didn't look so tough."

His father didn't even bother to look at him, just muttered, "And you don't look that stupid, but looks are deceiving, aren't they?"

I knew the expression on the kid's face. My old man was an asshole, too.

The Bowdens flanked me as we entered a corridor. To my left was the hallway to the trophy rooms. To the right of my cell were wooden doors, ten feet high and solid-looking as granite. Bowden gestured with his chin, and we turned that way. The doors swung open with a hydraulic "whoosh" and we passed through into a courtyard.

A short, paved path led away from the house to another structure. I looked up to see the moon, but although I could feel it goosing the Lycan energy and making my veins throb, the view was blocked by a roof clearly designed to provide shade during the day.

Shaggy wanted—okay, needed—to fight. Trying to think while keeping my Lycan side under control made it hard to walk, and I nearly stumbled twice. My ears thrummed with the watery beat of the two men's hearts, and I felt it would have been worth it to rip their throats out. Would have felt great for the thirty seconds before I died.

Like a march down death row, I shuffled towards a chain-link fence with a wide gate. As we got closer, I made out bright stadium lights on stanchions. Bowden wasn't kidding about televising this fiasco.

Fifty feet further out was a sunken bowl in the ground, like an empty swimming pool or a skateboard park, with steep sides and wooden benches set up on two sides. A rope ladder led to the floor of the pit, maybe twelve feet down. A ten-foot-high wooden fence surrounded it on three sides, blocking the view from everywhere but the house.

As the full pit came into view, Odin Torson was already down there, waiting for me. The big, hairy asshole stood stripped to just a loincloth. He looked up at me, staring and glaring, swinging his giant arms—big around as my waist—side to side, loosening up. He wasn't messing around. The look in his eyes as I neared the arena sent a shiver up my spine and Shaggy squirmed around in my guts. The urge to kill—Shaggy's urge—was lava hot in my blood. My own fury and need for violence added to the boiling emotions.

A couple more minutes, big guy. Then you'll get your chance.

I kept my eyes on Bear Guy even as Bowden drawled on. "Okay, here's how this works. You go down that ladder there. We pull it up. You two have at it. Only one of you comes out. Any questions?"

I wanted to make a smartass joke, but it died halfway up my throat. There was no universe in which this was funny. I was going to die, but at least I would have a chance. Then I saw two big guys with scoped rifles at opposite ends. Wrong again. It was obvious if Torson didn't kill me, these boys would finish the job. Either way, my head—okay, Shaggy's—was going on Bowden's wall.

I was screwed, but I wasn't giving these nimrods the satisfaction of admitting it. "Nope. Let's get this shit-show over with."

CHAPTER 27

There wasn't much of a crowd, but then I suppose this shindig was put together on short notice. It was the middle of the night, and most of the audience would watch on the Dark Web. Guards took up a position at each end of the pit, rifles and scopes at the ready. A half-dozen or so huge men, dressed just like the Bowdens, so probably their goon squad, gathered in the bleachers. Six heads rose in unison, appraising me as I was perp-walked naked into the arena.

My Lycan self was on red alert, sniffing and growling and itching for a fight. That desire to fight—No. To kill—was rising again and as much as it terrified me, I knew it was my only hope.

My Shaggy-powered ears picked up everything three hundred and sixty degrees around me while my eyes and attention were locked only on the huge Berserker. From yards away, I detected the laugh of a huge Hispanic guy and the voices dropped to whispers. Then three of the other men shook his hand. He must have been given pretty long odds to put his money on me. I wasn't sure even I'd take that action.

"Get moving, asshole." Junior slammed the butt of his rifle into my shoulder from behind, nearly sending me headfirst over the edge. With a little assistance from Shaggy, I whirled around, let out a growl and, still in Johnny form, backhanded the gun out of his hands. I felt a satisfying smack, and the weapon spun out of his hands through the air until it clattered on the concrete ten feet away. The jerk backpedaled so hard he fell back on his ass into the bleachers, his eyes wide as Frisbees. This drew huge laughs from everyone but Clive Bowden, who just dropped his head and shook it sadly.

Up on the wall, I heard the *snick-snick* of safeties being taken off of high-powered weapons. They trained every goddamn one of them on me. "It's time, kid, save your strength. You're gonna need it." Bowden waved his pistol towards the rope ladder.

A hail of bullets would be a lot quicker than what Torson had planned for me, and a ton less satisfying to the Bowdens and their ghoulish audience. They made refusing to cooperate almost worthwhile. Shaggy disagreed though, desperately craving battle.

He deserved to go out on his terms. And if I died feeling that rush again, well, things could be worse.

Screw it.

Saying nothing else, I gripped the railing and put my foot on the first run. Something occurred to me and I raised my eyes up at the cowboy.

"Exactly how many times has he fought like this?"

Bowden gnawed at the toothpick in his mouth. "Twice before. He fought a Chupacabra. That's him hanging in the trophy room. Took him about a minute and a half. Then there was the guy who thought he was a vampire or some shit."

"Was he? A vampire?"

Bowden took the toothpick out of his mouth and waved it at me. "Nah. Turns out he was just bat shit crazy. Torson didn't leave enough of him to stuff and mount, not that I'd have bothered. That room is reserved for the real thing. Quite the honor." The bastard had the nerve to give me a friendly wink.

Vampire? Now I had a million questions but couldn't go down that rabbit hole. I flashed on the monstrous head gracing the special trophy room and decided it was time to focus unless Shaggy was going to join the collection.

I looked down, sucked in a breath, then hand-over-handed until I hit the second from the last handhold and dropped into the pit. My bare feet landed on cool, smooth concrete. Running a hand up the wall, I felt fresh paint and a perfectly smooth surface. Slick with no handholds. *Great.*

A loud grunt drew my attention back to Torson. His face was red and his whole gigantic, hairy body was tensing and flexing. Clearly, he was holding in a change of his own, and barely maintaining control. I knew I could at least influence Shaggy when he was in charge. Could Torson do anything with his alter ego or was it in control? It was a good question. *Exactly how berserk would a Berserker get if a Berserker went berserk?*

He was bigger than me. Hairier. Definitely stronger. My only real chance was he wasn't smarter than me, and that was a crapshoot. Maybe I could rile him up until he did something stupid?

I waved hello. "Hey. Nice diaper." Torson squinted and his eyebrows met in the middle."You look like a Viking slept with a Sumo wrestler."

That was met with another growl, this time accompanied by chest beating and a foot stomp. I definitely had the better sense of humor. Not much use in a fight, but it was something.

My brain frantically searched for information about bears that might be helpful.

They're big and smelly.

They like picnic baskets.

They shit in the woods.

None of that was particularly helpful. I tried calling to mind all the animal documentaries I'd seen of Grizzlies in action. They fought on their hind legs, mostly, which limited their mobility but gave them plenty of leverage. Their claws sat on top of paws the size of my head and they took long, looping swings like a drunk in a bar. *Shit, that's actually useful.* They only used their teeth for close-up work, which was another data point. They were faster than they looked, but still slower than a wolf.

Just don't let him get you on the ground.

The amplified squeal of a microphone interrupted my game planning. "Okay, gentlemen. When you hear the horn, go to it. We'll count down from ten."

A metallic beep. *Ten.*

Nine.

Eight.

Torson let out a scream about then, and from the shaking and the sudden higher pitch of his screams, it was obvious his change had begun.

Seven.

Six.

Screw it. Let's go.

There was no time for a gentle transition. I just let it rip. Hearing nothing but my own howls, I shrank into myself, and Shaggy took over. Fire consumed my entire nervous system, both incredibly painful and incomprehensibly pleasurable. The world went supernova with white light.

My eyesight sharpened, my hearing became more acute, and my sense of smell sent a mushroom cloud of odors to my brain. Most clearly, I sensed the onrushing stench of meat and sweat and rot that could only mean a bear was close and getting closer.

Before the thought registered, I flew backwards and slammed into the wall behind me. I slid down the wall to my—Shaggy's—tailbone. Without thinking, I dodged low and to my left as a shadow passed over me. The thing that was Odin Torson collided with the wall with a force that would have reduced me to a pancake had I still been there.

In three bounds, I retreated to the other side of the arena and struggled to get my bearings. That offered enough time to determine what I was up against. While my eyesight and hearing were at peak levels, the details registered in my brain a beat slowly, like passing through a wall of water. What I saw wasn't encouraging. Shaggy, on the other hand, was beside himself. For him, this was playtime.

Torson's bear-self was massive. HIs body hair wasn't as long and thick as Shaggy although he was covered in a dark brown fuzz. His snout was more pug-shaped, flat against his face instead of long and pointy like mine, and two big fangs reached up in an under-bite. They were the teeth of a scavenger, not much use for attacking, so yay me. The bad news was his hands.

The problem was, they were *hands*. Instead of the big, padded, clawed pizza paddles that proper bears have, Torson stood flexing his fingers. They all moved independently. Long vicious claws, half as long as mine but thick and evilly sharp, glinted in the TV lights. I remembered Cree's description of Berserkers, and it made a kind of depressing sense. Without hands like that, there was no way a warrior could hold an axe or a sword. My claws were longer and nastier—better weapons, maybe. His hands could grasp and hold. If he got me in reach, with those mitts and his full weight, it would be game over.

Crap.

While I was taking inventory of all the ways this guy could kill me, Torson's bear-self was building himself into a frenzy. Roaring, chest pounding, stomping the ground. The big guy didn't have so much a plan as an objective, which was to get his paws on me and inflict as much pain as possible. It wasn't subtle, but at least he wasn't overthinking it.

Shaggy wanted to attack, to get his teeth on that big smelly ogre. *Wait for it. Wait. He'll come to us.*

He did. And he wasn't screwing around. Those arms, as thick as my torso, windmilled as he let out a roar that shook the concrete. At the last minute, I ducked low and took a good swipe at him as I passed between those redwood-sized legs. That left three long, satisfying gashes where his Achilles tendon was. Rather than cripple him, it did nothing but piss him off.

A move like that would have crippled anyone else I'd ever fought. It had in the past. All Torson did was howl and swipe at the air with those giant paws. He missed by a mile, but the breeze was enough to move me back. If he'd connected, I'd have been knocked senseless, Shaggy-powers or not.

My brain was full of disjointed images of blood, rage and a desire to kill at all costs. I liked where my Lycan alter ego was going with that. Torson turned to face me for another charge, and this time, I swiped both claws at his face. Before they could make contact, he blocked the blow. A shiver went up my arm as it slammed against his. Only one claw tip made contact, with his face leaving a streaming red gash down one cheek.

Torson gripped my claw in his left hand and damn near tugged my arm from my shoulder socket as he flung me away. I felt myself taking flight and slammed hard against the arena floor twenty feet from him. Strong didn't begin to describe the big bastard.

I spared a look around me. With Shaggy-eyes and ears I could hear the spectators shouting and whooping, the blood lust in the bleachers nearly matching that in the pit. Their cheers caught Torson's attention too, because he sniffed the air and let out a giant roar. The asshole was digging the attention. Well, he had the home-field advantage.

We met each other's eyes. I swear his lip curled in a sadistic grin before bellowing another challenge and lumbering towards me. That much meat moved slowly, but its momentum was hard to stop. This time I felt Shaggy crouch low to the ground, and, as the bear pulled his arm back to lower the boom, I jumped, targeting that bicep.

My cardinal rule in a fight was never to let Shaggy bite someone unless we were going to finish the job. After Kozlov turned, I swore never to bite anyone again, and certainly never leave them alive. But what was I going to do, turn Torson into a werewolf? He was already a fricking bear. At worst, he'd get an ugly case of sepsis. Staying alive was more important than the moral implications.

I allowed my teeth to sink into his flesh. Blood spurted into my mouth, exploding on my neuroreceptors like a fire hose full of happy juice. I clamped harder, refusing to let go and hoping to rip that arm clean off. Instead, I was lifted off my feet and shaken back and forth.

My brains were being scrambled in my skull as Torson tried shaking me off. I was determined to hold on and clamped my jaws even tighter. Another rush of blood in my mouth let me know I was hurting him, but not winning by any means. All that thrashing around just made me dizzy and confused, and Shaggy was less responsive to my thoughts.

There was no way to know which way was up or to do anything but hang on, literally for dear life. Finally, I felt my jaw cramp, and had no choice but to relax my grip just a little. That was enough for one good swing of his arms to send me flying end ass-over-teakettle into the pit wall.

I expected Shaggy to jump up and attack, but we sat on the ground for a moment, needing time to re-orient ourselves. While struggling to my feet, I felt a shiver run through my body. In the back of my brain I felt, more than heard, a sound I never expected to hear. It was a whimper. Of fear. From Shaggy. He was afraid, and that alone was the scariest thing I ever imagined. If he couldn't—or wouldn't—fight like hell, we, I, would be dead in a heartbeat.

The bear-thing charged, snorting and grunting like a hairy steam engine. Needing to clear my head, and give Shaggy time to recover, we ducked low and launched ourselves across the arena. That began a drawn-out game of tag, and Torson was "It."

Low to the ground, twice his speed, and dodging like crazy, we kept the game up for a minute or so. The Berserker kept swinging low and twice I was able to jump out of the way, one time actually leapfrogging over him. It was almost funny seeing the bewilderment on his fuzzy face when he found me standing behind him. The game continued until my senses returned.

The laughing, jeering men above had abandoned all sense of duty and congregated in the bleachers where they could get the best view of the action. I tried spotting the armed guards, but Torson's heavy breathing alerted me to another attack.

His claw whiffed over my head. I took a swipe of my own, clear across his abdomen. My arm's momentum slowed as the razor-like talons struck hairy, thick meat. Three inch-wide gashes ran the width of that huge gut. The Berserker might have been insane, but he possessed a healthy sense of self-preservation. Torson retreated to the far corner, panting and checking himself for damage.

I wish I could have used the break to my advantage and gone for the kill. Truth is, much as Shaggy wanted to finish the job, he was unsure he could do it and wanted to run. I didn't want to win so much as get the hell out of there. At least we wanted the same thing. The key to teamwork is alignment on the mission. I sat on my haunches, panting, looking around, waiting for a miracle that would never arrive.

The guards still sat with their compatriots, booing us for not fighting. Torson took it personally and roared up at them, waving those enormous arms in fury. He believed he should have killed me by now, and was getting frustrated. It looked good on him. He took deep breaths, glaring at me, timing the next rush.

There was just enough time between agonizing inhalations to study our position. Everyone had moved to one side of the arena for a better view. That left three sides unguarded. The problem was there was ten feet of fence even if I got out of the pit. Nobody could jump that high.

But maybe I didn't have to.

The corner farthest from me had about a four-foot slab of concrete pavers between the pit and the wall. It should have been occupied by one of the guards. It wasn't. If I could get up there, I might make it over the wall in two trips. Or Torson could catch me. Or one of those boneheads might suddenly decide to do their jobs and shoot my ass to bits. The possibilities were endless.

My muscles and lungs burned. The idea of leaping to the top of a twelve-foot wall seemed as ridiculous as my sprouting wings and flying out. Shaggy studied it for a minute and grunted. Okay then.

No more time to think about it. All six-five of Torson's body rose up on his hind legs and bellowed a challenge. Rest time was over.

Wait.

The wall is twelve feet. Torson is over half that height. I don't suppose I could ask him to give me a boost?

He wouldn't do it willingly, but a truly bat shit crazy idea occurred to me. I let out the loudest Shaggy-howl I could muster. The Berserker lowered his head and charged. Shaggy and I crouched as low as possible, muscles tensed and waited.

Come on, big guy. Come to Johnny.

The Berserker rose to two legs as he charged, arms outstretched. I think his plan was to grab hold and then flatten me. If I didn't time this exactly right, he'd get his wish.

Wait.

Wait.

And... now.

I ducked under his right arm. He rushed past me but quickly slammed on the brakes.

Now.

Before he could turn around, I jumped on his back with Shaggy's hind feet finding a place to dig in above his hips and fore-claws burying themselves in his shoulders.

Enraged, the bear-thing whirled round and round, trying to spin us off. When that didn't work, he did what I wanted him to do, try to rub me off against the wall.

The first time he did it, I almost abandoned my plan. Being on his back was good, being close to the wall was good. Having three or four hundred pounds of furious were-bear smashing me between the two was a decided disadvantage.

I'd only get one more shot at it. After I absorbed the first blow, he pulled back to smash me again. That gave me enough room to scamper higher on his back.

This time, before he smooshed me into a pancake, I sprung. Claws extended, I hooked the edge of the pit and pulled myself up. My legs pedaled like crazy, just out of reach of Torson's hands. Thank God bears can't jump.

I don't know who was more surprised when I found myself on the hard surface looking down at a furious, spinning, howling bear-thing. Across the pit, the men assembled on the other side just stared. For a second anyway. Then they got it together. Seeing them reach for their weapons, it was time to high-tail it out of there.

Bears I could outrun, not bullets. I turned to the fence, called on Shaggy for help, and sprung. Talons hung over the wall, supporting my weight. One more good pull and I was over, landing in a heap on the other side. There was no time to enjoy my freedom. A series of shots rang out. Holes appeared in the fence, perfect circles with TV light streaming through. This was no time to gloat.

I allowed myself one good howl of victory and took off into the desert.

CHAPTER 28

Christ only knows how far I ran before I slowed down and finally dropped, panting, in the lee of a big rock. Every inch of me ached. My bruises throbbed, open scratches stung, and shame burned through every inch of my hairy, abused body.

As the razor-thin, whitish-blue line of morning appeared far off to the East, I curled into a whimpering ball. Too exhausted to change, I kept my Shaggy form. Just my luck, my Johnny brain was in charge, for what that was worth.

The terror that wracked Shaggy earlier was gone, replaced by a dust devil of relief, confusion, anger, and regret. It was impossible to tell which of those belonged to which of us. The sky slowly lightened—it had to be after four-thirty but not quite five, yet. I tried making sense of it all.

We'd survived, which most people would take as a win. But what else had I accomplished? I hadn't gotten the egg back. In fact, I managed to lose the fake one as well, so a double screw up. My boss's worst enemy had it, which probably meant I'd be fired, and the entire world—at least a twisted, messed up corner of it—knew who and *what* I was.

Shaggy's ears picked up the far away mosquito-drone of small engines. ATV's most likely. Bowden had his men out looking for me. And they were the only ones. Cree would never know what happened to me, and the list of people who gave a damn got awfully short after that.

Really? She's the first you think about with everything going so spectacularly wrong? Prioritize, dummy.

The buzzing noise split in two, and I realized whoever—and however many there were—that Bowden sent after me had split up. My Lycan eyes saw paw prints leading like a neon sign to my hidey hole, but it was still dark enough the goons would miss them. The cowboys were doing a cross-sweeping pattern, hoping to find my trail.

The moon's pull on me was weakening, and it took some focus to stay Shaggy, since being naked in the desert seemed counterproductive. Normally, I had no problem maintaining this shape even after sunrise. Then again, I'd never been mauled by a bear before. I had about fifteen minutes before even those idiots couldn't miss the signs and come barreling down on my furry ass.

Shaggy's fear and desire to flee were turning to something darker. Fury, revenge, and most importantly, that sweet ache of wanting to kill someone. Something—I still had a choice in the matter. Whatever it was, my blood was boiling with the need to do... anything but sit there.

One sure sign that you're doing something stupid is when the last thing you say before doing it is, "fuck it."

"Fuck it," I said.

To have any chance of success, all I'd have to do is sneak back to Bowden's compound, break back into the trophy room, grab the Egg (and if the gods or spirits or whatever were with me my backpack) and get the hell out of Dodge. All while the sun was coming up, and I had no idea who would waited for me when I got there.

The only thing I had in my favor was that only an idiot would try it, and Bowden didn't think I was *that* stupid. He didn't know who he was messing with. I was way dumber than he gave me credit for. It was my superpower. That, and the Lycan body that was getting harder and harder to maintain. Fortunately, Shaggy's desire to rip something apart kept him present and motivated.

With no time to waste, I headed West. With any luck, I could loop around and avoid the armed rednecks on their glorified golf carts. Even with the sun directly to my back, my eyes burned with the flames of daybreak. My brain wanted to shed Shaggy and just rest, but I wasn't done. Yet. I motored through and focused on following the monstrous shadow in front of me, keeping my head down and shuffling through the rocky desert.

When it felt like nothing could make me take another step, I sent Shaggy a vision of Torson in full bear mode, and Junior Bowden's punchable face. That was good for another burst of adrenaline, righteous wolf's anger, and a few steps more.

Shaggy knew where to go better than I did. About the time I was sure I was lost, I saw the first outbuilding. They'd have been easy to miss in the rolling dusty brown landscape, except each sported a giant American flag. At least I didn't have to guess if it was the right place.

The doors to the biggest building were wide open, but it was empty aside from a battered pickup. Had they sent all hands out after me? My luck generally didn't run that good but at least there wouldn't be too many people around.

My Lycan-self took the lead in scouting the location. While we didn't see or hear—or smell—anyone, that wasn't the only problem. The giant gates around the arena were closed and a low hum meant the electrified fence was back in action.

Lovely.

Going through the fence was going to be painful as well as slow, but there was no way to climb over. Shaggy sprouted teeth, claws and fur, not wings. It's not like I could just fly. But I could fall. That would be more my style, anyway.

I was just about ready to collapse as it was. The moon's power had long left, and I was running on a cocktail of adrenaline, cortisol, and a desire to kick someone's ass.

The eaves of the farthest building hung over the far fence, sending long shadows all the way to the arena pit. A quick, moderately painful drop would at least get me on the right side of the electricity, and from there I could just force my way in. I sat back on my haunches and considered the plan, such as it was.

Easy-peasy—sneak past three more buildings, avoid being seen in the insanely bright daylight, climb onto the roof when I didn't know if there were enough reserves in the tank, land on the other side, break into the room, steal the crystal egg, and head out across miles of open sagebrush without getting shot or becoming bear food.

What could go wrong?

If I thought about the answer to that question I would quit, so I ignored it and got to work. Shaggy's aching body dragged me to the base of the last building, with a lot of sniffing, breath holding, and freezing at every puff of wind or creaking weathervane. It took an eternity, but I finally reached the shed nearest the fence and looked up at the roofline.

Goddamn, that's a long way up. I'd cleared a lot higher fence a few hours ago, but there was no way of doing it again with a body on the verge of collapse and no lunar help. Staring, panting, and wanting to quit, my ears picked up a flat, bored voice drifting over from the other side of the building.

It was Junior Bowden. Big shock, he'd decided to supervise from the comforts of home.

"Whaddya mean you can't find him? It can't be that fricking hard. How many seven-foot-tall coyotes can there be?"

Who's he calling a coyote? I should kick his ass just for that. Shaggy bristled at the familiar voice, and the urge to attack rose from my toes and made my claws tingle. It took some doing, but I tamped down my alter ego. We didn't have strength or time for anything else but the task at hand, no matter how tempting.

It took some scrambling to get onto the roof, daring the eaves trough to come off in my claws and leaving big scratches up the stucco from kicking like crazy to climb up. It left a telltale sign behind from my clawed feet. They'd know it was me. That seemed as silly as worrying about leaving fingerprints behind.

Of course they know it's you. Who else would it be? Just get it done.

Crouching on the roof, I saw Junior pacing around the pit area, shouting into his cellphone, just circling the hole in the ground. There was no sign of Senior, who worried me a lot more. Much as the kid was less of a threat, he had a hand-cannon strapped to his hip, so it wasn't like the chances of getting shot were zero.

When I was sure I was invisible, I shuffled to the edge of the eaves and looked down. It wasn't much of a drop to the concrete, especially with Lycan powers. My claws were more human than not, and the Shaggy part of me was receding further with each minute. The nails were shorter, barely visible, but enough to provide a solid grip while I dangled down and let go, dropping onto the ground.

A sharp pain shot up my ankle. *Crap. That should've been easy.* I had very little Shaggy-strength left. Partly it was the rising sun. Mostly, I was beaten to the point of exhaustion. After making sure my leg could bear my weight, I ran to the giant doors leading to the house.

Locked. With a keycard entry. Both my ankle and head throbbed; I couldn't waste any more time. Odds were, they hadn't had time to repair the French doors I came in the first time, and all the guards were somewhere out in the desert looking for me.

Sure enough, after limping around the corner, I slipped through the gaping hole I'd created hours ago. I hobbled through the normal trophy room and across the hall to Bowden's special, creepier version. For a moment, the keypad mocked me.

What the hell was that number? It was a war. Eighteen Twelve? Nineteen Forty-One?

With aching hands that were not entirely human, I seventeen-seventy-sixed my way past the door and bent with my hands on my knees, gasping for breath. There was hardly any Shaggy left. There wasn't much of me either, to be honest. The Chupacabra grinned down at me, and I imagined he'd have been proud of me for beating Torson. "Wish I'd kicked his ass for you, buddy." Then the empty plaque reserved for my head caught my eye, and I was determined to just get the holy hell out of there.

Summoning what strength I had left, I gave a giant, grunting, pull on the display case. It wouldn't open. It didn't even budge.

You've gotta be shitting me. Come on!

My backpack was still on the floor. I grabbed it, rummaging through until I found my Ruger. Without much thought, I grabbed the barrel and smashed the grip against the glass case. It shattered into a thousand satisfying pieces, and for a millisecond I thought I'd actually get away with it. Then the alarm shrieked like it saw me naked.

"Damn." I didn't bother swapping eggs. There was no time to be cute. I grabbed the Sky Egg, slipped some of the loose bubble wrap around it and threw it in the pack with the fake. Then I threw the strap over my shoulder. There was no way those eggs could weigh as much as it felt. Clearly, I was at the end of my rope. Energy leaked from my body through every cut, scratch, and bruise.

The claxon alarm kept "a-ooo-ga-ing" over and over, hammering spikes through my ears into my brain. I needed to get out of there. Spinning towards the door, I almost crashed into a very surprised, extremely annoyed Junior Bowden.

"No fucking way." We stared disbelievingly at each other.

Then he reached for his gun.

Normally, I'd have said something smartass or just tried to run. Instead, I flexed my hands as fury, frustration, and the urge to do some serious damage charged through me like an electric shock. I'd been insulted, hurt, fed to a bear and shot at. Plus, he'd stolen Cromwell's egg and hit a girl. There wasn't much left in the tank, but I leaped at him with everything I had.

I inhaled the scent of his fear, and it brought Shaggy back to me, at least what was left. It was mostly me that crashed into his chest, knocking both of us to the ground with me on top. My knee slammed into his right wrist, his gun hand. I was rewarded with the satisfying crack of bone. With clenched, bloody human fists, I rained blows onto the squirming, shouting figure. Each punch sent a blast of adrenaline and who knows what chemical soup through my brain. Shaggy was there, but it felt more like he was watching, cheering me on. I kept beating Bowden bloody.

And it felt good.

I was going to kill him, and it couldn't be blamed on my Lycan self. This was Johnny beating the ever-loving shit out of a man. *This feels amazing.* I bathed in the smell of blood, and his pathetic moaning. I reveled in the feeling of something I'd only ever felt second hand. The urge to kill. I grinned and looked down at the figure below me.

Bowden's face was bloody red meat, bruises forming where I'd broken his nose and probably a cheek bone. Each breath spat blood from his nose and mouth. From a distant corner of my brain, Shaggy bayed for me to finish the job.

"P-p-please."

He expected mercy? After what he'd done to me? To Karmen and Cree and Lemuel Collins, and–well—everyone? Was he crazy?

No. I was.

I caught a reflection in a piece of shattered glass. The face staring back was unrecognizable, spattered in blood, eyes bulging, teeth— human teeth, my teeth—bared. It was me, but it wasn't.

I'd been in more than my share of scraps. I'd never hurt someone this badly. He might make it, probably not. In the past, anything terrible could be blamed on the beast deep inside me, who was more than happy to accept responsibility. But he was dormant, hiding from the desert sun. This was all Johnny.

I lifted my head and let out a cry that was a hundred percent human. Rolling off the groaning lump beneath me, I lay on my back panting, gasping, probably crying. I don't know. There were tears and snot and blood. Inside my head, there were enough brain cells still firing to tell me I couldn't stay. I needed to run, to escape.

Staggering to my feet, I grabbed the backpack and slipped an aching arm through a strap, leaving it dangling to my knees. It took a ton of focus to step out of that room, through the hall to the other and out into the morning light.

Where in the hell was I supposed to go? How did I think I was going to get out of here? It's not like I had an Uber waiting.

Wait. Maybe I did.

Cree. She might not have given up hope. I felt an unfamiliar spark of hope.

My hands hurt so badly, I barely managed to pull the Velcro pocket open and take out my phone. It fumbled from my grasp, and I stabbed my finger at it while it sat on the ground. *Please have some juice left.*

My screensaver: Bill, Gramma, and me at Navy Pier appeared. There was a little battery life, although my eyes couldn't focus enough to tell me how many bars or even if I had a signal. I was debating whether to attempt a phone call when I heard the buzz of those frigging ATVs. There was no time. I needed to get the hell out of here. I half ran, half shuffled out into the morning sun. A red plastic flag gave me as much direction as I was going to get.

That way.

Safety.

Home.

On fumes and desperation, I jogged, then ran, then walked, then stumbled again. The few reserves Shaggy had left offered enough strength to stay upright and heading east. A laughing howl escaped my throat while Bowden's house faded away behind me.

Ha. Got your egg, you old bastard? Finders keepers.

CHAPTER 29

It took three tries, but I finally convinced my eyes to stay open. I was in a hotel room. Good so far. My hands touched both edges of the mattress, so it wasn't my room at Caesar's with the king-size bed. Other than that, I had no clue.

"Are you going to actually stay awake this time, or are you going to keep teasing us?" The voice was familiar, but it made no sense. The speaker should be in Chicago right now. I was reasonably sure my body was in Las Vegas.

"Bill?" I tried sitting, but my spinning head negated that silly idea. The motion caused a stinging in my arm, which turned out to be from a needle and a plastic tube leading to a bag hanging from a metal stand. "What are you doing here? And where's here?"

"You're in my room at Caesar's. Whoever you pissed off is probably watching yours. I came out to give you some good news. Thought it might be fun to surprise you."

I lifted my hands as high as I could and grunted, "Surprise." It wasn't a great joke, and it was clear Bill wasn't amused. This was his "you scared the shit out of me and it's not cool, dude" face. I used to get that a lot, but it had been a while. Bill sat in a stuffed armchair he'd pulled beside my bed, his cane over his lap. Obviously, I'd slept better than he had.

The needle pinched again, and this time I managed to sit up. I inspected my arm, trying to puzzle out what was going on. A terrible thought occurred to me. "You didn't take me to a hospital, did you?"

"No, figured it would raise too many questions you didn't want to answer. Cree brought you straight here. Then we called one of those Hangover Buses and hooked you up. It's just electrolytes, but we figured it couldn't hurt."

Crap. "Someone saw me like this?"

Bill got one corner of his mouth to smile. "This is Vegas. Guy said he'd seen way worse. This town is seriously messed up."

"You don't even know, man." I was about to ask the next of about a thousand questions when the door opened, and Cree blew in, glaring at her phone.

"That's like, the hundredth time Karmen's called. Is he...?" She stopped, seeing me sitting upright.

She dropped the phone on the bed and bent over me. A cool hand pressed against my forehead. Cree snapped at Bill, "You were supposed to let me know when he woke up."

Ignoring Bill's hurt-puppy face, she turned back to me. Her hand slid to my cheek, then up to my forehead. "How are you feeling? Jesus, you scared the crap out of me!"

"Us." Bill said, as if this was an ongoing argument. Over Cree's shoulder, he raised an eyebrow at me.

Cree nodded. "Yes, yeah. Us. Sorry. We're all totally freaked out."

All at once, too many images flooded my mind. The Egg, Torson's ugly bear's face, Old Man Bowden laughing, and the younger one spitting blood and pleading for mercy. Shaggy shifted at the back of my mind, enjoying that last visual more than I did.

My eyes darted around the room and I pulled my body straighter. "Where's my pack? The egg—"

Cree stood and wiped her hands on her shorts. "It's here. Well, they both are. We need to get them to Karmen soon as you're able. Mister Collins is waiting to authenticate the real one, and Malcolm

Cromwell is making a big stink about you being there, and him watching on video."

I'd completely forgotten about Lemuel since his disappearing act the night of the robbery. I was glad he was back in the picture. He would tell us which one is real. I could throw the crystal doo-dad in the Charger, then this whole fiasco would be over and done with. Sweet. Maybe this would have a happy ending after all.

Bill tapped his fingernails on the metal tubing of his cane like he always did when he got nervous. I owed him answers. Her too. I also knew there were Cree answers and Bill answers, and it was a little fuzzy who needed to know what.

Closing my eyes to focus, as well as to avoid their looks of disapproval and disappointment, I began. "Okay, after Cree dropped me off..."

The very short, cleaned-up version of the story was simple enough. I'd gotten to the compound, got as far as the trophy room, and got caught. Torson and I fought, which was true enough without going into the nasty particulars. I escaped, then went back for the Egg. There was a fight with Junior, about which I said next to nothing, and got the frick out of Dodge. After that, it was anyone's guess what happened or how I wound up here.

The end.

Cree filled in a few blanks on her end. After dropping me off, she'd driven around for a while watching the locator app. It went blank after an hour or so—Bowden must have turned my phone off after he caught me.

Her voice stayed fairly steady as she told the tale. "I didn't know what was going on. And then Bill showed up at the Museum looking for you..."

I closed my eyes, but it didn't help me remember. "Where did you find me?"

"Under a rock, hugging one of those gas company flags. You were all sunburned and dirty and—"

"Naked."

Her mouth lost the fight to keep from grinning. "Yeah. Naked. Bill came with me and we... both... got you into the truck."

Bill said, "Mostly she did it. I was pretty useless. As usual."

"No, you were great. Someone had to navigate." She was trying to make him feel better, not that it would work. Bill Mostoy was the only person I knew who was harder on himself than I was.

It was clear how worried she'd been, and Bill was barely holding it together. *This sucks. There aren't that many people who care about me and I manage to make them miserable half the time.*

Cree broke the silence. "Okay, I have to tell Karmen you're awake. Think you'll be okay to head over in an hour or so? It'll take that long to get everyone together."

"Yeah." I picked the wrong time to flinch at the pain from the bruises.

"No way." Bill said. "He needs more time."

I shook my head. "We don't have it. They'll be coming back. Sooner we get this wrapped up and get the hell out of town, the better. For everyone. Go ahead, call Karmen." Another twinge of pain stole my breath for a second. My blood hummed with Shaggy's healing powers doing their voodoo, but it still hurt like the devil. Would for a couple of days.

Cree left to make her call. Bill waited til she was gone before lighting into me. "What the hell are you trying to do? Get yourself killed?" Everything he'd been holding in spewed out.

"It's okay—"

"The hell it is! How bad was that fight, anyway? I mean, was it you fighting, or... him?" Bill referred to Shaggy in the third person like I did. It was his way of separating the normal me from whatever it was I became when all hell broke loose.

"Doesn't matter."

"Anybody hurt bad?"

"Maybe. I don't really remember." My head leaned back against the pillow and I stared at the ceiling. "Cree knows about me."

As far as Bill knew, he was the only person who knew the exact details of my secret. "She does?"

She did. Cree and God only knew how many weirdos watching on Bowden's Dark Web WrestleMania. There was going to be hell to pay, no matter how this shook out.

"Who is she? Really?"

"Not now, man."

"You should have seen her, dude. She never stopped staring at her phone. For like five hours she just kept hitting refresh and wouldn't go home or anything. Soon as it came back on, she took the truck out to get you. It was kind of impressive." That was a rave review coming from him. I know he was burning for more details.

Avoiding his questions about my personal life was an old game, even if I knew I owed him whatever answers I had. "Which reminds me, what the hell are you doing here?"

Bill struggled to get out of the chair and clomped over to the hotel room's desk. He picked up an envelope and tossed it onto my bare chest.

"Your name change is finally legal. You're not John McPherson anymore. Your last name is Lupul. Legal as a church wedding. You sounded so down last time we talked. I grabbed the first flight out of O'Hare. Figured we'd celebrate before you went home. Didn't really count on all... this."

I ignored the hurt in his voice and stared at the unassuming envelope with the earth-shattering news inside. My birth name was my own again. Like Jim and Eileen never happened. A fresh start.

"You still have to go to the DMV on your own. And the passport office. I'm not doing everything for you." Bill would always do more than he said he would. Or should have. It's what we did for each other.

"Help me up, will you? I have to get dressed."

Bracing his bad leg against the chair, he offered his arm. I pulled myself to the edge of the bed, then to a wobbly, naked standing position.

Bill let out the first genuine laugh I'd heard out of him since I woke up.

"What's so funny?" I demanded.

He pointed to my lower body. "Dude, you're sunburned everywhere. Like—everywhere."

I dropped my hand to cover my tomato-red shame. "Shut up and help me get dressed, will you?"

His laugh had reverted to its usual giggle. "She said you were sunburnt. But, dude."

"Wait, Cree saw me like this?"

"Who do you think put you to bed? I couldn't do it with this." He waved his walking stick at me.

Of course she did. Because I know how to impress a gal.

I was dressed by the time Cree came back into the room. She had washed her face, and if I had a single ounce of detective powers left, fixed her makeup. Her eyes looked greener somehow. I liked it.

She clapped her hands and was all business. "Ready? Everyone will be there soon. We have another show tonight. I can't miss another performance. Boudica will kill me. Mister Collins will come over after and we can do everything then."

I nodded my agreement, and Bill offered me his arm. I shook him off. "You don't have to come, you know."

He looked me in the eye. "Yeah. I do." Okay then, no arguing with him.

Cree furrowed her brow. "Are you okay to drive?"

Just as I was about to say yes, a spasm shot across my abdomen. "Probably not."

She picked the car keys off the pile of my belongings. "I'll drive."

Bill's mouth dropped open. "You're going to let her drive the Charger?"

"Not now, Dude."

CHAPTER 30

One night past full moon—waning gibbous.

It was a quiet ride over. Cree and I sat up front. My best friend stewed in the back about not being allowed to drive. Not that different from our high school days. The clash of the cold air conditioning and the steam emanating from Bill pouting in the back seat should have caused fog. I tried pointing out landmarks on the way, but my buddy just grunted and eventually I gave up. Trying to stop the conga line in my skull, I closed my eyes and rested my head on the window.

It was about five o'clock when we rolled into the packed Museum parking lot. Apparently, the rumors of the break-in and the witch-hunting vandals had only amped up the crowd's curiosity. There were a lot more Goth women in black tee shirts than on my last visit. Extra staff to help manage the crowds, I guessed. A couple of them had holsters on their hip. Extra security.

I don't know who hated the idea of going inside more, me or Shaggy. I stared at the door, hesitating. Cree took my hand and hustled us through the employee entrance and nearly into the waiting arms and bosom of the Mistress of Magick.

"That's her, right? Karmen Mystère? From TV." Bill whispered in my ear. I had forgotten his childish, fawning, celebrity fetish. There was no time to answer, because she came right at me, arms outstretched, boobs first. I braced for impact.

"There you are. I was worried sick. How are you, darlin'?" Now that we had the egg back, and she was out of Cromwell's bad books, Karmen was lathering the Southern charm back on. Her ice-cold cheek brushed mine. Shaggy growled softly in the back of my head. My inner wolf still believed she'd had something to do with our being set up. I didn't disagree.

"I'm good. Fine. Is Mr. Collins here yet?" *For the love of everything holy, let's finish this and get the hell out of here.*

"He's running late. I told him to come by later. It's almost show time, and the show must go on." She threw a dirty look at Cree.

"Oh, right. Damn." She gave my arm a squeeze and dipped out to get prepped for the show.

Her eyes landed on Bill. "And who's this charming creature?"

"This is my business partner, Bill Mostoy."

Karmen put on a flirty smile and held her hand out to Bill. My pal shifted his crutch to his left hand, muttered something incoherent and offered a slight blush as he shook it. I didn't expect him to fall under her spell for obvious reasons, but her fame and sheer diva-ness had him transfixed. Say what you want, Karmen Mystère offered something for everyone.

It took her two seconds to figure out she was barking up the wrong tree with Bill. "I have things to do before the show. You're invited of course, you and your fabulous partner. Meanwhile, why don't you show him around our little museum." She noticed the sag in my shoulders and added, "If you'd rather, you can always sit in my office if you're tired. Boudica has some of the coven members watching the Egg but they know to let you in."

A soft chair sounded good. Bill wiggled like a puppy at the thought of looking around, especially for free. It was the accountant in him. Aside from being tired, I felt reasonably human, and he'd flown all the way to Las Vegas with no fun to show for it. What the hell.

"Fine, I'll show you around. But I'm not buying you a tee shirt." His smile brought out one of my own. It made my face hurt a little.

We entered the first display room, which smelled of fresh paint and sawdust. Karmen had wasted no time getting the place operational again. It looked the same as it had before me and the bear had our first disagreement, except some items on display were in different places. A couple of them gave off creepy vibes I didn't detect last time. Or maybe I was still recovering from the ass-kicking and imagining things.

Bill "ooed," and "ahhed," and made snarky comments over the relics. Last time I was here, Lemuel had encouraged me to let Shaggy sense which items were legit and which weren't. This seemed like a good time to try the experiment again. I closed my eyes and called on Shaggy.

With each curio Bill pointed to, he offered his own nonstop commentary, but I mostly tuned him out. I got as close as I dared and let Shaggy sniff around. It was like that kid's game. They felt colder, warmer, colder, colder...

Red fricking hot!

"Don't get too close to that." I said, grabbing Bill's crutch arm. The World's Most Haunted Doll stared back at us.

"Dude, seriously?"

"As a heart attack. Yeah, don't screw with that one."

Bill shook his head. "What's up with you, man? You're actually believing all this now? You sound like Gramma. It makes no sense... I mean, what planet do you live on?"

The same one as you, only now I'm learning what's really out there. Whoever said knowledge was power knew nothing about werewolves, bloodsucking jewelry, evil witch spirits, or demonic kewpie dolls. What Bill and the rest of the world didn't know allowed them to sleep at night. Awareness was exhausting as hell.

Maybe it was because it was only two days after the full moon, or maybe I was getting better at it, but the ability to pick up Shaggy's feelings about these creepy doo-dads came easier. A lot more items set off alarm bells, and by the time we got through the exhibits, my head felt three sizes too big for my body and I needed to sit down.

"Come on, man, I want to see the show." Bill was being a bit of a baby, and I was in no mood to hear it.

"I've seen it. Enjoy the show. I'm going to see if I can lie down for a bit."

After assuring him I'd be fine, he headed for the showroom. I ducked through a hidden hallway and up the stairs to Karmen's office. There was a comfy sofa in there with my name on it.

Assuming, of course, I could get past the giant Nordic blonde in the hallway. A Valkyrie of a woman stood with thick, badly inked arms folded across humongous breasts. She wore what I knew now was the unofficial uniform of the coven—a black Museum of Magick tee and tight black jeans. What was her name? Valerie? She looked down at me in all senses of the word as I came to the door. She had to be six-four and a buck ninety.

A couple of other women appeared out of nowhere, flanking me. That was a professional security move. They might be part of Karmen's coven-slash-fan club, but there was no doubt Boudica trained them. They all looked straight out of Wonder Woman, like they were the Themyscira National Guard. If I wasn't tired, cranky, and sick of the whole thing, I might have handled it better.

"I really need to get in there." The Valkyrie almost pushed her palm through my chest. I maintained more composure than I felt. "Karmen told me it was alright."

"I was told not to let anyone in. Since the break-in and all." Well, it spoke. That was a decent start.

"Look, my name is Lupul, and—"

"*You're* the guy?" I heard the judgment and disappointment in her voice. I don't know what she expected, but attitude, I didn't need.

"Well, I'm *a* guy, which probably doesn't help my case." *Classy, Lupul. You didn't need to go there. Don't be a dick, she's just doing her job.* That didn't mean I couldn't play the Boss card. "Look, I'm sorry. Karmen told me to wait for her there. The only thing I'm going to do is fall asleep and maybe drool on her cushions. Please, there's no need for drama."

Four pairs of eyes asked each other if it would be alright, and I balled my fists up to prepare for a more robust argument. I had to deliberately relax them before she nodded and opened the door.

Get a grip, Johnny. Jesus.

"Boudica said you might be up here looking for a place to crash. Don't touch anything, and I'll be right out here if you need us." *Boudica? Since when did she give the orders around here?* Truthfully, I didn't care if the devil himself said to let me in, long as I got to take a nap.

I nearly tripped over my own feet in a rush to hit the sofa. My eyes were still closing as I fell into a deep, healing sleep.

CHAPTER 31

An hour's shuteye was all I needed to feel close to human. Shaggy's healing powers, barely on the downside of the cycle, were working nicely, and I ached a lot less now than before passing out. That weird German magician lady stared down at me from the wall poster, reminding me where I was. A sound like thunder shook the place, and it took a second of drama to realize it was the crowd in the showroom roaring for Karmen and her crew. The performance was ending.

I checked my phone and saw two missed messages from Cromwell. It would be a damn shame to go through all this and still get fired. I hit the button for a video call. A face loomed large on the screen, but it wasn't a cranky old man taking up the screen.

"Hey kiddo. How are you doing?" Nurse Ball's expression was serious. "Mister Cromwell isn't doing so well today. He asked me to set up the call so we can get the authentication done." Her tone flattened. "He's here with me now."

A voice like a chainsaw with laryngitis barked from somewhere behind her. "Lupul. Are we going to have any more trouble, or do I finally get my egg?"

Francine raised an eyebrow at the camera. Our boss was in a mood.

I shouted into the phone, like that would help. "Yes, sir. It's all good. I should get out of here tomorrow and head home."

Francine turned away from the camera and pointed behind her. "Okay, sir. Go lay down, I'll let you know when Lemuel does the authentication. *Now,* please." I heard Cromwell grunt and the bed creak. He knew better than to argue with her. *Smart man.*

It was good to see a friendly face, even if she was all business. Francine stepped out of Cromwell's room as we chatted. "You look like hell. Who was she?"

"It's not like that, believe me."

"Why not? I told you to come back with a decent bedtime story. Are you going to disappoint me, Mister Lupul? Maybe this'll hold you." She winked into the camera and then turned the phone and aimed it down the top of her uniform. It provided a momentary glimpse of her breasts trapped in that matronly, industrial-strength bra she only wore on the job.

The conversation was about to take an unprofessional turn when there was a knock on the door behind me. It creaked open and Lemuel Collins entered. He nodded to the giantess at the door. "Thank you kindly. You have a good day, Miss."

I hadn't seen Lemuel in a couple of days. I was still pissed at him for vanishing and going radio silent. He looked good, though. The man was dressed impeccably, as usual, and offered a smile that almost made me forget I was mad. "How are you, young man? Heard you've had some trouble."

With his arrival, I'd forgotten Francine was still on the phone until I heard her voice. "Is that Mister Collins? Let me speak to him." I turned the phone to the older man. She gave him a chipper, "Lemuel, so good to see you."

All his teeth showed in an enormous smile. "Miss Francine. Good to see you as well, thank you. How's Mister Cromwell doing?"

"About as well as can be expected. How are you feeling?" She was using her professional nurse voice, and I saw a cloud pass over Collins' face before the smile returned.

"Finer'n frog hair. Nice of you to ask."

I stood there like an idiot, holding the phone up, trying to make sure they could see each other. It was clear this wasn't their first meeting, and I wondered just how far back the relationship between her, Lemuel, and Cromwell went.

"You're sure?"

"Yes Ma'am. Fit as a fiddle." He said it in that way older people have of telling you whatever the problem, it wasn't worth talking about. I found myself worrying about him instead of being suspicious.

The social niceties handled, Francine and I agreed to reconnect when everyone was gathered together. I rang off, making sure to hide the screen as I got another glimpse of decolletage as a parting gift.

"Fine woman, Miss Francine."

I slipped my phone into my pocket. "Yeah, she's great. Are you ready for this?" I plunked my butt down on the sofa and gestured to a wing chair.

Mr. Collins nodded gratefully and sat down with a soft groan. "Bones are getting old." I wanted to ask him a bunch of questions, starting with where the hell he'd been hiding, but never got the chance. There was a loud babble in the hallway, then the door flew open and Karmen Mystère, in full show costume, blew into the room like a tropical storm in stilettos. Boudica followed, surrounded by a half dozen of the Coven members. Cree came next in her, although she'd changed into her boots. Limping along behind was Bill.

"Dude, you should have seen it. That was, like, the best magic show ever! You were amazing, Karmen."

"Thank you, sugar. Your friend didn't seem to enjoy it half so much," she threw me a dirty look.

God, I wanted to get away from her and this place.

She replaced her sneer with a smile for the clairetangentist, who put his hands together in a prayer sign and a sincere greeting.

"Can we just get on with this, please? Let's end this bullshit." Boudica sat on the edge of Karmen's desk, which didn't endear her to the boss. Karmen looked like her head would implode, but let it slide and went back to playing the gracious hostess.

The blond assistant griped, "Well? Let's do what we have to do here and get on with our lives."

Everyone looked at me, and I stared back until I realized they were all waiting for me to say or do something. "Oh, yeah. Right."

I got my phone out and Old Man Cromwell and his liver spots appeared on the screen. That was followed by a round of very strained but extremely polite greetings.

Finally, we were good to go. *Now what?* "Yeah, so... yeah."

Cree nodded her support, and I talked mainly to her, which helped. Bill leaned on his crutch, moderately confused but not saying anything. I wasn't scared of werewolves, ghosts, or even Gramma's temper, but public speaking made me wish I was back in the bear pit. I'd never emceed a sideshow like this before and wasn't sure how to start. I opened my mouth, a noise came out, and then my brain kicked into gear.

This was the first time I'd ever been in charge of a swap like this. I didn't know the protocol. There was a lot of money on the line, and this was significantly different from shaking gamblers down for their cash. I cleared my throat. "Okay, so what's going to happen is we need Mister Collins to authenticate the Paiute Sky Egg. When it's proven real to Mister Cromwell's satisfaction, I'll take possession of the object on his behalf. Miss Mystère will get the money sent to her account, and everyone is satisfied." There were lots of big words, and it sounded official as hell. I looked around the room for validation. "Right?"

It must have been okay, because everyone nodded or muttered agreement, except Boudica. She glared with her arms folded across her chest and emitted a peeved, "shyah," noise and nothing else.

Everyone stared at me. I wasn't entirely certain of the next step.

Finally, Cromwell's voice crackled through the phone. "What are you waiting for, Lupul? Christmas?"

Cree caught my eye and nodded to the backpack on the floor. That brought me back to the matter at hand. Shaggy growled a little as I picked the bag up and extended my arms to Lemuel. Sounding way too formal, I said, "If you would, please, sir. There are two eggs. Which one is the real one?"

Collins bit his lower lip and shook his head ever so slightly. "Maybe you can just hand me one, if you would?"

I reached into the pack, grabbed the first egg I touched, and gently passed it over to him. Everyone held their breath, and the tension was palpable, mostly because none of us knew what to expect. I focused on not dropping the damned thing and shattering it into a thousand pieces. Lemuel's dark, shaking hands moved at a glacial pace, but eventually he took a deep breath and took the crystal object into his palms. I let go and took a step back.

Nobody breathed except the evaluator. All eyes were watching his face for some reaction. If we expected drama, we were disappointed. After a second, the old man let out a long breath and shook his head. "This one is the fake."

"You're sure, Lem?" Cromwell demanded through the phone.

"Yes, sir. Nothing there."

Old man Cromwell sighed. "Alright, Karmen. That one's yours. Keep it for your dog and pony show there."

The look on the woman's face could have castrated someone at twenty paces. She bit her cheek and kept something like a smile on. "Thank you, that's very kind. Folks will love it."

Lemuel wiped his hands on his pants. "Well, then. Since the other egg must be the real one..."

I wasn't letting him off the hook. "No, sir. We've got to confirm this once and for all. Isn't that right, sir?" I wasn't going to give my dick of a boss a single reason to complain. I was an I-dotting, T-crossing son of a gun. Even Bill seemed a little impressed by my impression of a grownup.

"Damn right. Come on, Lem. Get on with it and let me go back to bed."

Unhappy but resigned, Collins nodded and steeled himself. I pulled the second egg from the bubble wrap and dropped it ever-so-gently into the shaking, upturned hands of the evaluator.

Then nothing.

Nada.

Zilch.

No response at all. *Is this one a fake too?*

Lem Collins stood with his eyes closed in complete silence. We all looked from him to each other, wondering who was going to say something first.

Of course, it was the old gnome in Chicago.

"Is this thing working? I can't hear a god-damned thing." The phone was working fine. It was Lemuel Collins who appeared frozen, standing stone-still. A statue in a Brooks Brothers suit.

"Lem? What is it?" Karmen asked, reaching out a hand to touch his shoulder.

His only response was a thin line of drool out of the left corner of his mouth.

"Mister Collins? You okay?" I asked. His eyes were still closed. Saliva now ran in a small stream, staining his shirt. I slipped the phone into my pocket and put both hands on the man's shoulders. His muscles locked up tight.

"What's happening? I can't see anything." Cromwell shouted from inside my pocket.

Mister Collins' eyes flew open and nearly bulged out of his face. His lips fluttered a bit before I heard the faintest voice.

"So. Many. Stars."

Then the old man's knees gave way, and he crumpled to the ground. He hugged the Sky Egg to his body, cradling it as if afraid of fumbling a football. Cree, Karmen and I nearly crashed our heads together, bending over him and checking him out.

I was one body too many, so I stepped back as Cree and Karmen shouted at Mister Collins, getting no response. They ran their hands over him, trying to figure out what was wrong. Without a thought, I pried the Egg from his quivering hands and stepped back, watching in horror.

Shaggy whined at the presence of the real Egg, and did a lap around my head. While there was no physical sensation, my body felt like someone had dipped it in ice water. I set the genuine Egg on a chair, wrapped it securely in plastic, and shoved it into the backpack. As soon as the zipper closed, I felt a lot better and so did the thing inside me.

A female voice from my pants shouted, "Johnny, what's wrong with Lem? Let me see what's going on."

I pulled my phone out, and Bill shouted at me. "Really, dude? Not a great time for pictures."

"Francine's on the phone." That appeased him, but everyone else needed an explanation. "She's a nurse. Let her take a look." I faced the camera to the body on the floor. Karmen stepped away immediately, wiping her wide, frightened eyes with her sleeve. Cree stood and began backing away, but Nurse Ball ordered her to stay.

"No, I need someone to check him out. Is he breathing?" Cree served as Francine's proxy examiner, checking for respiration and pulse, answering questions as best she could. Karmen dialed nine-one-one and shouted profanities at the operator until we knew an ambulance was on the way.

I picked up the pack and moved closer to Bill, who jerked his body away from mine as I got closer. Poor guy, he wasn't ready for this level of crazy, and the strain and lack of sleep showed on his face.

I gave him my best smile. "It's cool. We got this."

We didn't have this at all and he knew it, but it bought me time.

A few minutes later, EMTs showed up with a gurney. We all stepped back, each of us lost in our own thoughts, until the patient was loaded onto the stretcher and wheeled out.

I gave Francine the news. "They're taking him to University Medical Center. They have no idea what's wrong with him, but they're hauling ass."

"Okay. Keep us posted, please." She hesitated, then asked, "How are you doing? Really?"

Whether it was Shaggy's powers or adrenaline, I actually felt surprisingly good, other than being worried sick about the nice old man in the ambulance. Oh, and the fact that I possessed whatever caused the problem in the first place. Cree stood behind me. Her hand rested on my back as I wrapped things up with the nurse in Chicago.

"Okay, I'll let you know what happens next. I imagine I'll be heading out tonight... well, tomorrow, now, I guess." Even I heard the exhaustion creep into my voice. Those stress hormones cause a hell of a crash when they quit working.

"Get some sleep. Who's that behind you?"

She was talking about Cree. "Oh, that's Cree. She's... Karmen's assistant."

Francine's voice softened a tad. "Cree? You did real well there. Nice work."

"Oh, thank you. I'm sorry, who are you?"

How would I explain this one? "Uh, she's..."

"I'm Francine Ball, Mister Cromwell's private nurse. Johnny and I work together sometimes." Francine was saving my bacon once more, even if she didn't know it.

I didn't have time to work out the logistics of this conversation. Cree gave my back one more rub and went to help Karmen.

I looked at the screen, and Francine was grinning smugly. "Cree, huh?"

I squirmed. "Yeah. Lucrezia, really. She's great. A big help." Uncomfortable silence hung in the air. "Listen, I have to finish up here. I'll keep you posted soon as we hear anything."

Francine was like a dog with a sock and wouldn't let go. "Good head on her shoulders in a crisis. She was a big help. Kinda cute. I like her."

I rubbed my forehead. "Yeah, me too."

SHIT. Why did I say that?

Francine chuckled. "Mister Cromwell is worried about Lemuel. They go back a long time, so keep us up to date. He also wants you to know he wants the egg back here ASAP."

No rest for the wicked. "Yeah, I'm going to load it up right now. Maybe I'll head out tonight."

"Don't be an idiot. Get some sleep. You look like ten miles of bad road."

She wasn't wrong. I turned to see Karmen, Boudica, Cree, Bill and half a dozen freaked-out coven members waiting for me to get off the phone.

"Yeah. I guess I still have some work to do." I thumbed the phone off and plopped back onto the sofa.

Everyone plainly expected me to say something. *Who died and left me boss of anything?*

I looked right back at them. "Okay, so now what?"

CHAPTER 32

Karmen leaned back in her chair, ran her hands through her raven black hair, down her cheeks, and finally across her eyes. In a voice that was pure exhaustion, she said, "I don't care what you do with the damned thing. I want it gone. Tonight. Now."

Boudica's voice was far more emphatic. "Finally."

Cree summoned up enough courage to bark at her. "Why are you like this? After all, Karmen's been through tonight—after what we've all been through. And what does she have to show for it?"

Boudica pointed at her boss. "She's got absolutely nothing, which is what she deserves. We should have never fucked around with that thing to begin with."

Cree's mouth dropped open. "How can you say that? This thing... whatever it is.... it's amazing."

Boudica got right up in her grill, towering over the shorter woman. "That's the problem. We don't know what it is. Not really. It might really be alien, in which case we're taking something incredible and turning it into a cheap laser light show for tourists. Here's what we do know... it has absolutely nothing to do with magick. Or the work of the Coven. She got greedy—"

Boudica ranted as if Karmen wasn't sitting in the room. The Mistress of Magick slumped in the chair and rubbed her temples. "It's like most of the rest of the crap here. Interesting, but not the real thing. Making a joke out of what we do. What we all do. It's a... a disgrace to the coven. To the Mothers. What we should be standing for. We could really help women instead... argh."

Bill and I both backed up. There was more going on here than we understood, and it made zero sense to get in the middle of it. As long as I had the Egg, I was staying out of this family quarrel. I motioned for him to join me on the couch and out of the line of fire.

Karmen slapped her hand on the table. "Wait just a goddamn minute."

Boudica shook her head. "No, this is all your fault. All of it. You should have just sold the Sky Egg in the first place. Or returned it to the Paiute Nation, which was probably the more honorable thing. But no. You had to play your little reindeer games—again—getting between two rich old assholes. You almost got us killed, and what do you have to show for it?"

Karmen stood, her eyes shooting lasers. "You can't talk to me that way. This is still my coven. And my museum."

Boudica took a step closer to Karmen. "Museum? Is that what this is? This place is a joke. You flounce around like Vampira's white-trash sister, flashing your tits for tourists and let all these kids and wannabes worship you. This isn't about magick. You don't give a shit about us. You almost got people killed over a stage prop. Do you realize that, you selfish bitch?"

Karmen's lip curled. "You don't seem to mind the money on payday, do you? Not such a purist."

Boudica put her hands on her hips. "You think I enjoy strutting around like this? Soon as I have the money, I am out of here. You can find another set of tits and ass to amuse the tourists." She looked around and nodded at the Security Women. "And I won't be alone. It's time we got serious about our power, with you or without."

Cree's head was about to explode. "You can't talk to her that way." She took a couple of steps towards Boudica, but one of the armed security women held up a warning hand. Shocked, the redhead halted in her tracks.

Boudica laughed. "Anything else you want to say, Newbie?"

The hair bristled on the back of my neck. The tension was palpable and my Lycan self was itching to protect my friend. Someone needed to take control of the situation, and no other adult being available, that left me. With a Shaggy-assisted shout I yelled, "Hey." Everyone turned to look at me. "There's obviously more going on here than just the thing with the Egg. And it's none of our business. We're going to take it now and leave you to your drama."

The blonde Amazon shook her head. "Look, you're pretty bad ass and all. But you're in no shape to drive out tonight. And that thing is safer here than in the parking lot at Caesar's. I want it gone as much as everyone, but let's do this right. We can take care of the Egg until tomorrow."

I was developing a serious dislike for this woman. Karmen may have sold me out, but at least she was the boss. What was this chick's deal? "Like you did the other night? In case you forgot, that's how this all started. How do we know Bowden won't come back and try again?"

Bill's eyes widened in fear at the idea. The poor guy had come out to deliver some news and have a good time. "Hang with your friends," was supposed to be just an expression, not something that could really happen.

Boudica bit her lip as she thought about it. She pushed some papers from the corner of Karmen's desk to make room and parked herself on the corner again, completely ignoring Karmen's horrified expression.

She locked eyes with me. "We weren't ready then. And I wasn't in charge of the arrangements." She may as well have just backhanded her boss across the face and didn't even spare her a glance. "No, first of all, this time we have more armed security. Second, Bowden knows we're expecting him, and he's not stupid enough to come for it in broad daylight. In a few hours you'll be rested and, on your way, back to Chicago in your stupid macho car and we never have to do business or see each other again."

That was below the belt. The poor Charger had never done anything to her, and I wanted to rise to its defense, but Boudica had a point. Not about the car. The other thing. I was healing pretty well. Another night's rest and I'd be damn near human again. The Egg was safer here than anywhere else for the next ten hours or so. No sane person wanted to mess with Boudica's army—it was clear Karmen wasn't in charge anymore—so why not?

I crossed my arms to maintain a little of my manhood. "Ten O'clock. That way, we can get it out of here before the museum opens at noon. Work for you?"

"Great. Whatever. Soon as you and it are out of here, the better. I promise, we'll keep it safe til then. Last thing I want is any more trouble from the creepy old men."

We both nodded, and Cree picked up the backpack containing the egg. "It's fine, Johnny. I'll stay with it and..."

Boudica's voice was flat and offered no room for argument. "No, you won't. We've got six women with weapons. That's plenty. We don't need you." She looked back over her shoulder at Karmen. "Or you."

In a contest to see which woman was more upset, it was impossible to pick a winner. Karmen and Cree looked absolutely shattered. I wanted to defend them, especially Cree. The blood pounded through my veins. Part of me longed to put a hurting on the person being needlessly cruel. Realistically, a wounded Shaggy in daylight against six armed women and Boudica, who was a lethal weapon by herself, would not be productive. Thank God for Bill, then.

Using his crutch, he stood up, then clapped his hands once. "Okay, it's been a long night for everyone. Why don't we see Cree and Ms. Mystère out and leave you... ladies... to your work? My partner and I will take final possession in the morning. Agreed?"

Whether it was surprise because Bill spoke up or just a desire to end the night for everyone, Boudica nodded and rose from the edge of the desk.

"Fine."

"Move." Cree elbowed the security woman aside and ran to Karmen. She wrapped her arms around her boss. Offering a hand, she helped her boss to her bare feet. The killer stilettos had long been kicked off. Karmen's aura of invincibility was shattered. The Mistress of Potions tried to console her coven mistress. Bill offered what help he could.

In a daze, Karmen shuffled barefoot out of her office, holding onto Cree's shoulder and Bill's arm. I studied the remaining women and their ringleader, wondering just how ugly this would get before it was over. What was it Gramma always said? "Not my circus, not my monkey?" This wasn't my circus, but it was one big, hairy, stinky monkey.

I needed to be on the road before the poo started flying.

CHAPTER 33

As much as I just wanted to go back to the hotel and crash, it took a while to get out of there. First, there was the call to Old Man Cromwell. I told him I'd set out in the morning, since it was so late. He was surprisingly okay with that. Honestly, he seemed more concerned about Mr. Collins, which was a little weird. They left my friend and the redheaded witch talking amongst themselves while I played big boy and took care of business.

Boudica agreed to have some of her team stay with the Egg until the morning. In about eight hours, we'd be done with all this.

Meanwhile, Cree spent some time talking Karmen off the ledge and making sure the boss was okay to drive before sending her home for the night. The rebellion in the coven—nobody thought it was funny when I called it a Boudi-coup—could wait another day. I couldn't imagine what the stage show would be like for a while.

Finally, Cree, Bill and I dragged our carcasses into the Charger. I was feeling better and got behind the wheel. Bill called shotgun, which left Cree in the back seat. This arrangement seemed to work for everyone, as the two of them got into an animated discussion about Karmen and how the coven worked—or was supposed to—and what exactly Cree believed in, given it was the twenty-first century and all. Meanwhile, I drove and organized my thoughts, or as sorted out as the rabid squirrels in my brain would permit.

Bed beckoned. "Okay, so we'll drop Cree off at home and then back to the hotel."

Her voice sounded tired, but she said, "No, I don't want to be alone right now. Can I go back to the hotel with you guys for a while?"

To my surprise, Bill was all for it. "Yeah, cool. I'm not ready to crash yet. I haven't played any blackjack, and Gramma gave me some table stakes." Like all accountants, he thought he was better at counting cards than he was. God knows he regularly beat the snot out of me at cards, but that was a low bar. His talent was honed by all those nights at home, getting fleeced by the old lady.

Bill gave Cree a grin I didn't understand, but wasn't going to analyze too closely. They were playing nicely, and that was alright with me. Gave me precious time to think.

Somewhere about Oakey Street, a thought occurred to me. "Dude, when's your flight home? Jesus, I never even asked."

Bill looked a little embarrassed. "I didn't book a return flight. I didn't know what was going on with you, and I kinda thought we could drive back together. If that's okay."

I was surprised, but agreed in a heartbeat. "Yeah, that'll be great." He'd come all this way, we'd spent almost no time together, and he might need therapy, or at least a ton of conversation, to get over what he'd seen. Plus, it might be fun to have someone share the driving. There was only so much damage he could do on a straight, flat interstate. For sure, it would prevent a repeat of that shitstorm in Amarillo. Shaggy was always on his best behavior around either of the Mostoys.

"Sounds like fun. All that male bonding and testosterone," Cree piped in from the back seat. That set the two of them off again as she asked how long we'd known each other, all about Gramma Mostoy, the whole ball of wax. She learned more from Bill in three miles than I'd told her in four days. It was also more than I'd asked about her. I felt like a jerk. Totally exhausted and still on an expense account, I sprung for the valet. The three of us staggered into the fake-Roman vomitorium that was the lobby of Caesar's Palace. At that hour of the morning, we were still in better shape than most of the people around us.

Bill pulled a wad of bills out of his pocket and waved it at us. "Alright, I'm headed into battle. Wish me luck. You guys okay?"

Cree's hand pressed ever so slightly on my back as I said, "Yeah, we're good. Have fun. Win something or Gramma will have your ass."

Cree smiled at my friend. "Have fun. I wish I was good at that lucky charm stuff, but I'll send you what juju I can." She wiggled her fingers, all magick-y at him. He grabbed her hand and made sure the waves of witch-luck hit the money directly.

Bill leaned in to give me a bro-hug, shifting his cane to his other hand. He whispered, "Don't be a noble idiot about this." There was no chance to ask what the hell he was talking about. He waved and headed for the tables.

I watched him go with this weird feeling in my chest. It took me a second to realize what was going on and what that odd sensation could be. Was it... fun? I'd almost forgotten what that felt like.

Cree's arm slipped around my waist as we watched him limp off. "What happened to his leg?"

"A street fight."

"He doesn't seem the type."

My arm moved of its own volition and reached around her. She fit quite nicely against my hip. "It wasn't his idea."

"You saved him, didn't you?"

"A little late, but yeah."

To my surprise, she turned to me, her hands resting on my hips. Those green eyes gazed up into my face, her overbite just so adorable. It took willpower not to just bend down and kiss her right there.

She took the decision out of my hands. "Let's go up to your room."

That would not help my resistance any. "That's not a good idea."

Her hands slid up to cup my face. "I disagree." She pulled my face down to hers and softly kissed my lips. "Can we discuss this upstairs?"

Hell yes. We can discuss the shit out of it. I knew if we went to my room, there'd be precious little conversation. I could already feel

Shaggy chasing his tail in anticipation, and that was precisely the problem. "No. It's too soon."

"I know, but you're leaving tomorrow and—"

"That's not what I mean." Her eyebrows did that cute, scrunchy thing. *That's not helping, either.* I tried to sound patient. "What was Tomas like for a week or so after he... changed?"

Understanding crossed her face as her smile faded ever so slightly. "I know but—"

"It's not safe. Trust me." I couldn't look at her anymore and turned my face away.

Her hands cupped my cheeks and pulled me back to look at her. "I have a plan. You trust me, right?" She'd saved my life, helped me in a hundred ways, and was the only person in Vegas who'd been half-way decent to me. Of course, I trusted her. It was me and Shaggy I didn't have ten cents' worth of faith in.

She brushed her lips against mine again with a wicked grin. "Let's talk about it upstairs. If I can't convince you, I'll admit defeat gracefully. I'm a good loser. Coach says that's my problem, remember?" She was talking about MMA fighting, not romance, although in my limited experience, one could be as brutal as the other.

Before I could offer any more resistance, she took my hand and pulled me towards the elevators. Our fingers were warm where they laced together, and it felt great. For all the wild monkey-sex Francine and I had over the last few months, we had never just held hands, or just sat and talked. I wanted this... maybe more than actual lovemaking with Cree, although Shaggy was making sure that thought wasn't far away. I really, *really* wanted it and it couldn't happen and if we weren't in public, I'd scream in frustration.

In the crowded elevator, we said nothing, what with her trying to play it cool and me trying to figure out how I'd politely refuse the thing I wanted more than anything in the world. Drunken partiers surrounded us and we just stayed quiet; hand-in-hand and hip to hip. About the twelfth floor, she stood on her tiptoes and whispered in my ear. "Relax. It's a really good plan," and offered a cute, very dirty chuckle.

The minute the door to my room clicked shut behind me, she put her arms around me and kissed me, more insistently and with serious intent to suck my tongue out of my head. I was inclined to let her, at least for a while. We made out for a minute or two before I got all responsible and grown up about it.

"Hold it. Wait." I wiped the evidence of our make-out session from my lips with my sleeve. "Look-"

She put her hands on my chest and pushed me back into the stuffed chair. "Sit down and shut up, okay? Let me talk."

Talking back occurred to me, but she held a finger up in a way that only a woman can do that meant "disobey at your peril." I sat. Even Shaggy backed off for the moment.

Running a hand through her spikes, she looked out the window for a second to gather her thoughts. "Sorry, don't mean to be all bossy-pants, but hear me out." She faced me, her grin twisting up in one corner. "I really like you. And I'm pretty sure you like me too... Fuck, this is sounding too much like middle school."

In some perverse way, her discomfort made me feel better. "No, go ahead, counselor. Make your case."

"Okay, let's try this again." She sank onto my lap and wrapped her arms around my neck. "The only reason you're not all over me right now, despite my being a shameless ho, is that you're worried about what will happen because of... you know, *him*. Right?"

"Yeah. Absolutely, I mean..." I was babbling. *So much for looking cool, but that ship has long sailed, and she seems okay with me, anyway.*

The finger came up again, and I shushed. "So, if it weren't for that thing inside you, we'd already be in that big old bed, right?"

To avoid saying something stupid, I nodded and motioned for her to continue.

She leaned forward and gave me another long, slow kiss. We both emitted little moans as our lips touched. Her voice dropped to a whisper. "But what if he wasn't there? Just for a while?"

Nice idea, except for the reality of the situation. "But he is."

"We've sent... him... away before. Temporarily, I mean."

She was now miles ahead of me, and it was taking a lot to keep up. "Huh?"

She dug in her bag and pulled out a plastic bottle with a familiar brown sludge inside. She waggled it in front of me. "Think of it as kicking your roommate out for a bit while we do it."

That stuff again? She was serious. Her eyes held mine, demanding an answer.

"I don't know. It feels weird, taking chemicals so we can—you know."

"What? People do it all the time. Old guys use Viagra. Sorority girls use tequila. Big deal." For a chemical engineer, she made a hell of a lawyer.

"But last time it made me so sick. I mean, not exactly romantic, right?"

She got that hot nerdy look in her eye. "Right, so I put three milligrams of ginger and fennel seed in there, along with a little essence of peppermint. They're all natural anti-emetics. Like, anti-puke agents. Sorry, I know that doesn't sound very sexy." *Maybe not, but the amount of thought she's put into this sure as hell is.*

"What if it doesn't work, and I throw up?" If this was a trial, my client would get sent up the river at any moment.

She grinned. "You have a toothbrush, right?"

A gavel banged in my head. *Case closed, your honor.*

Ten minutes later, and after one case of the dry heaves and a quick brush and floss, we stood, both topless, next to the giant bed. Shaggy was wherever that guck banished him to, and I was a little wobbly on my legs and awkwardly hollow inside.

Being so close to the full moon, he should have been front and center. Instead... nada. Another kiss stabilized me enough to wrap her in my arms. Her breasts pressed against the hair of my chest. She wiggled against me, and I let out a little growl.

I did. Not Shaggy.

Me.

Cree looked at the enormous white duvet and laughed. "Think it's big enough?"

"Please tell me you're talking about the bed."

Her hand trailed down past my chest and conducted a quick inspection. "That too. Remember, I've already seen it."

"Careful, it's sunburnt." I chuckled and leaned in to kiss her neck. My lips landed right above all the tattooed religious symbols. I sucked in a breath and was a little disappointed that there was no Lycan-assisted scent. My very human nose worked, though. Taking another good sniff, I sensed what anyone would; soap, some kind of vegan-holistic-wicca-approved body oil, a day's sweat. It was amazing. My lips tasted that skin, and she let out a soft sigh. Shaggy-powered ears would have sent wild, electric tingles throughout my body, driving me dangerously crazy and sending me for the soft flesh of her throat.

Instead, it felt... nice. Not a white-hot acid burn, but the happy heat of warm cocoa seeped through my veins, beginning in my chest and spreading to my extremities. All of them. She pressed against me with a little wiggle and a hungry moan of her own.

Soft fingers trailed through my chest hair, followed by her lips, pillowy soft and wet. Giggling, she pinched my nipple just to see what happened. Instead of the electric jolt my animal senses usually experienced with Francine, it actually hurt a bit and made me jump. I pulled away for only a moment. Cree took that as a challenge and treated the other one the same.

"Wimp."

"Oh, yeah?" I returned the favor and heard her growl. She threw her head back, exposing her throat. It was too much to resist, and I pressed my lips there. I couldn't hear her heartbeat or feel the veins throb as when Shaggy was present. Normally, I'd be tenuously trying to control him and had to divide my attention. This time, all I tasted was her, and the only thing I wanted was more.

Alone in my own body, I smelled, tasted, felt exactly what anyone else would. There was no fear of hurting her—because there was no desire to. My body relaxed—well, most of it. Other parts of me were tensing up in the most delicious way.

This is what normal people feel. No wonder they like it so much.

We faced each other on the bed now. My hands were guided by only my own mind, which meant I was a little clumsy, and apologized occasionally, but every time I did, my protests got cut off by her sweet-tasting kiss. I lingered wherever I—and she—wanted. Cree wasn't shy about letting me know what worked for her by putting her hands on mine and pushing against them. She needed more. I was happy to oblige.

Unlike with Francine, there wasn't the tension of maintaining control. I was just Johnny.

I was awkward as hell. It was like being a virgin again, experiencing so much for the first time without holding a slobbering, violent murder machine in check. All the most common sensations were brand new. And so very welcome.

I was holding back too much. Cree didn't have the fierce, sometimes scary, need Francine had, but she was a woman who knew what she wanted.

"I'm not made of glass, you know." She raked her fingernails down my back and ground harder against me.

"I don't want to—"

"You won't." Cree hooked her leg over mine like a wrestling move and was suddenly on top, grinning as I felt her warmth surround me. "You can't. Do it."

I ran my hands softly down her spine, letting her set the pace. She let out a frustrated moan. "Goddammit, Johnny. Please."

Cree nipped at my shoulder, and instinctively, my teeth caught her skin in retaliation. I froze, worried I'd gone too far but instead heard. "Thata boy. That's better."

I had never really let myself go before, but she asked so nicely. My arms wrapped around her in a bear hug and mashed her tighter against me, feeling her soft skin against my furry chest. It still wasn't enough. For either of us. I gripped her harder, grinding my body against hers, feeling the friction and heat.

"Is that all you got, tough guy?"

I always loved a challenge. We rolled over with our mouths locked together. My body pressed into her, pinning her to the mattress until I worried it was too much. The fighter in her would not tap out, and a little competition always made everything more fun.

And man, was it fun.

This wasn't frenzied, animal passion, it was less than that. And more. At one point, I felt tears build, and it took a valiant effort and some misdirection to keep her from seeing that. *Jesus, Johnny.*

The tension built as we urged each other on. The word "Yes," panted in my ears, was both a confirmation and a request for more. Rather than worry I was too much for her, I began to feel inadequate and stepped up my game. That was met with more, louder yesses.

With my brain undistracted, and the sensations so powerful and new, our lovemaking—and that was something I'd never called what Francine and I did—didn't set any duration records. It didn't have to.

When we were done, Cree brushed a sweaty lock of hair from my forehead. "You okay?"

"That's my line." Running a fingernail along her neckline, tracing every line of the inked ankh and then the Star of David, I asked. "I didn't hurt you, did I?"

Cree shook her head. "No, it was nice. Wait, that sounds lame, but it was…"

"Nice. It's a good word for it. Nothing wrong with nice." Nice was an unfamiliar feeling, but I did like it. A lot.

Cree got up on one elbow. "What about… how do you feel?"

"It's weird. I feel like I'm in a big echo-y room. Kind of alone in there, if that makes any sense."

"Do you feel him at all?" She was all business now, the scientist checking on her experiment. This was probably a massive ethics violation or something.

"I don't think so. How long do you think I'll be like this?" *What if he never comes back? What if I was just me for the rest of my life?*

Would that be so awful?

I looked into Cree's face and thought that might not be such a bad thing at that.

"I'm not sure. Do you miss him?"

"A little. Yeah." I struggled to make sense of the sensations. This was a lot, and feelings weren't something I was used to dealing with. "How long was he gone the last time—in Karmen's office?"

"About thirty, maybe forty minutes. Why?" Then she smiled a broad, naughty smile.

I wasn't thinking about sex so much as just being here with her. Alone. Just us. "So we still have some time left."

"Yay," she said, and rolled on top of me, straddling my hairy belly, pressing her lips to mine and kissing me like our lives depended on it. "And no more Mister Nice Guy."

CHAPTER 34

Three days past the Full Moon- waning gibbous

It turns out Cree had one glaring character flaw. Other than her taste in men, obviously. Being an understanding and sensitive guy, I was willing to overlook the fact she didn't eat breakfast. Like, ever. Dabbling in the dark arts was easier to get my head around. Still, it gave me a chance to have breakfast in the coffee shop alone with Bill.

My buddy poked at his egg white omelet while giving the stink-eye to the syrupy stack of pancakes and six pieces of bacon in front of me. I wasn't sure what he was so disgusted by. I let the server put the plate down before attacking it. Her fingers were never in real danger.

After the first fatty, salty slice of heaven, my hunger was tamed enough to carry on conversation. "So, did you get lucky last night?"

Bill dropped his fork and looked down his nose at me. "Seriously, dude. You're just going to serve that one up to me on a plate?"

"Blackjack. You know what I meant."

"Not really. Lost all Gramma's money but broke even on mine."

"Funny how that works, huh?"

Bill grinned. "The secret to great money management is account assignment." The old lady was going to tear a strip off his pale, hairless hide but he was in a pretty good mood. Losing usually made him grumpy as hell. "Now, how'd it go up in the honeymoon suite?"

I was never much for morning-after guy talk, mainly because I seldom had anything to talk about. On those rare occasions Francine stayed over, she provided loud play-by-play commentary that everyone on the block could hear. There wasn't much left to be explained.

"It was nice."

"Nice. That's what you're going with?"

It was all he was going to get. I hadn't wrapped my head around the night—well, early morning—before. Certainly not enough to coherently share anything with Bill and his insistence on salacious details. And there was more.

In a couple of hours, Bill and I would be on the road, back to Chicago, and not likely to return any time soon. Most guys would see that as a big plus. Surprisingly, I found myself wanting to stay. Las Vegas held no charm for me. Cree did.

Bill gave me a minute alone with my thoughts before asking, "What about... you know? How did you keep him under control?" We knew pretty much all each other's secrets. He was aware of my struggles to control Shaggy when there was a woman involved.

"We used a magic potion."

He snorted. "Is that what the cool kids are calling it?"

"Dude, seriously. It kind of... I don't know. Sends Shaggy away for a while."

"What's that feel like? I mean, you've always had him in there, right?"

"Yeah. It's like I feel, I don't know. Hollow, kind of."

"Do you like it?"

I shrugged. There were too many answers to that question. *Imagine being able to just be with Cree—or anyone. And the notion of getting on a plane, or even a crowded elevator, without experiencing the urge to slaughter everyone, was appealing. On the other hand...*

"I kind of miss him when he's not there. It's messed up." Shaggy was still pretty much gone. If I paused and focused, I sensed his presence, but a long way off. Normally, the clatter of dishes and all the morning noises in a busy diner would have my teeth on edge. It wasn't bothering me at all, at the moment, at least. Chalk up another one for normal, human hearing. *So, this is what everyone else feels? It doesn't quite suck. It's just... boring*, as if everything was in sepia instead of color.

A cool, soft hand touched my neck, and I jumped. Nobody should have been able to sneak up on me. I usually heard them coming a mile away. Cree placed a soft peck on my cheek, and I stopped worrying about it.

I sniffed and got a hint of generic hotel-brand shampoo, but not much else. It was as if my nose was turned down to a one or two, instead of stuck on ten like usual. Still, it wasn't bad, exactly.

"You okay?" Cree asked as she sat next to me, her leg brushing against mine.

"Yeah. Great." Shaggy knew she was there. I felt an uptick in my energy level, but he was a long way off still.

She gave me a sweet smile that had just a hint of sadness to it. Maybe I was imagining things. Probably was. Certainly, she sounded chipper enough. "Good. Big day. We probably need to get going."

Bill rose from his seat. "Yeah, I'll go get my stuff and meet you at valet." He pointed a finger at me. "And this is a business expense. Charge it to Cromwell."

Cromwell. Shit. Yeah, let's get this over with.

Half an hour later, we were on our way to the museum. This time there was no argument about who sat where. Cree rode next to me while Bill claimed the back seat. He said his leg was hurting, and he wanted to stretch it out across the seat. That's a good friend right there.

The two of them were getting along famously. As I drove, they yakked away. About what, I had no idea. My thoughts were everywhere but on the road. The Charger was pretty much on autopilot. Between working out the logistics of collecting the egg, occasionally checking to see if Shaggy was back, and thinking about saying goodbye to Cree, I was lucky not to wrap us around a light pole.

Eventually, we pulled into the lot at the Museum. It was a couple of hours before opening, and the covered parking was almost empty. I recognized Karmen's midnight-blue Mercedes and a couple of dusty beaters that belonged to maintenance staff. The only thing out of the ordinary was the desert—brown Hummer squeezed into a Handicapped parking spot near the entrance.

Other than being a much bigger vehicle than anyone actually needed, there wasn't anything about the Humvee that should have triggered a response, but I was uneasy anyway. First, nobody was supposed to be there until the place opened. Second, I felt a faint trembling in my belly. Shaggy was still not completely present, but he didn't like it either.

Cree used her electronic key to let us in. I held the door for her and Bill, alert for anything out of the ordinary. Something was off, but damned if it didn't look like Bowden's truck in the parking lot. *Couldn't be.* Everything was as normal as a building full of creepy relics could be. Emo music played over the stereo as we crossed the lobby and headed for Karmen's office.

I knew something was funky when there was no one standing guard. Boudica was supposed to have guards around the Egg all night. I expected Valerie the Valkyrie to be on duty. Instead, it was eerily quiet. The whole place was empty.

The hair on my arms started dancing. Shaggy nudged at the back of my head. Something was seriously wrong. Where was everyone?

Putting my ear to the door, I listened for a moment. Someone was moving around in there, but nobody was talking. I gently rapped on the door. "Karmen?"

A soft, strained Southern voice said, "Come in."

I held my breath, and the three of us passed into the bright, sunlit office. Cree and Bill ran into my back and bounced off as I halted.

Crap.

Karmen sat at her desk, stiff and uncomfortable. Boudica was on the sofa, leaning forward and hugging her knees. She looked up at me with watery eyes and a dark purple mark on her cheek. Those lethal hands of hers were zip-tied together.

Against the far wall stood two familiar figures. Clive Bowden leaned on his cane with an insufferably smug look on his face. His big-ass Stetson sat back on his head and mirrored shades hid his eyes. Beside him stood Torson, dressed in camo gear with a Glock strapped to his hip.

The old bastard gave me a nod. "Howdy, Johnny. We have some unfinished business."

I was almost out of here. So goddamn close.

CHAPTER 35

For a few seconds, it was deathly quiet. Bowden smirked while Torson stood there, terrifying, but immobile. Karmen had her hands flat on her desk, eyes wide and biting her lip. Her normally perfect raven hair was a wig, sitting slightly askew on top of her head. Cree stood behind me, her hand barely touching my hip, and Bill behind her. Boudica hung her head, stewing in a big pot of defeat and shame. She glanced up at me, and I noticed a bruise forming on her swollen bottom lip. Apparently, the badass Amazon was no match for a were-bear at close quarters.

Shaggy went on the alert, and a growl came from my mouth. He wanted Torson badly, and it was obvious from the giant Icelander's eyes the feeling was mutual. This would not end well. I winced at the small muscle spasms that signaled Shaggy's full return and desire for action, but otherwise stood as still as I could until I knew what was going on.

Trying to gain control, I turned to Karmen. "Are you okay?" She sniffed and nodded. Then I looked at Boudica and lifted an inquisitive eyebrow. She took a deep breath and turned away from me. "It wasn't supposed to happen like this."

Karmen hissed like a cobra. "What did you think was going to happen, you backstabbing bitch?"

If she expected an apology from her coven mate, she was disappointed. Boudica just glared back and said nothing.

Bill's voice came in a whisper. "Dude, what's happening here?"

Bowden frowned as he noticed Bill. "I don't know who you are..." then he turned to Cree. "Or you. But what's happening is apparently nobody around here can do as they're told. The only person supposed to be let in here was him."

Meaning me.

Boudica's eyes shot daggers at him. "Then you should have left Valerie there, shouldn't you?" A stifled noise and a kick against the closet door answered the mystery of the missing security woman. Torson had been a busy boy. At least Val the Valkyrie was alive.

Karmen stiffened in her seat. "Just take the damned Egg and go. It's what you want, isn't it?"

Bowden shifted his weight to his good leg and grimaced. He didn't even look at Karmen, just kept his eyes locked on my face. "It was. Just business. This one..." he pointed to Boudica, "tells us where the egg is, for a pretty healthy price, I might add. We grab it. Scoreboard. Game over. Fuck Cromwell. Should have been simple. But no, you had to come and fuck things up."

Meaning me. Again.

Bowden removed his sunglasses. Those old eyes were rimmed with red, and his lip curled into a Grinchy sneer. "Just business. Best man wins and all that. Hell of a show you put on back at the house. I could respect that. But then you had to go and make it personal."

I was hoping Junior was okay. That's what you get for hoping.

"He came at me with a gun." It didn't sound as convincing coming out of my mouth as it did in my head.

The cowboy's voice was ice-cold gravel. "You killed my boy. That changes things."

Somewhere behind me, Cree gasped and pulled her fingers away like she'd touched a hot stove. My heart sank into my guts.

Shaggy knew how much shit we were in and how deep it was. My pulse pounded as he slowly clawed his way closer to the surface, waiting for his chance. The growling voice coming out of my mouth sounded more like him than me. "Just let the women—everyone—go, and you and I can do whatever the hell we have to do."

"I've got no desire to hurt anyone else. Christ, I'll even let Blondie keep the money. After all, I got the egg and I have you, so it's worth it. Unlike some people, I am a man of my word."

Boudica shrieked at him. "I don't want your stinking money, you old bastard." *Great. Now. I wonder how much she got for setting us up.* And I thought it was Karmen all this time.

"That's not what you told me a week ago. Take the money, start your own coven or whatever feminazi bullshit you called it. Kiss this place goodbye. Isn't that what you said?"

Boudica's hands strained against the plastic restraints. "You said you'd take the egg and leave. Nobody was supposed to get hurt."

"What the hell have you done?" Cree asked her. "After all Karmen's done for—"

I interrupted. "Uh, not really the time and place." The angry look she shot me roiled my guts, but we needed to keep the situation under control. I could only handle one crisis at a time, it was clearly going to get ugly. Cree's emotional state and disappointment in me weren't the first priority.

I saw the way Karmen and Boudica looked at each other. *Or maybe it could, but first things first.*

I needed to get Bill, Cree and Karmen safely out of there. Boudica too, if I could. She had a ton of Karma heading her way, but Bowden and the Berserker were Job One. "Let them go, Bowden. I'll do whatever you want."

HIs voice was gravelly. "No. They will bear witness. I want them to tell Cromwell and everyone who gives a crap what happens to you. I am not to be fucked with. Ever."

Stall, Johnny. "Just out of curiosity, what is going to happen to me?"

"Oh, Torson's going to kick the shit out of you. I don't know if you know this or not, but Berserkers aren't impacted by the moon like you are."

"Well, that doesn't seem very fair."

Torson flexed his hands into ham-sized fists, and his mouth turned up into a grin. Bowden put his sunglasses back on.

"It's not, really. But then, neither was you and Junior, was it?" *Touché.*

I looked around. This office was too small for any kind of fighting. I didn't mind getting my ass kicked. At least not too much. It was what I'd signed up for. But in this small a space, other people would be at risk, and it played to the advantage of the less mobile party. The parking lot would give us plenty of room, plus there was the chance someone would see us and call the cops. Sounding way cooler than I felt, I cracked my neck and asked, "Shall we take this outside?"

The old guy was crazy, but not stupid. "Nope. Too much attention. This is a private show." He snapped his fingers. "You know, that's what we'll do. Let's make it a genuine show. Would've been nice to have a bigger audience, but beggars can't be choosers."

"What do you mean?"

He coughed and spit on the carpet. Charming. "There's a perfectly good stage down the hall. Comfy seats for everyone to watch. We'll do it there."

It wasn't a terrible idea. First choice was not to do it at all but I didn't get a vote. At least this gave me and Shaggy plenty of room to operate. That was going to be important against Bear Boy. Better yet, there was enough space between the stage and the seats that the others would be safely out of the way.

"Onstage? Really? Bowden, anyone ever tell you that you're a big ole drama queen?"

Bill snorted at that, which I appreciated more than the old guy did. His gun hand moved a little to the left, right at my buddy. "Got something to say?"

I stepped between them. "Hey, hey. Let's figure this out. I'll fight your boy here, winner takes the Egg and all. But no matter how this ends, you let everyone else go. They'll never say a word about this." I turned and looked at the others. "Right? This is all between us. A private matter. Just business." I was appealing to his ego and bullshit Western code of honor. He didn't have to go for the deal. But he backed off. I took the win.

Karmen and Boudica nodded quickly. With Cree and Bill, I had to make some serious crazy eye contact to get even a nod, but eventually everyone agreed to the idea.

I clapped my hands together. "Alrighty then. Shall we?"

Torson, who had said nothing until now, grunted, "Your ass is mine, Ulfhednar."

"Come and get it, Yogi."

Bowden shook with another wet, phlegmy cough. "Cut the bullshit. Let's go."

The old man nodded and waved his gun around the room. Karmen stood, then she, Bill, Cree and turned and walked towards the door. Boudica struggled to stand with her hands tied like that, and Torson grabbed her elbow and flung her forward, nearly into the door. Those two didn't like each other, and my guess was she'd managed to put up a fight before he finally lassoed her hands. I hope she got some shots in. True, she'd sold me out and messed up this entire deal, but the enemy of my enemy is my... whatever the hell she was. Finally, Bowden motioned me towards the door.

Cree walked right beside me towards the showroom. She turned those green eyes on me and spoke through a clenched jaw. "Is it true?"

This was no time to play dumb or to deny reality. I nodded. "It was an accident." That was the first lie I'd ever told her, and my stomach turned to acid. It felt horrible. Worse than actually killing a guy.

As we marched silently to the showroom, the squirrels in my head began circling each other.

You killed a guy. You have this coming.

The others didn't. And he tried to kill you first.

All this over a fricking glass egg and nobody really knows what it is. Stupid thing to die over.

I thought about the Paiute Egg. What was it that old men were willing to fight and die over? Or did that even matter? It was the possessing, not what was possessed. Rich dicks like Cromwell and Bowden didn't seem to care who got hurt as long as they won. It was a crappy way to live your life.

And what was that damned thing, exactly? The last time I saw the egg in action, it had crippled Lemuel. In the showroom, those lights and that horrible noise brought me to my knees and had my brain leaking out of my ears. I never wanted to see that thing again and here I was, ready to die over it.

Again.

Torson maintained the stoic look of a stone killer. He may have taken a bit of joy in putting his hand on Boudica's back and shoving her along when she was too slow, but otherwise was all business. I felt his eyes on my back, burning holes between my shoulder blades. He wanted this rematch badly.

Shaggy was fully back now, which was good, but probably would not be enough. Without lunar assistance, it was going to be as much me fighting as him, and Torsson had nearly killed us the last time. The presence of the Paiute Egg was going to complicate things. Those lights and sounds drove Shaggy crazy. I wondered what effect it would have on the Berserker over there?

I slowed my walk as a question occurred to me.

Were bears as sensitive to sounds as Lycans?

I turned to Cree, who was making a point of not looking at me. I leaned in anyway and whispered, "I have an idea to get us out of this."

She slowed her walk but still didn't look at my face. *Goddammit, Johnny.* I felt worse about disappointing her than killing Junior.

Her voice was positively Arctic. "What?"

God, I know you don't owe me any favors, but *don't let Bowden hear us.*

I told her, in as few words as I could, and as far as I thought it out. Her eyes widened. She even gasped a little, and I felt a glimmer of hope that disappeared when she shook her head and sped up to avoid me.

I couldn't blame her. It was a really terrible idea. But it was the only one I had.

CHAPTER 36

"Alright. Everyone sit there. You two... up there." Bowden directed traffic with his pistol. Cree, Bill, Karmen and Boudica stood in the front row and then, after a not-so-subtle command, sat. I took my time climbing to the right-hand side of the stage, while Torson lumbered up the left, flexing his hands in anticipation of ripping my throat out.

Bowden himself leaned on the stage apron, keeping his eyes on the folks up front, although with Boudica bound up and Karmen pretty much shell-shocked, there wasn't much to worry about. He hadn't figured out who Bill and Cree were, but assessed them as an annoyance, not a threat. He looked like someone enjoying the sheer power tripping asshole-ness of the situation.

I decided to play to my only actual strength. Bowden kept underestimating what an idiot I really was. "It's kind of cool from up here, isn't it?" I sounded like a moron, but it bought time.

If my half-assed idea was to work, there were three things that needed to happen. First, the Egg needed to be out in the open. Second, Cree needed access to the sound and lights. Finally, I had to avoid getting dismembered before I could give her the signal. Technically, I needed to figure out a signal, so maybe there were four. Math was never my best subject.

I surveyed the scene. My side of the stage was clear and empty, leaving a ton of room for Torson to chase me around, but not much for me to work with. Behind the Berserker, the big props for Salem's Revenge—the fire stake, the rock drop and the noose—were shoved together near the back curtain. A soundboard and mixer sat on a table back there, along with maybe a dozen crates containing all Karmen's illusion secrets.

The women obviously performed some of their coven duties up here, because a folding table was draped in black with some half-melted candles, tarot cards and other witchy paraphernalia.

Perfect. I grabbed one of the thinnest candles, snapped some burned wax off, and shoved the chunks into my pocket.

Thankfully, Shaggy was on full alert, and I was glad to have him back even if it meant struggling to keep him controlled. It would take both sides of me to pull this off. Teamwork makes the dreamwork, etcetera, etcetera.

Bowden slapped his hand on the stage. "Okay, let's do this."

Okay, Johnny. Try not to screw this up too badly. Step one...

"Whoa, whoa, whoa. How do I know you're not going to just sneak it out of here while I'm busy with Winnie the Pooh here?" Before Bowden could protest his innocence and pure intentions, I poured it on thicker. "Nah. I want the Egg here where everyone can see it. Once he kicks my butt, you can carry it off like we promised, but let's at least pretend you're not full of shit, okay?"

My little dig at his twisted honor must have hit the spot, because the old man's eye twitched. "Fair enough. Winner takes the prize. Like I said." After another wet cough, he took the egg from the backpack at his feet and offered it to Torson.

The big man bent over the edge of the stage, accepting it from his boss. Those hands trembled as he held it at arm's length, worried he'd drop the damned thing. He looked around, a little bewildered. "Where do I put it?"

From the corner of my eye, I saw the stand they used for the Egg during the stage show. I dragged it to center stage. "Right here, big guy. I'll take good care of it once I kick your fuzzy behind again."

For a second I worried I'd overplayed my hand, because his face twisted with the onset of the change, and it seemed he was going to drop it and charge. Luckily, Torson hadn't gone full Berserker yet. He took a deep centering breath, nodded and placed it carefully on the table for all to see. "Good enough?"

I shrugged and took a few steps back. One whole stage of the master plan accomplished. That was further than most of my schemes got, so I was on a roll. On to phase two.

I moved to the front of the stage with my hand shading my eyes, acting as if I could hardly see. Honestly, Shaggy's powerful vision added to mine was making me blink, but this was mostly an excuse. "Can we turn these bad boys down a bit?"

Since my body was upstage from Torson, he turned into the brightness and had to shade his eyes. Bowden barked from the floor, "What do you think?"

"It is kind of bright," the big man was almost apologetic.

"Doggone it. Yeah, fine. Turn'em down a bit."

"Cree, you've got a remote back here—for lights." I looked out to where she was half in shadow. "And sound, too, right?" *Please say sound. Come on, lady. Work with me...*

"Yeah, sound and lights. On the mixer board, it's about nine by six." *Good girl. I could kiss you. Not that you'd ever let me do that again. What kind of vegan kisses a killer?*

I scooted over, grabbed the remote control, and brought it to the edge of the stage. Bowden trained his gun on Cree, decided she wasn't up to anything nefarious, and nodded. She slowly took three small steps to the apron, her hand out.

My eyes locked on hers as I passed it over. Pretending to lose my balance a bit, I grabbed her hand and leaned forward. Like a ventriloquist trying not to move his lips, I hissed out, "You'll know when."

I checked her eyes for understanding. Somewhere between the revulsion, disappointment, and general terror, I thought I saw a glimmer of understanding. Her eyes were greener and prettier than ever. Must have been the stage lighting.

Priorities, dipshit.

Almost two steps along, and my plan hadn't imploded. Even in Las Vegas, there was no way this hot streak was going to last. Time to just get on with it.

The lights dimmed a bit, giving me some relief and a chance to scan the front row. Cree stopped fiddling with the remote and cradled it in her lap. Karmen quietly nipped at a once-perfect cuticle, nervousness outweighing vanity. Bill sat with his crutch gripped firmly across his lap. He was white with fear. Boudica just glared straight ahead, burning with shame and frustration.

"Okay, so how do we do this?" I asked as I kicked off my shoes and tugged my socks off. I wasn't going to strip down all the way. It wasn't modesty—everyone there knew about Shaggy, even if they'd never seen him. I couldn't let Shaggy completely take control, though. He couldn't run the show if there was any chance of success. The inconvenience and discomfort of clothes would give me some leverage over his darker instincts. If I stripped off, there'd be less stopping him from taking over. At the same time, claws were good, and there was going to be a lot of jumping and dodging going on. Bare feet were more useful than dress shoes.

There was another, bigger problem. Fury and blood lust were building up inside me, coming to a boil under my skin. My Lycan brain-mate wasn't the only one that wanted to kill Torson. I was feeling it too. And Bowden, while I was at it. That smug old face. I wanted to strip the wrinkled face right off of his head. Boudica probably could use a lesson while I was handing them out. A good old killing spree might make me feel better.

Stop it. Controlling the normal homicidal side of me was tough enough. I really didn't want to surrender completely. That was going to take more than I had in reserve.

Breathe Johnny. That isn't you. You can beat him without killing him.

Except I couldn't. At least not if my half-assed scheme didn't work perfectly, and I damn well knew it. There'd be no going back. Cree had already written me off. I wondered if this was a bridge too far for Bill. *Fuck it. Let's get it over with.*

I scanned the people in the seats once more. They were all depending on me. One old man, even uber-motivated and heavily armed, wasn't the real problem. If I could get the giant bear-thing out of the picture, we'd be fine. If.

I didn't want Torson dead. Well, I did, and that was another problem entirely. I'd do my best, though, if only for the sake of what remained of my soul.

Turning to Bowden, I asked, "So how does this happen? Do we... Oh crap." Torson had run out of patience. The crazy sonofabitch already ripped his khaki shirt off and had half-changed so that he was covered in brown fuzz and those lethal hands were flexing open and closed. The walls shook with his bass-amp roar and those heavy clomping footsteps as he charged around the stage. I clearly heard the gasps from the audience. Bowden's cackle sounded even creepier alongside everyone else's fear.

Going half-changed seemed about right, but it would take a couple of seconds—time I didn't have. The way Torson moved, it wouldn't matter much if I moved left or right, he'd at least clip me going by. If I took him head on, I'd be a smudge mark on the stage before we even began.

Come on, come on, annnnnnd...

I dropped into the tightest ball I could form and dropped to the floor, hugging my knees to my chest. Torson's massive shadow passed over me with a confused grunt. It would have been nice to see the look on the jerk's face, but I needed to get away. Fast.

Assisted by Shaggy, I sprung towards the far edge of the stage. Claws and fur replaced my own hands and feet. My body wanted to complete the change. Hell, I wanted to go full Shaggy at that moment, but it wasn't the time. Not if I wanted to pull this off.

It was my face, but Shaggy's eyes I saw through. I needed Torson angry—out of control. Problem was, I couldn't let him actually get his hands on me. On the other side of the stage, Torson threw his head back and bellowed again, beating his chest. Well, the first part of the plan was going nicely. He was pissed.

Speaking clearly wasn't possible. The words stuck in my throat, but the concentration necessary to talk kept Shaggy from taking over. "Come on, Yogi. I haven't got all day."

Apparently, the other guy had all the time in the world. Rather than charge at me, which was the goal, he slowly, methodically, stalked me. Uh-oh.

Torson inched forward; his amber eyes watched my feet to gauge my intentions. He crouched low, arms outspread, claws wiggling in anticipation of wrapping them around my throat.

With my Lycan hearing, I could hear the audience's sniffles, gasps and moans. Somewhere under all that sound, like a quiet, killer bass line, I heard a mumbling voice. Sparing a moment I didn't have, my eyes shot to the right.

It was Karmen's voice. Her eyes were closed while her body rocked back and forth in her seat. She was praying, or whatever witches did. To whom or what, I had no idea, and there was no time to figure it out. I had a couple of hundred pounds of pissed-off Icelandic berserker heading my way.

Under the circumstances, the stupidest thing I could do at that point was charge right at him.

Naturally, I charged right at him.

A burst of Lycan muscles in my legs propelled me straight into Torson's huge gut. I didn't knock him off balance. I barely slowed him down, in fact. His oak tree arms crushed me against his chest. The air left my lungs in one tremendous *whoosh*. I would have loved a do-over.

Up close I smelled his sweat, his bear funk—hell, everything he'd eaten for the last week. But it also gave me access to one vulnerable spot. I pulled my fist back and put everything I had into a quick jab at his exposed throat.

With a panicky gasp, his arms flew open. I dropped to the floor, taking in what air I could. Torson staggered backwards, clutching his throat.

Bowden's voice barked from the floor. "Christ, you big asshole. Finish the son of a bitch." He turned his gun from the front row seats to me. I was happy to be a decoy, but this wasn't going to remain a fair fight for long, judging from the look on his face.

Torson flailed around, trying to get enough in his lungs to come at me again. It was time for Step Three. This was uncharted territory; I'd never gotten this far into a plan without it blowing up before, but this was no time to get cocky.

I reached into my pocket and felt the chunks of candle wax. My fingers rolled them into balls, softening the paraffin. This was going to require just a couple of seconds more. I shouted to Bowden, "Hey, you old fart! Last chance to take your boy and just get the hell out of here. No harm, no foul."

It was silent except for Karmen's mumbling and Torson's ragged breathing, which was normalizing faster than I hoped. In my pocket, there were now two balls of soft candle wax. Hopefully, they'd do the job.

"Not til you pay for my boy." The voice was devoid of emotion. There was no room for negotiation. That sucked for me.

He might not have been a hundred percent, but the Berserker was out of patience and wanted to end the nonsense. He charged once more, slaughter in his eyes. His immense body stood between me and where I needed to be. Dropping to all fours, Shaggy howled a challenge, and went at him as well. I misjudged the distance, because his fist, heavy and hard as granite, caught me on the top of my skull. I face-planted face on the stage floor.

Stars went supernova in my head. The world spun out of control. My hands clawed at the floor, hoping to drag my ass to the corner where the stage props were. The Berserker grabbed my ankle and dragged me backwards. My talons cut ragged lines into the stage floor as I tried to resist.

I kicked out blindly with my clawed feet and got rewarded by the rip of cloth and a fiery rush of blood. His huge hands released me long enough for me to crawl, stumble, and roll to the far corner. My back was against the pile of Styrofoam rocks used for Karmen's escape trick. Time to see if I had a snowball in hell's chance of making it out alive.

My fingers were swollen and almost useless, but I needed to hold this form for one more task. Taking the candle wax between my thumb and finger, I grabbed the first ball of wax and shoved it in my ear. The world got a little muffled on one side of my head, which was exactly what I wanted. Before I could put the other makeshift ear plug in place, though, Torson was on me.

Without thinking, I hurled one of the fake boulders at him. Clearly, he'd never seen Salem's Revenge, because he pulled up short and braced himself for a heavy rock to the cranium. Instead, it bounced off his skull with a pathetic "boink." The look on his face would have been hysterical if I weren't fighting for my life.

It gave me time to stuff the other ball of wax in the other ear. I could still hear, since something as simple as a pair of earplugs could not foil Shaggy's ears, but it would have to do. Before I could give Cree the signal, everything went into shadow. The stage lights were blocked out by Torson's body flying through the air and dropping on me. For the second time, every atom of oxygen deserted me. Those damned killer hands wrapped around my throat and tightened.

I tried calling for Cree, but all that came out of my mouth was a gurgling "C-c-c" that accomplished nothing but depleting my air supply.

It was Shaggy time.

233

My hands shifted, and I swung with all I had. The claws caught the bear-man across the face. Torson roared and reached for his face with one hand. His other hand still held me down, but at least I could breathe. After a couple of pathetic gasps, I looked out through blurry eyes to where the audience sat.

Shaggy's vision had no problem picking Cree's face out of the darkness. There wasn't enough air in my body to make the sound, but my lips formed the word "Now."

Torson was on me again, and for a moment I was too busy trying to stay alive to wonder why nothing was happening. Another slice across his face, to the left side this time, put him in a towering rage and I knew I was really toast this time.

Except I wasn't. Through my wax ear-stoppers, I detected the screaming guitar notes that masked the Egg's activation signal. A shudder ran through me, and Shaggy protested. It wasn't as awful with my ears plugged, and I could maintain a tenuous control.

Easy, easy.

It all came down to this. How would the monster react to the lights and sounds from the egg?

At first, he was just frozen in confusion as his animal brain tried to decode what was happening. Then the first ray of frigid light shot from the Egg. Even through my plugged-up ears, the blood-curdling high-pitched shriek beat against my brain. I tried shoving my fingers into my ear canals as well, but that would have driven six inches of Lycan claw into my brain. Instead, I ducked and covered, cupping both hands over my ears.

Torson wasn't so lucky. He did not know what was going on. Blindly, he clutched at his head as I had the first time, roaring his confusion and agony. He held his head in his hands and spun crazily around the stage, his eyes nearly popping out of his fuzzy head.

From off to the side, I heard a craggy voice yell, "What the hell's that? Knock that shit off. Stop it."

Since he hated the sound so much, Shaggy wasn't at all reluctant to cede control. My hands and feet were all mine again, for all the good that'd do me. I needed something I could use to kill Torson now that he was so badly weakened. I wanted him dead. Shaggy doubled down on the idea.

No. I can't kill him. I mean, I want to but...

Torson understood little of what was happening, but he had enough working neurons to know I was responsible. Staggering from the pain in his head, but determined to end me, he lumbered forward, swinging wildly.

A quick look around didn't provide any simple answers. Fake rocks, a water tank. I really could have used some of the fire Karmen used for the burning stake routine, but that was a nonstarter.

There was just a tall wooden pole on a rolling platform. Great.

The longer the music played, the more freezing rays of light shot around the room. Cree had killed all the other lights now, so the room was in pitch blackness except for the Egg's beams.

This was not part of Bowden's master plan. He shouted and fumed, audible even through my stopped-up ears.

As furious as he was, it was nothing compared to what was going on between Torson's ears. If I was in pain and hated the noise, at least I knew what was happening, and was protected by the earplugs and my hands. He was unprotected and under audio assault.

I struggled to my feet. That underlying signal was drilling itself into the back of my head, but I gritted my teeth and moved towards the stake. Torson's hate-filled eyes followed me. I looked behind me and saw what I prayed would be there. *Son of a gun, this might just work.*

Hiding the fact that your brain is about to explode isn't easy, but I faked a smile and stood as tall as possible. I crossed my arms across my arms and gave him my cheesiest smile. "Hey, ya ugly bastard. How's it going?"

If the Berserker ever had any fucks to give, they were long gone. He growled and ran at me, just as I hoped he would. This time, I took a half step to the side and stuck my leg out. It caught his ankle, and he fell face first to the floor. Impact stunned him for only a second, but that's all I needed. The Velcro cuffs Cree and Boudica used to lash Karmen to the post came in handy. I jumped on the big guy's back and bound his hands behind his back. It probably wouldn't hold him long, but I only needed a second.

I took two. I allowed myself the satisfaction of putting an NFL-class kick to the side of his head before strapping the second set of cuffs to his ankles. He thrashed around like a landed marlin. Clearly, he was out of commission for the moment. I collapsed on top of his squirming body, panting and groaning.

The music stopped suddenly, the final power cords echoing off the empty theater walls. That probably wasn't good. I yanked the plugs from my ears and looked over the edge of the stage.

Bowden held the remote in one hand, his gun in the other, and was screaming incoherently at Cree. She might have been a head shorter, but she was in no mood to take any more from him. I watched her plant one foot behind her and shift her weight, ready to launch a punch.

The old guy had been in enough fights to back up out of Cree's range, looking around for any other trouble. He snarled when he saw the soles of Torson's giant boots and his pet berserker flat and useless, lying on his gut. "This ain't over. It's not, goddammit."

Next to Cree, Karmen was doubled over, still praying. Chanting. Whatever the hell she was doing. Near as I could tell it wasn't doing a goddamned thing except to annoy Bowden. That didn't mean it was useless.

"Knock that shit off. Stop it." Even as angry as he was, the old cowboy could only shoot one person at a time. Poor guy was having a bitch of time figuring out who it ought to be. He waved his gun at me, then to Cree, to Karmen, and back at me. That was just fine. Confusion was a weapon.

Bowden knew he'd lost, but that didn't mean he wouldn't want to take a couple of people with him. Starting with me, of course. That wasn't so bad. What worried me was when he saw the look on Cree's face as I came nearer. A nasty sneer and another hacking cough attack, and he wiped his sleeve across his mouth.

"Give me the egg or your girlfriend dies."

"She's not my girlfriend. Let her go."

"Yeah. Yeah, she is. Now hand it over."

Before I could respond, a strange look passed over the old cowboy's face. He waved his free hand across his face, as if shooing away a fly. I couldn't see anything there, but he waved at it a second time. "Just give me the... what the hell?"

He began flapping his arms around, as if an entire swarm of flies, or mosquitoes, or something small and nasty was attacking. His glasses fell off his nose. His watery eyes were wide with fear.

No, it was more like terror. He moaned and slapped at himself, ridding himself of something that nobody else could see. The gun slipped from his hand to the floor as he rubbed his arms, rubbing his face against his sleeve. His voice went up an octave. "Get'em off! Get'em off me!"

For the life of me, I couldn't figure out what was going on. Bill sat in stunned silence. Boudica's eyes were on the old man, a gleeful, evil glint in her eye. I heard Cree's voice. "Karmen, no."

Mystery solved. Karmen was the cause of whatever this was. Still muttering, she lifted her pale face and focused on Bowden. Her makeup was smeared with sweat, her hair wild, and there was something feral in those eyes. Her lips never stopped moving. Bowden's voice was just shrieks and babbles now, as he jerked and spun. He believed himself covered in an invisible swarm of something hateful and vile.

The smile the Mistress of Magick gave him was pure venom. Her eyes were wide now, her nostrils flaring, and something far nastier than a giggle came from her mouth. She was clearly enjoying this.

She shrugged off Cree's first attempts to stop her. "Karmen." Cree put her hand on the witch's arm. "Karmen, this is wrong. Stop." The only answer was an orgasmic moan from somewhere deep inside the older woman.

Boudica's voice boomed from down the row of seats. "About time. Fucking kill him. Do it." Her own eyes blazed now, reveling in the unleashed magick and its use on an enemy. She chuckled. "Show him what we can really do. Use your power."

Cree grabbed Karmen's arm again, ignoring the vicious nails that swiped at her. "No. Do no harm. Ever. To anyone. You said that."

Boudica shook her head and nearly bounced up and down in her seat. "This is what we could have done all along. What's the point of power if you don't use it? Now do it!"

Whether it was Cree's pleas, Boudica's voice, or sheer exhaustion, something penetrated the mystical fog in Karmen's head. She shook like a wet dog for a second. Then she blinked. Her eyes cleared, and she collapsed back into her seat. Clive Bowden was a whimpering, shaking, heap on the floor. Whatever attacked him had let up.

Shaggy had a better idea of what the hell was going on than I did. The feeling he got around magic phenomena had him in a howling, gut-churning frenzy. His disorientation prevented me from moving too quickly.

Karmen let out a series of sobs, and Cree wrapped the woman in her arms, rocking her slowly back and forth. That girl's heart was too soft for her own good. I watched quietly, proud of her. Not that I had any right to feel that way. She wasn't mine. After today, she wasn't likely to be.

Crap.

Bowden had enough wits left to realize he'd dropped his gun. While everyone focused on Karmen, he found it and rose to his feet. "You killed my boy."

The old bastard clearly decided. If he was going to kill one of us, it was going to be me. Fine. Probably the right answer. I lifted my hands. "Great. Do it."

"What did that witch do to me?"

I shrugged. "Why ask me? I don't know what the hell's happening either." I was killing time, but it was also a fact. There was no use even pretending to be in control of the situation.

Clive Bowden whirled and pointed at Karmen and Cree. "She's a... an abomination."

I tried regaining his focus. "Hey, John Wayne. I'm the one you want."

He was desperate to kill someone, but uncertain just who. He swiveled to face me, then the women. As he shifted his weight to take aim at me, a blur from behind him caught my eye. The old guy must have seen the look on my face, because he stiffened and turned to see what it was. It was too late.

A hollow metallic *ping* filled the room, and Clive Bowden hit the ground with a groan and a thud.

I couldn't believe my eyes. "Holy shit."

"Holy shit," Bill's voice had more surprise in it than mine did. He stood, a little wobbly, over the unconscious cowboy with a slightly dented crutch still clutched in his hands.

"Dude." I couldn't think of any higher praise, and Bill accepted it with a weak smile.

CHAPTER 37

Cree turned the house lights up. Everyone blinked at each other, not saying a word. The audience was too stunned to say or do anything. I wasn't so lucky.

The air was thick with scents that drove Shaggy crazy with the urge to kill something. Fear and sweat were the most prominent odors. The remnants of Karmen's magick hung in the air, smelling of pumpkin spice and rotten meat. Surprisingly, the stench of bear was nearly gone. Torson had returned to human form and laid face down on the floor, hands and feet velcroed together. All the Berserker energy faded away and all the fight was out of him.

Since he was no longer Berserker-sized, I ran over and tightened the cuffs, just to make sure he stayed put. "You stay down, okay?"

"Is Mr. Bowden alright?" Aw, that was kind of sweet. He was more worried about the old cowboy than the other way around.

"Yeah, he's fine. But it's over."

Torson nodded and relaxed, panting, face down on the stage. "I'm bleeding."

The copper scent filled my head. Shaggy wanted to get in on this, but it wasn't his show any more.

I looked over my shoulder. On the floor, Bowden removed his Stetson and rubbed the goose-egg on the back of his head, glaring at

Bill. I patted Torson on the shoulder. "He's going to have a hell of a headache, but he's okay."

Headache or not, the old bastard was still feisty as hell. Karmen had picked up his gun from the ground and held it with two fingers like someone had handed her a cobra.

Bowden might have been beaten, but wasn't going down without a fight. He threw a punch at Cree, whose MMA skills kicked in. He swung wide, and she ducked, then threw a body punch that doubled him over. Her hands flew to her mouth.

"Are you..."

Bless her heart. She was going to ask if he was okay, and he must have been, because he snarled and backhanded her across the face. Shaggy and I reacted as a team. In two bounds, we were across the stage. I grabbed Bowden and pulled his face close to mine. My teeth extended, and it was Shaggy's eyes that bored into the old man's skull.

I knew then that Shaggy considered Cree part of his pack. That's a big deal for a primarily lone animal. I don't know exactly what to call what she was to me, but she was under my protection. Plus, I was tired, injured, insulted, and sore as hell. It wasn't even a decision, so much as a foregone conclusion. Bowden had to die.

I pulled his face to within inches of mine. His mirrored shades were askew, and I could see one of his red eyes, his pupil wide as my fist. I let out the most terrifying roar I could, and was gratified to hear a pathetic little whine, then a series of body-shaking, mucous-y coughs.

"Johnny." Cree's voice came at me from a million miles off. Shaggy and I ignored her. She didn't understand. I was doing this for her. Bowden'd hurt her. He'd hurt other people. It would be so easy. Not to mention solve a lot of problems.

My nails poked holes into his camo jacket as I pulled him close. The stench of fear was my reward. My stomach growled. Shaggy was doing a victory dance. Just for the joy of it, I took another deep sniff. It wasn't just his fear this time. There was something else there. Something wrong.

Under all the intensive odors in the room, I detected something foul. Putrid. It oozed from the old man's pores and wafted on the air along with his breathing. It was the stench of sickness. Probably cancer. I was a werewolf, not a doctor. One thing was obvious: Clive Bowden was a dead man walking.

Shaggy sniffed again, just to be sure.

Bowden's jaw tightened, and he pulled himself straight. He looked into my eyes. "Do it." He meant it, too. He was ready. More than ready, he wanted to die.

"Dude, don't." Bill pleaded.

"Johnny. You can't." Cree was still defending him. Didn't she realize this was for her? I growled again. Shaggy panted expectantly.

Bowden shouted in an unsteady voice. "Go on. What are you waiting for?" My mouth watered as I realized I'd be doing him a kindness. Nothing like rationalization to scrub the guilt away.

But he didn't deserve kindness.

I let out an angry howl and shoved him five feet into the first row of seats. Then I sank to my knees and cradled my head in my hands. Whether it was relief I didn't kill him, or anger at myself, there was no way to tell in that cyclone of confusion and rage.

"Somebody cut me loose, damn it." Boudica was on her feet, hands still zip tied together. Her wrists were bloody and bruised from her attempts to escape. I waved her forward. Biting her lip, she held her hands out expectantly.

I looked at her and for a moment thought she'd be a decent substitute for Bowden in the killing department. After all, this was her fault. She'd set me up when I went to the compound. She tried to betray me and Karmen both by selling the egg out from under her. Plus, that look in her eye was more defiance than regret. I felt the claws growing on one hand. Shaggy bayed for her blood.

It took a couple of attempts to saw through the plastic manacles. Her hands parted and Boudica flapped her hands to get the blood going. Then she wheeled around and put a kick right in Clive

Bowden's breadbasket, knocking the wind out of him. From the sound of it, she cracked a rib as well.

"You son of a bitch." She shouted.

A low, nearly unrecognizable voice came from off to the right. "You're the bitch."

Karmen had risen to her feet and glared at her betrayer. She had that wild-animal look on her face again, her eyes half shut, her teeth bared and a low growl coming from her. Boudica backed away, but from the way her eyes widened, she was more surprised than frightened.

"You don't want to do this." The Amazon's voice had just enough threat in it to make Karmen pause.

Cree put herself between the two women. "She's right. This isn't how we do things."

Karmen put her hand on Cree's face gently, giving her a soft smile. "Yes. Yes, it is, honey. Now get the fuck out of my way."

The witch raised both cupped hands. Her lips moved silently again. A bitterly cold wind blew through the room. Boudica's blond hair tossed like in a breeze.

Boudica's eyes widened, then a slight grin emerged. "You know I'm stronger than you. Always have been."

Karmen was sweating. Whatever she was doing took a lot of energy, and she'd already cast the freakout spell on Bowden. If Boudica was telling the truth, this would not be much of a fight.

"It's my coven. Mine. It's not your time yet. But you couldn't wait, could you? And you turned the Mothers against me."

Boudica twisted her head left then right, making her neck crack as she loosened up. "And you've been a waste. With all this power, we could have done real good. I'm done waiting for you to get your shit together."

From my spot on the stage, I watched, horrified, as Boudica lifted her hands in a mirror image of Karmen's. The temperature dropped even lower, and an invisible, cinnamon-scented wind circled through the room, blowing everywhere, first one way, then the other.

Shaggy whimpered in my skull, smart enough to know this wasn't our place and wanting nothing to do with the power struggle in front of us.

For a minute, it looked like nothing was happening except that crazy wind. Karmen's hands trembled slightly, then shook more violently. Boudica let out a wicked laugh.

"See, you old cow? You're weak and pathetic. It's my time. Give in. just say it."

"No! Cree, give me your hand." Karmen's hand flapped and flailed until her nails dug into Cree's wrist.

Cree knew what to do. After a moment's confusion, she dropped her head. Her lips began the same quiet muttering as her leader. The wind shifted slightly towards Boudica.

"If you're relying on this one for help, you're more pathetic than I thought." Boudica raised her hands higher, and the wind reversed yet again. Cree and Karmen squeezed each other's hands higher and chanted louder.

Bill looked up at me. "Dude, what's going on?" I didn't have an answer to give him. Before I could speak, Cree shouted at him.

"Bill, help us. Give me your hand." Without giving him time to think about it, the redhead grabbed Bill's hand and squeezed.

Bill's face changed. When Cree had grabbed him, he was merely confused. Then his entire demeanor changed. He got paler, and his eyes darted around the room. He seemed to track something that darted from side to side, with no kind of natural rhythm.

"Johnny, what the hell, man?" He tried yanking his hand away, but Cree's grip was too tight.

I tried making sense of what was happening in the empty theater. "What is it? What's going on?"

In a matter-of-fact voice, Bill said, "It's... they're so angry."

He didn't seem terrified anymore. I'd gotten him into this, and there had to be something I could do to get him out of it. I jumped from the stage to the floor and grabbed his free hand. He clamped onto mine, way tighter than I expected.

A surge of something like liquid electricity shot from his hand to mine with an eerie hum. Shaggy tried to bolt like he always did when he sensed magic, and I heard myself roar til the walls shook. It burned like hell and I couldn't shake it off. But I couldn't get away either. I watched everything through a thick fog, along with fire running through my entire body.

Bill wouldn't—or couldn't—let go of my hand. I backed up and yanked my arm back harder. This time, though, something grabbed hold of my free hand. Long, sweaty, pale fingers took possession of mine before I could make sense of what was happening.

The minute Karmen took my hand, the circle was complete, and everything in the room changed. The pain was still there, and my sight was blurry, like watching through a rain-covered windshield.

We were no longer in a dark, cheesy showroom, but in some place entirely other. Someplace I knew I had no business being but had been before.

We were in the gray nowhere I'd been with Karmen before we projected to Bowden's house. Shapes like dark thunderclouds shot through the air. I was the only one who seemed to be in any kind of pain. The others looked completely normal. Standing apart from our circle, Boudica was an outline in a fuzzy green aura. It was impossible for me to break away. The four of us held hands. Again, they seemed perfectly comfortable. My hands burned where Bill and Karmen touched me. Everything was blurry and kept coming in and out of focus.

Karmen's head was still down and her prayer, chant, whatever the hell it was, continued. Cree's eyes were wide open. Awe filled her eyes, and she was glowing with more than just that aura. *That's right, she's never been here.*

Bill was just confused and disoriented, but seemed otherwise fine. Every part of my being was desperate to get the hell out, but I couldn't leave him. Nobody dared let go. Whatever—wherever—whenever this was, we were here until the close of business.

A shrieking voice—no, several of them—filled the space and passed right through our bodies. There were half a dozen gray blurs shooting like comets across the space. Two of them broke off from the rest and changed form. Their shapes changed multiple times until they settled on something my pain-addled brain recognized. I knew who they were.

The Mothers.

The old one, the Crone, darted from Karmen to Boudica and back, shouting incoherent, angry words in a language that made no sense. The other one, the younger and less hideous form, hovered inches from my face. Her voice was sibilant. She reeked like pumpkin spice and skunk cabbage. Her hatred sent shivers racing up and down my spine.

"We told you before. You can't be here, intruder."

Like any of this was my idea, but my hands couldn't break free of the circle. Humility seemed like the best plan. "I don't want to be here. Please, send me—us—back." The ghostly form ignored me, and had already moved on, studying Bill's blank face.

"This one... his women have much power. He has it in his blood. It's a shame he's a man."

Bill stood calmly. The only thing he could manage was, "No. Way." He looked at me for an explanation that wasn't forthcoming. I had no damned clue.

The younger Mother focused on him. "Listen to your women, lad." He nodded. Whether out of politeness, agreement, or sheer terror, I had no clue. Either way, Bill always picked his fights more wisely than I did.

The form moved on to Cree. The Crone left Boudica and joined her. For an eternity, there was silence except that damned wind. Pain and my hazy, magic-resistant brain made it hard to concentrate.

Cree's body language had changed. She stood with her head down meekly. Her eyes were watery, and her bottom lip quivered. "You're the Mothers. Aren't you?"

The Crone reached out a hand to her chin and tilted Cree's face up. In an unexpectedly tender voice, she said, "You are welcome here. Why have you not joined us before, child?"

Cree's voice was barely a whisper. "I have wanted to for so long, Mother. But, I don't have the gift. My magic is too weak. I don't deserve the honor."

"Nonsense." The older spirit screamed until the air itself shook. "Who filled this child's head with such lies?"

The younger Mother pointed to Boudica. "This one. This liar. She tried to keep us apart from her." Her form flew right up to Boudica. The blonde avoided the gaze as best she could. The spirit continued. "You kept denying her entry."

Cree let out a gasp. "Is that true?"

Boudica crossed her arms across her chest and lifted her chin in defiance. "She's weak. Nothing. She's unworthy. You said I was the heiress. I was next. You promised, both of you—"

Karmen's hand tightened on mine, ramping up the electric burn and nearly making me bite my tongue off. She glared with palpable hatred at Boudica. "You couldn't wait, could you? I told you the coven was yours after... after..."

She never got to finish the thought because the Crone got up in her grill.

"And you. Selfish. Vain. Useless. Such a waste of the gifts you were given." Karmen looked like the old witch slapped her across the face. Tears welled in her eyes.

"I tried. I—"

The young one shook her head and pointed at both of them. "Useless. The pair of you. A shame to the Mothers who came before. Unworthy to lead." She drifted back to Cree again, inspecting her with no further words.

Cree stood a little taller, breathing deeply and her eyes lifted to meet the specter's. It didn't look like it was out of fear so much as respect.

"But this one. You know herbs and potions, yes?"

Cree uttered a barely audible, "Yes, Mother. But I lack other powers."

"What you lack is training. You're strong, girl. So strong." The crone looked from Boudica to Karmen, then back to an awe-struck Cree. "All of their strength, none of their wicked natures."

The two Mothers met in the middle of the space, huddling up about something. Finally, the old crone nodded and pointed at Cree. "I claim you, girl. To train and lead. Do you accept?"

Cree's lips opened, but nothing coherent came out. "I... I.... ummm"

The young spirit whispered in Cree's ear, insistent but not unkindly. "Choose. Now, child."

Cree gave a deep sniff and nodded. "Yes. I mean, please. Yes." She looked like an eager eight-year-old. Like Christmas came early.

The wind stopped. The cloud things mercifully stopped spinning around the room. Everything was still. The pain in my body and brain moved from excruciating to merely awful. Everything was still blurry, but the scene riveted me and I quit trying to flee.

Boudica's furious voice cut through the calm. "You said you'd teach me. You said I was the one who—"

The Crone's mouth opened three sizes too big for her face and screamed. "Silence. Traitor. Liar. This is the last you'll ever see of us."

For the first time, I saw real fear on Boudica's face. "No, please. I'll do better. I swear."

Both Mothers shook their heads. The younger one lifted a hand. "Too late."

With those two words, Boudica vanished. No sound, no trace, just one less person in the spirit-space.

Bill looked like he was about to say something, but I squeezed his hand and shook my head. *Not the time dude. Whatever this is, this has got nothing to do with us. We're just extra batteries.*

We had a whole cross-country car ride to talk about this. An entire lifetime. For now, shut the hell up and let the women do their thing.

The Crone turned on Karmen. "As for you. Payment is due. Your time is up. You will have no more access to this world unless through her." Her meaning Cree, apparently.

Karmen couldn't muster up words. She lowered her head and emitted a single, body-shaking sob. Finally, she nodded her concession.

The young Mother said just one word. "Go."

A breath later, we were back in the theater. Finally able to free my hands, I collapsed in a chair as the pain slowly seeped from my body. *Note to self. Don't mess with magick.*

Boudica hadn't bothered to stick around and wait for us. I only hoped that she'd remembered to untie Valerie the Valkyrie and take her, too.

Torson and Bowden were nowhere to be seen. I suppose I should have been a little more concerned with just letting them go like that, but hell. Bowden was a beaten—and dying—man. He was headed home to lick his wounds. After what he'd seen, I highly doubted he'd mess with Karmen or the Museum again. He might come for Cromwell, but I doubted it, and not for a while. As for Bear Boy, Torson was big and not terribly bright, with a monster trapped inside him. He needed someone to be the boss. Preferably someone rich and smarter than him.

That sounds like you, Lupul. The voice in my head could be a real dick.

I heard a grunt and a seat cushion give a little. Bill was a little dazed, but not hurt. He saw how worried I was, because he held up a hand, took another deep breath and said, "I'm okay. Really. You?"

I ignored the question, since the answer was too damned complicated. I was fine, confused, pissed off, nauseous and disoriented from all that magic and sore as hell from fighting Torson.

Bill looked at this damaged crutch, then back at me. "I guess I owe Gramma an apology, huh?"

"I think she'd settle for some of those winnings the other night, but yeah. Probably. We both do."

He wasn't done talking. Probably the nerves. "And it was all so clear. Like in high-definition. What was that about?" His experience was obviously different from mine. Clearly a conversation for another time.

"Karmen. Karmen. Look at me." Cree was bent over her former coven leader, so I couldn't see anything except her back and her butt. "Johnny, is she…"

I sidled up beside her and checked Karmen's throat for a pulse. "Karmen, are you okay?"

The woman had both hands clutched to her face. She rocked back and forth, wailing incoherently like a banshee.

Cree gently took one hand in hers. I took the other, and we slowly pulled them down so we could look her over. Cree softly shoosh-shooshed her the whole time, ever the caretaker.

The Mistress of Magick looked up at us with eyes spider-webbed with red. Dark circles hung under her eyes. Worse though, her face had aged twenty years. Deep crow's feet reached out from the corners of her eyes, like cracks in concrete. Her cheeks sagged a bit. Most striking of all, her wig had fallen to the floor, revealing her natural locks. A thick, jagged streak of white ran along the part in her once-black hair.

She clutched Cree's hand in hers. In a childlike whisper, she pleaded. "How bad is it?"

I guess the answer was clear in the way we looked at her—or rather tried not to—because Karmen Mystère, the Mistress of Magic, rolled up into a ball, arms around her waist and screamed from the depths of her soul. "No. No. Nooooooo."

CHAPTER 38

I safely stored the Paiute Sky Egg in the Charger's trunk, and it was time to get the hell out of Las Vegas. Way past time. Besides finally finishing the job for Cromwell, I was looking forward to two or three days on the road with my best friend.

There was one last thing I needed to take care of. Two, actually, but I had to file Cree under "permanently unfinished business." I needed to check on Mister Collins before hitting the road.

Bill waited for me in the hospital lobby while I wound my way to the seventh floor of University Medical Center. Cathedral-sized windows bathed the place in sunlight, and the floors practically gleamed. Having only seen Chicago public hospitals, it was impressive. The place looked more like a resort than a hospital. Every time I turned a corner, I expected to run into slot machines.

This nice Midwestern boy had never been in a private hospital suite. Especially not in a town like Las Vegas, which was used to taking care of stupidly rich people. No way was I prepared for what I walked into. Lemuel's room was double the size of a standard hospital room, with a bed equally out of proportion. The scent of a dozen kinds of flowers assaulted me before I even got inside. A beautiful Pinoy nurse brushed past me as I stood gaping in the doorway.

"Johnny Lupul, come on in, son."

He sounded good, and his smile lit up the room. The nurses had cranked the mattress up so he could watch a cooking show on the giant flat-screen TV. Instead of a flappy hospital gown, he wore fresh paisley pajamas with a crisply ironed crease in them. I'll say this for the old man. He made being a hospital inmate look good.

I resisted the urge to shake hands, but walked as close as I dared. "You must have some killer insurance."

"Nah, my insurance would have sent me home already. This is Mister Cromwell's doing. Wants me fully probed and tested. Plus, he's always taken good care of his people."

"Malcolm Cromwell? Cranky old guy in Chicago? That Mister Cromwell?"

He nodded and waved to a very comfortable-looking chair beside the bed. "He and I've known each other for a long time. You'll see. He might surprise you some day." When I was settled, he asked, "What brings you by?"

"Just wanted to check on you and say goodbye. I'm heading back to Chicago this afternoon." *Oh, and I have about a million questions I need answered before I lose my mind, so that too.*

"I'm finer than frog hair and twice as waterproof. Thanks." He wasn't going to make this easy.

"The tests they did—did they, I don't know, find anything?"

He ran his tongue over his lips and took a sip of water through a straw. "Nothing I didn't already know. But that's not what you're really asking, is it?"

"Mister Collins, I..."

"Please, it's Lem to my friends. You want to know what happened that night." It wasn't a question.

I leaned forward and dropped my voice so nobody would hear our discussion. "I mean, of course I care if you're alright. But yeah."

He shifted to sit up taller. "First, you tell me. What are you going to do with that thing?"

Sure as shit not touch it. "Keep it safely tucked away until I get to Chicago. Turn it over to Mister Cromwell and pretend I never saw it."

"That's a mighty good plan. What do you suppose he'll do with it?"

Who knew? Cromwell never actually seemed *to do* anything with his collection. It was about having those things so nobody else did, near as I could figure. "Put it in a vault with all his other weird stuff, I guess. He doesn't exactly fill me in on the details."

"That sounds about right. Gives me the creeps thinking about all those things—all that power—in one place."

"Is that bad?"

"Who knows? Most of them, at least the things I know of, are harmless. Some have really positive energy. But a lot of it is—"

"Evil?" The word sounded childish and corny, but I thought about the Anubis Disk, and a couple of other items I knew of.

Lemuel nodded. "Good a word as any. Keep an eye on him, Johnny. He doesn't always consider the consequences of his actions. He needs smart people like Miss Francine to watch over him. And you."

The old guy is screwed.

We sat in uncomfortable silence for a bit after that. It was clear I was going to have to ask if I wanted answers. "So, that night. With the Egg. What happened?"

Lemuel Collins looked up at the ceiling with an odd smile curling the corners of his mouth. "The first egg was a fake."

"Yeah, I know." I hated playing games. *Just tell me, already.*

"The second wasn't." I knew that too, but it was his story to tell.

"What was it? What did you see?"

The old man steepled his fingers as if in prayer and looked across the room at something I couldn't see. "it was dark like I've never seen, but then stars. A million, maybe a billion stars, brighter than they should be. And just me, alone in the middle of it all."

"That sounds scary."

He shook his head. "It was the most beautiful thing I'd ever seen. And then the sound—like music, but not *our* music. It got inside me and filled me up til I was fit to burst. I was just floating. In awe... that's the word. I've heard people say it before, but now I know what it means."

Whatever he was describing, it wasn't what I expected. "How did you shake loose?"

Lemuel Collins turned to look at me and placed his hand on the bed railing, close to mine, but not quite touching. "I didn't. I'd have never left if I had my way. It sent me back."

"You mean you'd have stayed? Where were you?"

"I don't really know. But somewhere better than here. It was so beautiful I didn't want to leave. Why come back? What's here for me? I'm sick and old and everything hurts. But up there..." He went back to looking at the wall. Everything was quiet except for the guy making tofu fajitas on the TV.

I had to ask the big question. "Is it dangerous? Is it... you know... evil—bad—whatever?"

The old man took a long time answering. "I don't know if it's good or bad, exactly. It just doesn't belong here, if you see my meaning. Heck, I don't know what I mean by that, but there you go."

That was all was going to get. At least as much as would make sense. I stood to leave.

"Well, I guess I should get going."

He held his hand up. "Wait. I have to tell you something. And you can take it for what it's worth because I'm just a crazy old man. But that thing you have... Inside you."

"It's evil. I know."

"No. That's not what I was going to say. Well, I mean it is, but that doesn't mean you are. Look at it as a gift."

Okay, now he was clearly delirious. I had a homicidal werewolf inside of me, as well as my own violent streak. Neither were anything good. It was time to leave.

"Seriously. You can learn from it. Like in the museum. It can tell good and evil. That will help keep you safe. Listen to it."

I remembered Shaggy sensing magic long before I could, and how he could tell good from bad. Still, nothing good happened with Shaggy in charge.

"Look at me, son."

I did.

"I said listen to it, not obey it. There's a difference. You know that. You're a good man."

It was really time to go. "I'm not. But I appreciate you saying that."

"You are. Or can be. If you want to be. It's up to you. But listen to me. You have to let it out. Like releasing steam from a valve. Keep all that hate inside you, and it will poison you. Turn you into something awful."

Yeah, ask Junior Bowden. Was my ability to control Shaggy the reason I was losing control of myself? What the hell are my options, and can I live with myself if there aren't?

It was too much to process. I needed air and a safe place to scream. I mumbled some excuse and a lame hope he got better soon and made my escape. All the way down the sun-drenched corridor, to the polished brass elevator, and down to the lobby, I kept thinking about what he said.

Listen, but don't obey. Yeah, I'll get right on that.

Bill was where I'd left him, parked on a bench in the waiting area. But he wasn't alone. A medium-sized redhead in cargo shorts, a tank top, and Doc Martins sat beside him. Both stared at the elevator as the door opened.

Bill stood, a little embarrassed. "Uh, I'm going to wait in the car." He gestured behind him and never gave me a chance to say anything. I half-expected him to rescue me. Instead, he just said, "Car keys? I'll just listen to the radio or something."

I tossed him the keys, and he clomp-clomped his way across the lobby.

"How did you know I'd be here?"

Cree gestured to the seat beside her. "You're not the type to leave without saying goodbye."

I sat in the seat with a heavy sigh. "Actually, I'm exactly the type. Cree, I don't know what to say."

"No, me first. I don't know what it's like to be you—I mean, I know better than most but, it's not the same. I'm sorry I got all judge-y. You should have told me."

I really didn't deserve anyone this good. It was just as well I couldn't have her. "Killing someone, that's the sort of thing you're allowed to be judge-y about. "

She reached over and put her hand on top of mine. I pulled my hand away like she was a hot stovetop. "I can't get you involved in all this."

Her crooked grin damn near killed me. "It's a little late for that. If I didn't mention it, I had a good time the other night." Jesus, it was only a day ago. It already felt like a million years.

"I did too, Cree. I really did, and I wish…"

"The timing sucks, I know."

A lot of things suck about this: timing. Distance. The fact I'm a stone-cold killer. "I'm not the guy you think I am."

She took my hand in hers. "Actually, I kind of hope you are. We just haven't had time to find out yet. You never know."

"I don't… we have to leave." I rose, and she got up with me, pressing her face into my chest, then looking up at me.

"I know you can't stay. Don't worry, I'm not going to get all girly about this. I can't leave either, even if you wanted me to. Karmen needs me if we're ever going to get the show up and running again. And I have so much to learn about… everything."

Yeah. Makes two of us.

She smiled. "You know, there are these things called airplanes. They go from Chicago to Las Vegas and back. They're kind of cool." Her hands slipped around my waist. God, it felt amazing.

"I don't fly. You know… I have this thing." I grinned down at her. Those lips were so damned kissable.

"Yeah. About that." She pulled away just long enough to pull a bag out from under her chair. "You might find a use for this sometime. Like, when you want to come visit." There were half a dozen plastic bottles full of Shaggy-be-gone.

I kissed her quickly. Too quickly for my liking. "I don't know. Turns out you're some kind of scary Wiccan goddess or something."

"Nah. Just a hedge witch with a chemical engineering degree." She kissed me back, harder. I and wrapped her up in my arms, trying to absorb her into me.

I finally came up for air and realized we were being stared at. I tapped her back. "Ummmm, this probably isn't a great place."

She smoothed her clothes and touched my face. "Bill's waiting. Hit me up when you need to refill your prescription. It's only renewable in person." Then Lucrezia Jensen turned and walked across the lobby to the revolving doors. She paused, and I thought for sure she was going to turn around, but she hunched her shoulders and walked out into the blinding desert sunlight.

Her image wavered like a mirage and then vanished.

Double crap.

CHAPTER 39

Bill stood at the edge of the Grand Canyon with tears in his eyes. It was my fault, and I didn't feel bad about it. In high school, he talked nonstop about hiking the canyon, or taking one of those whitewater rafting trips. Now, with his bad leg, that would not happen, but I made damn sure my best friend got the chance to see it for himself. I left him alone with his thoughts and the fresh air.

For the third time since we left Vegas, I popped the trunk to make sure the Egg was still safe and untouched. It lay innocently in the bubble wrap and that cheap Raiders backpack, just a cool glass tchotchke. Except it wasn't. It had cost at least one life, disrupted half a dozen more, and I still didn't know what it really was. Except cold fire and stars. It was those things, certainly, which told me exactly nothing.

Sitting alone in the Charger, I laid the seat back, cranked Zeppelin, and tried to pull my thoughts together. Cree, Lemuel—okay, *Lem*—Karmen and Torson, wherever he was. It was a lot to process. Fortunately, we had at least two more days ahead of us before I had to report to Cromwell.

I pulled the envelope with my legal name change out of my suitcase and looked at it for the thousandth time.

Lupul, John Michael.

Not McPherson. Jim and Eileen were in the rear-view mirror, but what was ahead? Updating my driver's license, obviously, along with my gun permit and PI license. It was a lot of paperwork, and the state of Illinois would probably make that drag out. Finally, my whole life would be up to date. But there was more. I could finally get a passport like a grown-ass man. Thanks to Cree's magic guck, I might even be able to get on an airplane. Where would I go?

The first place that occurred to me was back to Las Vegas. Kind of ironic since I couldn't blast out of there fast enough. There was that giant list of cities on Cromwell's list—places I'd never been like New York and Miami. London and Istanbul.

And Cluj, Rumania. Did I really want to open that can of worms?

I picked up my phone and looked at the last pictures I'd taken. Cree beside the truck. Cree and me looking goofy and making silly faces. The golden days before she knew I was a murderer. Was that really only five days ago?

Out the window, I watched a family of elk make themselves at home amongst the picnickers and Asian tourists. Everyone oohed and ahhed, snapping pictures while the animals pulled at weeds and looked annoyed. They were cute, but all that meat on the hoof made my stomach rumble. Shaggy would have to wait til we got somewhere more isolated. I knew better than to make him wait indefinitely.

I heard Bill approach and put the papers back, then tucked my phone away.

"You good?"

Bill nodded. "Thanks. It really is amazing. I appreciate you stopping."

There was no need to say anything. He was my friend, and it made me happy to give him this moment. Plus, he paid the park fee. Another business expense. He promised I wouldn't go to jail for claiming it.

He pulled out his phone and opened the map app. "What do you say? Albuquerque tonight?"

"Sounds good. Let's do it."

"And Amarillo tomorrow?"

No goddamn way. Add it to Yankton, South Dakota, to the list of places I was never going back to. "We can get further, all the way to Oklahoma City, probably."

Bill put on his pouty face. "But this hotel has waffles in the shape of Texas. And they have cowboys in Amarillo."

Now his real motivation emerged. "They have cowboys in Oklahoma, too."

He gave me a leering grin. "Promise?"

"Slut."

"You should talk. I'm not the one that tore up a hotel room with a witch. Someone I very much approve of, by the way."

"Duly noted." To his disappointment, that was all I was going to say on the subject. I put the Charger in gear and pulled out of the parking lot. Bill continued fiddling with his phone. He'd fulfilled his yearly quota of nature.

As we pulled onto I-Forty, he held up something on his phone. "Did you know that last night there were over fifty reports of UFOs in Las Vegas?"

I barked out a laugh. "That's about thirty less than usual. You know they've made a whole industry out of that Area Fifty-One crap, right?"

He put his phone away and put his seat back to get a nap. "You're probably right. You don't think it has anything to do with the Egg and all?"

"Nope." *Nothing to say it was.*

But so many stars...

He shrugged and closed his eyes. I aimed the Charger towards Chicago and switched to AC/DC. Beating the hell out of the steering wheel, I drummed along with Phil Rudd as we headed East and let out a happy little howl. I was with my best friend. We had the open road, great tunes, and a paycheck waiting when we got home. And I was officially Johnny Lupul once and for all.

I'd be lying if I said I didn't check the sky in the rear-view mirror behind us.

THE END

OBLIGATORY AUTHOR STUFF

Thanks for reading about Johnny's latest adventure. I really hope you enjoyed it and are eagerly awaiting book three: Johnny Lycan and the Witchfinder General.

When you write a series, you never know how people are going to respond. Especially with this book. In reviews of "Johnny Lycan and the Anubis Disk," people talked about how much they enjoyed the authentic Chicago feel, and so many of the characters. Naturally, for this book, I took our boy out of Chicago and left most of the characters at home.

I'm an idiot.

I sincerely hope I've captured how a native Midwesterner looks at my new hometown. After three years, I still love Las Vegas, but I don't have any illusions. As Bill Mostoy says, "Dude, this town is messed up." He ain't wrong. Now Johnny's back in Sweet Home Chicago where he belongs.

The two characters I'm most happy with may appear again if you ask nicely. Cree Jensen is just a badass, and a shocking number of my women readers have a girl crush on her. The character of Lemuel Collins appeared in a short story called "The Clairetangentist," first appearing in Storgy.com back in 2019. Both have a bigger place in the Johnnyverse. More to come, if I live long enough.

Not for nothing, but if you want to read more of my short stories, you can find them at www.WayneTurmel.com under Short Stories and Other Pieces.

I'm especially grateful you found this book because it was too long between the launch of "the Anubis Disk" and this book. A lot happened in between, including writing two non-fiction books for the day job, a global pandemic, and the near collapse of the Republic. Throw in buying a house and moving, and it turns out existential dread is not great for the creative process.

Book 3 is already under construction. I promise. I've already cracked myself up twice while writing it. That's a good sign.

One great thing about Sin City is the high number of talented and giving writers who live here. This book wouldn't have been possible—or at least legible—without my friends and critics in Sin City Writers and the Purgatory Town online group. Thank you all.

Finally, I'd be completely lost without The Duchess, Her Serene Highness, and Mad Max, Defender of the Realm and Most Manly of Poodles.

OTHER NOVELS BY WAYNE TURMEL

The Count of the Sahara (2015)

In 1926 "Count" Byron de Prorok was the most famous archaeologist in the world, splashed across headlines and beloved by audiences. By the end of that year his career, his reputation and his life lay in ruins. From the scorching Saharan desert to the frigid American Midwest, this tale is based on the real life of one of the 1920s most colorful characters.

Acre's Bastard: Part 1 of the Lucca Le Pou Stories (2017)

The Holy Land-1187. Lucca the Louse is a ten-year-old orphan running the streets of Acre—the wickedest city in the world. When a horrific attack forces him to flee his orphanage, he finds himself thrust into a world of leper knights, Saracen spies, and holy war. Can one lone boy save the Kingdom of Jerusalem from defeat at the Horns of Hattin?

Acre's Orphans: Part 2 of the Lucca Le Pou Stories (2019)

Lucca narrowly survives the worst disaster ever to befall the Crusader army, but he's not safe. His beloved city of Acre is about to fall to the Saracens. With the help of a determined Druze girl, a leprous nun, and a Hospitaler knight with a tragic secret, Lucca must get a message to the last Crusader holdout at Tyre. Can he and his friends fetch help before it's too late?

Johnny Lycan & The Anubis Disk (2020)

Johnny Lupul is riding high. He's got a PI license, a concealed carry permit, his first big payday and a monster of a secret. After rescuing a bookie's daughter from Russian mobsters, the newly-minted PI catches the attention of a rich, mysterious client. At first, it's easy money. But while chasing an Egyptian relic, an obsessed enemy from his past emerges. Johnny learns that the world is much stranger—and more dangerous—than he ever suspected. Being a werewolf may be the most normal thing he has to face on this case.

ABOUT THE AUTHOR

Wayne Turmel is a former standup comedian, car salesman and corporate drone who writes to save what's left of his sanity. Originally from Canada, he writes and lives in Las Vegas with his bride, The Duchess. This is his fifth novel.

www.wayneturmel.com

NOTE FROM THE AUTHOR

Word-of-mouth is crucial for any author to succeed. If you enjoyed *Johnny Lycan & the Vegas Berserker*, please leave a review online—anywhere you are able. Even if it's just a sentence or two. It would make all the difference and would be very much appreciated.

Thanks!
Wayne

If you enjoyed *Johnny Lycan & the Vegas Berserker,* make sure not to miss the first book in the series:

Johnny Lycan & the Anubis Disk

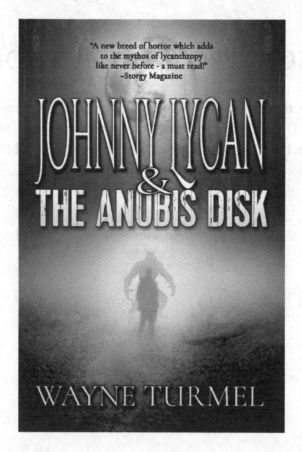

"A new breed of horror which adds to the mythos of lycanthropy like never before - a must read!"
–Storgy Magazine

JOHNNY LYCAN
& THE ANUBIS DISK

WAYNE TURMEL

"A new breed of horror which adds to the mythos of lycanthropy like never before - a must read!"
–Storgy Magazine

We hope you enjoyed reading this title from:

www.blackrosewriting.com

Subscribe to our mailing list – *The Rosevine* – and receive **FREE** books, daily deals, and stay current with news about upcoming releases and our hottest authors.
Scan the QR code below to sign up.

Already a subscriber? Please accept a sincere thank you for being a fan of Black Rose Writing authors.

View other Black Rose Writing titles at
www.blackrosewriting.com/books and use promo code
PRINT to receive a **20% discount** when purchasing.

CPSIA information can be obtained
at www.ICGtesting.com
Printed in the USA
BVHW080916170822
644751BV00001B/8